Empowered By The Earl

Second Sons of London
Book Three

Alexa Aston

Dragonblade Publishing, Inc. is an imprint of Kathryn Le Veque Novels, Inc.
P.O. Box 23
Moreno Valley, CA 92556
ceo@dragonbladepublishing.com

Produced in the United States of America

First Edition March 2022
Trade Paperback Edition

ARE YOU SIGNED UP FOR DRAGONBLADE'S BLOG?

You'll get the latest news and information on exclusive giveaways, exclusive excerpts, coming releases, sales, free books, cover reveals and more.

Check out our complete list of authors, too!

No spam, no junk. That's a promise!

Sign Up Here

www.dragonbladepublishing.com

Dearest Reader;

Thank you for your support of a small press. At Dragonblade Publishing, we strive to bring you the highest quality Historical Romance from some of the best authors in the business. Without your support, there is no 'us', so we sincerely hope you adore these stories and find some new favorite authors along the way.

Happy Reading!

CEO, Dragonblade Publishing

Additional Dragonblade books by Author Alexa Aston

Second Sons of London Series
Educated By The Earl
Debating With The Duke
Empowered By The Earl

Dukes Done Wrong Series
Discouraging the Duke
Deflecting the Duke
Disrupting the Duke
Delighting the Duke
Destiny with a Duke

Dukes of Distinction Series
Duke of Renown
Duke of Charm
Duke of Disrepute
Duke of Arrogance
Duke of Honor

The St. Clairs Series
Devoted to the Duke
Midnight with the Marquess
Embracing the Earl
Defending the Duke
Suddenly a St. Clair
Starlight Night

Soldiers & Soulmates Series
To Heal an Earl
To Tame a Rogue
To Trust a Duke

To Save a Love
To Win a Widow

The Lyon's Den Connected World
The Lyon's Lady Love

King's Cousins Series
The Pawn
The Heir
The Bastard

Medieval Runaway Wives
Song of the Heart
A Promise of Tomorrow
Destined for Love

Knights of Honor Series
Word of Honor
Marked by Honor
Code of Honor
Journey to Honor
Heart of Honor
Bold in Honor
Love and Honor
Gift of Honor
Path to Honor
Return to Honor

Pirates of Britannia Series
God of the Seas

De Wolfe Pack: The Series
Rise of de Wolfe

The de Wolfes of Esterley Castle
Diana
Derek
Thea

PROLOGUE

Portugal—August 1813

MAJOR OWEN HASBURY awoke and stared across the tent at the new officer who had replaced Everett Wayland, Owen's best friend practically from birth. He and Ev had grown up on adjoining estates and had attended school, university and, finally, war together. As second sons, it had been their only career choice, especially with England at war against Bonaparte.

He missed Ev something awful. His friend, who had received a shoulder wound during last month's Battle of Vitoria, had received a letter once the battle had ended. A letter which had changed the trajectory of Ev's life.

Major Everett Wayland was now the Duke of Camden. One of the highest peers in the land. No longer a contemporary of his soldier best friend. Owen had also lost his second closest friend, Major Spencer Haddock. A second son like Owen and Ev, Spence had inherited the title of Earl of Middlefield with the death of his father. Spence had left them last year and had quickly found his countess in Lady Tessa Foster.

With his two dearest friends gone from his life, Owen was selfishly relieved that he still had the cousins on the warfront with him. Percy and Win had rounded out their group of five. They called themselves the Second Sons of London. The trio from schoolboy days had met Percy and Win at university and the five men had become inseparable during those carefree years. They had all entered the army, commissions bought for them by their respective families, and had thought to spend their careers together.

He supposed that he and the cousins would continue in the army until the Little Corporal was finally defeated—and beyond. Second sons didn't have the luxury of inheriting titles and living off the wealth of their estates. They forged their own paths in the world, the army their true constant, whether during time of war or peace.

Owen rose and his new tentmate, Captain Peters, did so as well, no conversation between them. It wasn't that Owen didn't like Peters. He merely missed his friends and did not want to become attached to anyone else who might lose his life in battle. Owen found his heart hardening more as each day passed. Seven long years at war would do that to a man.

He went through some drills with his men and attended staff meetings of officers. Wellington had marched his forces into Madrid after last month's Battle of Salamanca and plans were afoot for a siege against Burgos soon, most likely next month. Owen hoped the battle would take England one step closer to defeating Bonaparte and his allies.

After a quick evening meal in Win's and Percy's company, he parted from them and returned to his tent. On his cot lay a letter and he wondered if it might be from Spence since Ev wouldn't have had time to reach England and dash off a letter so soon after his recent departure.

He picked up the letter and sat on his cot, seeing it wasn't Spence's handwriting and curious as to who might be writing him. His mother had written him regularly from the time he had entered the army. His father never bothered to send a single missive. Both she and the earl had died during the years he'd been at war. His brother, Lawford, the Earl of Danbury, never corresponded with Owen. In fact, they hadn't spoken in years.

The two brothers had never been close, mostly due to the large age gap between them and the fact that Lawford would inherit the title one day, while his younger brother would spend his life in the army, most likely traveling the world in the crown's defense.

Breaking the seal, he immediately glanced to the bottom of the page, where he saw it signed by Mr. Sellers. Owen knew the name. It was his father's longtime solicitor, the man who had purchased Owen's army commission and seen him off to war since the earl had been too busy to be bothered with trivial matters such as telling a second son goodbye.

His eyes moved to the top of the page and he saw the letter was dated the eighth of May. It had taken over three months to catch up to him, just as the one Ev had received last month from his family's solicitor. That letter had borne news of the death of Mervyn, Ev's only brother. It had been brief, saying Mervyn had been grievously injured and had died from his wounds. Since Lawford and Mervyn were peas in a pod, both Owen and Ev had speculated on whether or not Lawford had been with Mervyn when the accident had occurred. In fact, Owen had encouraged Ev, once he reached London, to call upon Lawford and get to the bottom of the story in case his family's solicitor continued to remain vague.

His eyes returned to the beginning and he began to read.

Dear Major Hasbury,

I am writing to you on behalf of your brother, the Earl of Danbury. Lord Danbury was in the company of the Duke of Camden when both men were viciously attacked. Unfortunately, His Grace died from his injuries, while Lord Danbury was severely hurt. Part of those injuries included one to his head.

I regret to inform you that Lord Danbury has yet to awaken.

This situation leaves his care and the estate in limbo. I would ask that you take a leave of absence from the army and come home to manage the estate and see to your brother's care.

You may reach me at the address below. Please come to London as soon as possible, as that is where Lord Danbury is recuperating.

Yours Sincerely,
S. Sellers

Owen snorted. The last thing he would do is ask his commanding officer for an unnecessary leave of absence, which he doubted would even be granted in a time of war. His place was commanding troops in the thick of battle, not playing nursemaid to a selfish brother. That's what servants and solicitors were for. Besides, he owed Lawford nothing.

He stepped outside his tent and moved to the nearest campfire. Tossing the letter into the flames, he watched it burn until nothing remained and then returned to his tent.

EXHAUSTION FILLED OWEN as he returned to his tent, too tired to even eat, though satisfaction filled him. England and her allies were one step closer to defeating the Corsican Fiend. Thanks to Wellington's brilliant battle plan, the combined Anglo-Spanish-Portuguese Army had claimed a decisive victory over Marshal Nicolas Soult's Imperial French army in southern France at Orthez. Soult's forces were outnumbered, though they repelled several attacks on their right flank. Eventually, the left and center flanks were overrun, resulting in Soult's retreat. The orderly retreat had turned chaotic, becoming a mob that scrambled for safety.

Not only had over five hundred French soldiers been killed in battle, but Wellington had just shared in the meeting Owen now came from the early numbers. Over two thousand more French bastards had been wounded and over thirteen hundred taken prisoner. Others who had been conscripted into service were said to be deserting by the dozens.

Wellington wanted to strike while the iron was sizzling. With Soult and his decimated army in retreat, the French commander would not be able to defend both the port of Bordeaux and the city of Toulouse. Intelligence revealed defending—much less holding—Bordeaux would be difficult, mainly because of the lack of food in the area. Scouts had reported that Soult now marched east toward Toulouse and Wellington had told his officers minutes ago that that would be the site of their next battle, most likely in the next six to eight weeks.

Thank God it had been a British victory. Because of it, Owen actually believed the final stage of this lengthy war would soon unfold.

Back at his tent, he collapsed onto his cot, wishing one day he could have a hot bath and sleep once more in a feather bed, knowing the first would eventually happen and the latter never would, thanks to his career in the army. He pillowed his hands behind his head and let his thoughts drift far from today's bloodshed. He wondered what Ev and Spence were up to on their new estates and hoped they appreciated the lives they now led.

Sensing the presence of someone entering the tent, he opened his eyes, seeing a young private bearing a stash of letters in his hands.

"Major, a letter for you," the soldier said, handing over one piece of mail and then exiting the tent.

Owen looked down and let out a long breath of air, recognizing Mr. Sellers' handwriting. The solicitor had written to him three additional letters since the first one Owen had burned six months ago. All asked the same thing—for Owen to return to London and manage the estate and his brother's care. It seemed after the first few lines that Owen never bothered to finish reading the solicitor's letters and subsequently burned them as he had the first. This one would be like all the others, he surmised, but opened it anyway.

Dear Major Hasbury –

I have yet to receive a reply from you and can only hope my letters have reached you, despite this being a time of war and the British army constantly on the march. Knowing your father frequently mentioned how stubborn you were, however, I have taken the liberty of writing to your commanding officer.

Owen cursed loudly. What right had Sellers to insert himself into Owen's life? Anger simmering through him, his eyes returned to the page.

The physicians hold little hope for Lord Danbury's recovery. He could be in his current state for days, months, even years. Though his physical wounds have now healed, the traumatic injury to his brain has still left the earl unconscious all these months. It is unknown if he will ever awaken, much less have his faculties when he does. Since Lord Danbury never wed and produced an heir, you—upon his death—would become the new earl. It is imperative for you to return and take charge of things. I have explained this in detail to your commanding officer.

I look forward to seeing you in the near future, Major Hasbury.

Yours Sincerely,
S. Sellers

Owen wadded up the parchment, squeezing it tighter and tighter as his wrath grew. He was angry at Lawford and Mervyn for being careless enough to have been caught in the Stews at four in the morning. That, he had learned from Ev, who had written to Owen shortly after his return to England. Ev shared that Mervyn's throat had been slashed in a robbery attempt and Lawford had also been attacked, barely surviving.

Ev told him the robbers had never been found. If they were, they would certainly hang for Mervyn's murder. When Lawford did die of his injuries, that would be a second murder charge.

It finally sank in to Owen that he eventually would become the Earl of Danbury. Of course, Lawford could linger for years before Owen could claim the title. When Owen finally did, the estate might be in ruins if he didn't act quickly. Much as he did not want to, it seemed he would have to leave the military. A formal separation would be necessary, which meant selling his commission. He did not know if that would be all he would have to live on or if the estate would be allowed to pay him a salary as he managed it. At least he would have a roof over his head and warm meals in his belly. Though he had never been destined for the earldom, he could not see his family's name and Danbury ruined by his pettiness. He slipped the letter inside his coat and headed to Colonel Dixon's tent, hoping his commanding officer had not yet seen Mr. Sellers' letter.

He approached the tent and the sentry in front of it nodded curtly at him, holding the flap open. Entering, Owen saw Colonel Dixon at his makeshift desk. Correspondence was scattered across it and the man wore a deep frown as he looked up.

"Major Hasbury, I was just about to send for you. I have been reading a letter from a Mr. Sellers. It proved to be most interesting. He claims to have been writing to you since last spring."

Owen knew the temper Dixon had and produced the letter from inside his jacket.

"I, too, just received a letter from Mr. Sellers. It is the first I have received, Colonel. You know with an army on the move, it can take a while for correspondence to catch up and be delivered. I am certain Mr. Sellers' previous letters went astray but I can tell from the content of this one that my brother has been incapacitated by some injury."

Colonel Dixon's eyebrows arched and he said, "More than incapacitated. Mr. Sellers writes that there is no hope Lord Danbury will recover. If he ever regains consciousness, he is likely to be a vegetable. It is your duty, Major, to return to England and see to your family's estate and your brother's care. I will accept your letter of resignation and can help you in handling the sale of your commission."

The colonel rose and offered Owen his hand, which he took and shook.

"You have been an exemplary leader, Major Hasbury. I hope that you will make for as good an earl as you have an officer in His Majesty's army. Now, sit and write that resignation letter for me so that we might get things into motion."

"We are so close to defeating the French, Colonel," Owen pleaded. "I would ask that I be allowed to remain and participate in those few remaining battles and see us march victoriously in Paris. Surely, that will occur in the next couple of months."

"Out of the question!" roared Dixon. "If you were to die in battle, what would become of your poor brother and the estate? Your duty to your country has been fulfilled by your outstanding service. Now, your duty is to your family and the title and estate which will one day be yours." The commander's eyes narrowed. "Is that understood, Major?"

Owen nodded, knowing his course had now been set. "I understand, Colonel."

He took a seat and composed a brief letter of resignation and then handed it over. Colonel Dixon skimmed it and nodded brusquely.

"We will do our best to find you transportation in the next couple of days, Major Hasbury. In the meantime, think of the officers under you and which one might deserve a promotion to your position."

"Thank you, Sir," Owen said and exited the tent.

He traveled across the campsite a good distance until he reached the tent Win and Percy shared. Going inside, he found the two cousins playing cards.

"Owen," Percy said jovially. "It is good we all survived today's battle. But then again, you have always been the luckiest of the Second Sons."

Win shot him a concerned look. "Something has happened since we saw you at Wellington's staff meeting. What is it?"

"I have just spoken with Colonel Dixon and have submitted to him my letter of resignation. I will be leaving as soon as I can find a way back to England."

"What?" both cousins cried in unison and Win added "Tells us everything."

"You know when Ev received the letter telling him of his brother's passing? Well, I received one shortly after that from Mr. Sellers, our family solicitor. My brother, Lawford, was with Mervyn. They were attacked in the Stews. Mervyn died immediately, as you know, making Ev the Duke of Camden. Lawford had severe injuries, including one to his head."

"Has he died?" Win asked solemnly.

"No, he actually has recovered from his physical injuries, though I am not aware of what they were. It is his head injury that has not healed. He has been unconscious all these months and Mr. Sellers has sent me letters, pleading for me to come home and handle estate affairs on Lawford's behalf, since he is unable to do so."

He raked a hand through his hair. "I selfishly ignored these letters, preferring to stay on the battlefield and do my duty to king and country."

"But you have a new duty now," Percy said quietly. "One to your family—because at some point you will become the new earl."

"Yes, you're right. While Lawford has lingered, I have let down the tenants and others. Apparently, the estate is in disarray. Knowing Lawford, he was profligate in his spending. Who knows what I will find when I return? The thing is, it will be mine eventually. This year. Five years. Ten years from now. Whenever Lawford expires. If I am to save it for future generations, I must go home and take care of things now."

"Who knew that another Second Son would be leaving our fold?" Win asked.

Percy said, "This calls for a drink." He rummaged under his cot and produced a bottle and then found three tin cups. Pouring a generous amount into each, he dispersed them and lifted his high. "To Owen—and to Second Sons everywhere."

"Hear, hear!" said Win.

The three men clinked their tin cups together and downed the brandy.

In that moment, Owen wondered what would be waiting for him in England.

And when he would finally gain the title Earl of Danbury.

CHAPTER ONE

Danbury, Kent—June 1814

OWEN OPENED HIS eyes. For a moment, he was confused as to where he was. Then he remembered that Strunk had moved his things into the earl's suite yesterday.

He was officially the Earl of Danbury.

Actually, he had been Lord Danbury for a week now. Ever since Lawford's death. His brother had never awakened from the coma he had been in ever since he and Mervyn had been attacked by footpads in London. No witnesses to the crime had ever stepped forward. The only reason he even knew there were two assailants is because when the two injured lords were found, it was the last thing Mervyn said before he died.

Owen had sat by Lawford's bedside every night once he returned from the Continent, hoping his brother would awaken and be himself again, removing the heavy burden of responsibility that came with being a future peer of the realm from Owen. He hadn't been raised to inherit the earldom and didn't know the first thing about it. He certainly didn't want to be in charge of the vast estate and holdings. More than anything, he longed to return to the army. It was all Owen had known his entire adult life.

Instead, he would remain in England and handle all the duties and obligations that came with being an earl. At least he wasn't a duke as Ev had become. That would have been even more shocking.

He had kept his presence in England a secret from Ev and Spence, not writing to either of them during the time Lawford lived. Neither had he written to Percy or Win, knowing they had been far too busy to write him with the recent events ending the long war.

As he had predicted to Colonel Dixon, the allied coalition marched into Paris at the end of March. Bonaparte abdicated a week later and one final battle had occurred at Toulouse. The Bourbons had been restored to the French throne and Bonaparte exiled to Elba, his wife and son fleeing to Vienna. Europe would be in chaos until the upcoming Congress of Vienna met and ironed out solutions to the many problems the Little Corporal had caused.

Owen had no idea where Win and Percy would be stationed. They had his address in Kent and he would wait to hear from them before he shared the news of Lawford's death. In the meantime, he had written to Ev and Spence in London once Lawford passed. Owen had brought his brother back to Kent because after his meeting with the family solicitor, he learned his brother had neglected the estate for some time. If Owen were to right things, it would begin at Danfield and he needed to be there in order to supervise the necessary changes.

He sent a footman to Cliffside once he arrived there to inquire if Ev was home and had received a message from Arthur, Ev's butler. It informed Owen that the Duke of Camden was in London for the Season. He couldn't imagine his shy friend gallivanting about in Polite Society but determined that Ev, always conscious of duty to a fault, would have gone to look for a wife. Ev would want to provide a ducal heir, knowing it was his duty, and the Season would be full of young women eager to take on the title of duchess. He only hoped his friend wouldn't be overwhelmed with all the attention he would receive.

Spence had already wed upon his return to England but Owen believed his friend and new wife would also be in town for the Season, partially to socialize and also to support Ev in his endeavors. Owen had dashed off quick notes to both his friends and sent them to London, along with the obituary to be placed in the newspapers announcing Lawford's death. It was what Lawford would have wanted, the last way Owen could honor a brother he didn't know and now never would. Nothing truly happened in the *ton* unless it was made public in the newspapers. That included births, marriages, and deaths.

Rising, Owen padded naked into the enormous dressing room, looking about to see the few clothes he possessed folded and sitting on the shelves. He had made do with purchasing a handful of items before he left London since he had no civilian clothes, only his military uniforms. There had been no need for them since he had left England years ago and spent his time on the march. Now, however, he was the Earl of Danbury and would be expected to dress as befit his station. He would wait until Ev returned next door after the Season and ask who his tailor was. Owen had no idea exactly what he would need to wear in Polite Society. At least here in the country, he could get away with a much smaller wardrobe.

Strunk suddenly appeared. "My lord, I have asked for you to ring for me when you rise each morning."

The valet had made that request but Owen had forgotten. Strunk had been the one who cared for Lawford during the past year. With his master's death, the servant had assumed he would become Owen's valet. Like the title and the estate, Strunk was inherited. At least the man gave a good shave.

"I apologize, Strunk. It is taking me a while to get used to everything."

"I understand, my lord. Life at Danfield must seem rather tame after what you have been through since your university days."

"It is quite different. And not exactly a life I am yet comfortable in," he admitted.

The valet placed the steaming bowl of water down. "Shall we shave you first and then dress you?"

"Yes."

Owen took a seat and closed his eyes, letting his thoughts drift as Strunk handled the shave. The quiet life of the country was getting on his nerves. At least his days were filled, making himself useful about the estate and then spending evenings trying to make sense of all the numbers in the ledgers. If he had a steward, the entire process would be much easier, but Danfield's steward had retired shortly before Lawford was attacked in London. No replacement had been hired, much to Owen's dismay. Sellers, the solicitor, seemed too timid to make even the slightest decision for the estate.

Because of that, Danfield was in disarray. He had taken it upon himself to act as the estate's steward but he would still need to hire a good one in the near future. In the meantime, he was out and about every day on the land, meeting tenants, monitoring the fields, making notes of what he thought should be done. He dearly wished Ev would find a bride and return to Cliffside. Surely, in the time since his closest friend had been home, Ev had gleaned some ideas about how to run an estate. As the Duke of Camden, he must have a good half-dozen or more of them.

Once dressed, Owen proceeded to the breakfast room, one of his favorite places at Danfield. It was sunny and the perfect way for him to begin his morning. He entered and footmen immediately jumped into action, fetching his coffee and bringing his plate. He dug into the meat and eggs, dipping his toast into the yolk rather than smearing it with butter or jam.

A third footman entered and whispered something to Croft. The butler nodded and the footman stepped back.

Croft approached and said, "You have a visitor, my lord. The Duke of Camden has come to call."

"He is here? Now?"

"Yes, my lord."

"Show him in at once."

The footman left, apparently to retrieve Ev. Excitement filled Owen. It had been the previous summer since he had seen his friend and he looked forward to their reunion.

Ev strode through the dining room and Owen rose to meet him. They threw their arms about one another, heartily clapping backs.

He stepped back. "Lord, it is good to see you, Ev. Come and sit. Coffee? Tea?"

"Nothing for me. I have already breakfasted."

They returned to the table, Ev taking a seat on Owen's right.

"Ah, so you are still keeping military hours and rising before the breaking of dawn?" he asked.

"I don't suppose you can ever take the military out of the man," Ev observed. "We received your note in London yesterday and happened to be making our way home the same day."

"We? Have you already wed, Ev?"

His friend beamed. "I have. I cannot wait for you to meet my Addie. She is the best thing that has ever happened to me."

"That was certainly fast work, you sly devil."

"Addie is Tessa's cousin," Ev explained. "Spence and Tessa took me under their wings and have helped me with Cliffside and then making sure I had bit of town polish on me before the Season began. Addie had a bit of a reputation as a matchmaker and so I put myself in her hands."

Owen whistled low. "I don't know what to say."

"Oh, I thought I had things all planned out. Addie insisted that I make a list of the attributes I was looking for in my duchess. She would use the list to guide her in making the appropriate introductions to ladies who displayed those specific qualities."

"And recommend herself?" Owen asked, chuckling. "I suppose she recognized herself on your list."

"Far from it. My list included the things I thought the Duchess of Camden should be. Dignified. Staid. Restrained." Ev shook his head. "Addie is none of those things. She is vivacious and full of light and life."

"Then how on earth did you wind up husband and wife?"

Ev shrugged. "I knew the moment we finished composing the list that what I thought I wanted—and what I truly wanted—were two very different things."

"You wanted her," Owen guessed.

"I wanted her. Very much."

It was hard for Owen to picture his reserved friend with a bubbly, animated woman but he could already see that Addie was good for Ev.

"We wed rather quickly—and then I did not recognize the woman who was my duchess."

"Why not?"

Ev shook his head. "Because unbeknownst to me, Addie thought she had to act the part of my duchess. She tried to embody all the qualities on my list. It was a dismal failure, her trying to hide her natural exuberance and zest for life. Fortunately, we cleared up the brief misunderstanding and are now as happy as clams. You'll see for yourself when you come to tea this afternoon."

"I am coming for tea?"

"That is the purpose of my visit. To invite you to Cliffside so that we might catch up and Addie can meet you. You are the two most important people in my life, Owen. It is imperative you get to know one another, especially now that you are back from the war and will be living next door to us in the country."

"I would be happy to come around for tea and meet your duchess," Owen said.

Ev's smile lit up his entire face. Owen couldn't recall the last time he had seen Ev look so happy. Perhaps never.

"Don't worry. Just as Spence and Tessa took care of me, Addie and I—along with Spence and Tessa—will make certain you are taken care of both now and next Season."

"You think to introduce me around then?"

"Of course. Hopefully, you, too, will find a wife."

Owen shook his head. "That is the last thing I need now, Ev.

You know me. Of all the Second Sons, I am the least likely to want to settle down."

"But you will need an heir," his friend insisted.

"I know that. I am still trying to get used to being an earl, Ev. Being a husband is the last thing on my mind, quite frankly. And when I do go to London for the Season, I have no plans to wed for several years. I want to enjoy the society there. You know a pretty face has always been my weakness."

When Ev's face darkened, Owen added, "I will do my duty in time. A wife, however, is not a concern. Just because you seem besotted with your wife doesn't mean I have to behave the same way."

Ev frowned. "You don't understand yet. Neither did I when Spence tried to tell me. Oh, I saw how in love he and Tessa were but I never dreamed of that for myself. Love wasn't something I really believed in—until I met Addie."

"Well, I am still part of that school of thought," Owen declared. "I neither need nor want love, Ev. When the time comes, yes, I will do my duty. I will marry and hope my wife produces the needed heir and spare. But I am certain I will have a marriage as my parents did—as most members of the *ton* do. My wife and I will lead separate lives and be quite happy in doing so."

Ev shook his head. "No, I thought the same and would have been miserable if I had wed anyone but Addie. You must open your heart, Owen, and let yourself find love. Sometimes where you least expect it. You are a good, honorable man. You will find a woman to love and keep your wedding vows. I know it."

"Whatever you say, Ev."

They talked a few more minutes about Danfield and his need to find a steward, with Ev promising to ask Painter, his own steward, if he knew of anyone who might serve in the same capacity for Owen. Ev left and Owen mentally rearranged his day in his head, making certain he would have time to return home and bathe before he appeared at Cliffside for tea with the new Duchess of Camden.

It had slightly surprised him when Spence wed so soon after returning to England but, then again, his longtime friend had always been the responsible type. His conversation with Ev shocked him, though. Ev had wed hastily and still showed signs of the bloom of being a newlywed. He seemed more open and relaxed than Owen had ever seen him and supposed the changes were thanks to his new wife.

Despite what Ev said, though, Owen had absolutely no plans to pursue a wife of his own when next Season arrived. It was as he said. He enjoyed the company of women. Now that he had returned to England and Polite Society, he would most certainly take advantage of that. He would flirt with all the pretty new girls making their come-outs and seek out the beautiful widows to satisfy his appetites. His father had never been faithful to his wife. Owen heard the rumors of Danbury's infidelities throughout his school and university years. Why, the randy old goat had been seeing a woman half his age just before his death. Owen knew because his mother had written of it to him. As usual, most of her letters to her younger son voiced complaints about her husband or older son. He couldn't remember a time when she had written him and spoken of only what she did or asked him about his time at war. Every piece of correspondence denigrated her husband and heir apparent.

Owen certainly didn't need a wife, much less a harpy such as his mother. When the time came, he would wed a young, malleable girl making her come-out and do his duty by getting an heir off her. He had no desire to go about with stars in his eyes as Ev did or Spence seemed to do. It saddened him that his two closest friends, both having taken wives and doing the foolish thing of falling in love, would now have more in common with each other than with him. He hoped the two wives wouldn't estrange him from Ev and Spence.

He would know more once he met the new Duchess of Camden and formed his opinion of her later today.

Chapter Two

OWEN ARRIVED AT Cliffside in his carriage. In the past, he would have ridden over on horseback but he was fresh from his bath and wanted to make a good impression on Ev's bride.

Exiting the vehicle, he walked to the front door, a bouquet in his hand. Every woman he knew enjoyed receiving flowers. He hoped his gift would put him in Addie's good graces.

Before he could knock at the door, it opened. A smiling Arthur stood there beaming at him.

"Good afternoon, Arthur," he said pleasantly. "It has been a good while since I have seen you."

"Come in, my lord," the butler said. "It seems right having you back, along with His Grace. You boys were always together."

"Causing trouble?" he joked.

Arthur grinned. "Perhaps just a bit, my lord. But what boy hasn't in his youth?"

"How is Mrs. Arthur?"

"She is well and still Cliffside's housekeeper. Hopefully, she and I will continue in service for several more years. Let me escort you upstairs to the drawing room."

In the past, that never would have happened. Whenever Owen showed up on Cliffside's doorstep, he had been admitted and then told where Ev was. He had headed there on his own. Of course, Ev was now a duke and Owen an earl. He supposed not only for Polite Society's sake—but the servants'—that certain conventions must be observed.

"Wait here one moment, my lord," Arthur said before he stepped into the drawing room for several seconds.

Owen heard his name being announced. Or rather the Earl of Danbury's. It still struck him as odd that only a handful of people, close friends, would ever call him Owen again. For the majority, he would be Danbury or my lord.

He sailed through, his eyes immediately drawn to the woman who rose, Ev by her side. The new Duchess of Camden was a striking woman, with honey-blond hair and eyes the blue of a summer's sky. She was slightly on the thin side, with an average bosom and nice height.

As he moved toward her, though, her eyes lit with excitement. No, mischief. He could see why his friend had been taken with her.

Claiming her hand, he raised it to his lips and kissed it. "I am Danbury, Your Grace."

"Oh, we'll have none of that," she proclaimed. "You are to call me Adalyn and I shall call you Owen. It is only right to do so, seeing as how Ev looks upon you as a brother."

He kept her hand in his and asked, "Not Addie?"

A low growl came from Ev's throat and he said, "Give my duchess her hand back."

Owen released it, chuckling.

"As for informality, I am all for it," Ev proclaimed. "But she is *my* Addie—not yours. Not anyone's but mine." His hand slipped possessively about his wife's waist.

"Don't be such a grouch," Adalyn gently chided.

"Well, you are my Addie," Ev said.

And he kissed her.

Shock rippled through Owen. While Ev had been no stranger as far as the fairer sex went, Owen had never seen him display any kind of public affection in regard to a woman. The kiss wasn't a light peck, either, but one that lingered for a moment. He worried now that the new duchess had somehow bewitched his friend. The old Ev would never have behaved so outrageously.

It was Adalyn who broke the kiss. Placing a hand lightly on her husband's chest, she said, "We have a guest, Ev. We will finish this later."

Turning to Owen, she said, "Won't you please have a seat?"

Before he took the chair she indicated, he handed her the bouquet, saying, "These are for you. I hope you enjoy flowers."

Adalyn accepted them, inhaling deeply. "Oh, they are lovely, Owen. Sweat peas are one of my favorite blooms."

He sat as a maid rolled in a teacart. Adalyn gave the bouquet to the servant, asking that she find a vase for it and set it next to her bedside. For a few minutes, they were busy placing items on their plates as Adalyn poured out for them.

"Tell me about growing up at Danfield," she urged. "What did you and Ev like to do?"

"Riding year-round. Swimming in the summers. Skimming rocks. Catching tadpoles. Roaming the woods between Danfield and Cliffside. Graduating from playing marbles to draughts to finally chess."

She smiled. "Ev has promised to teach me to play chess."

Adalyn looked to her husband, a look passing between them. A look that told Owen all that he needed to know.

This was a couple enamored with one another. Deeply in love. Two people who already shared a brief history together that they would build upon during the years as they started a family. A couple who would enjoy growing old together.

And for the first time in his life, Owen experienced jealousy.

He had always been athletic. Intelligent. Handsome. He did everything as well as or better than most. He had never envied anyone anything.

Until now.

Maybe there was something, after all, to what Ev had spoken of. Yet the notion of love was so foreign to Owen, he couldn't fathom it. Oh, he loved his brotherhood. The Second Sons were family to him. But true familial love with blood relatives? He had never known it. Danbury ignored him in favor of his heir. His mother treated him as a pesky fly to be shooed away. Lawford had barely acknowledged he had a brother.

As for women, Owen had never taken any of them seriously. Women had been good for one thing. Once he had pleasured them and taken his own pleasure from them, he discarded them quickly.

Yet a hunger now built within him.

He wanted what Ev and Adalyn had.

"Chess is an interesting game," he finally managed to say, causing Adalyn to glance from her husband back to her guest. "If Ev doesn't have the patience to teach you, I certainly can."

A womanly smile appeared. "My husband will find the time to do so. When we are not doing other things."

Owen had an excellent idea what those other things might be.

They talked some about the recent Season, which the couple had left early, as had Spence and Tessa. He asked about them and heard a few stories, including some about Analise, Spence's daughter who was four months old and whom Spence seemed to carry around whenever she was awake.

"You should see Spence with Analise," Ev said. "I never saw a man take more to being a father."

He wouldn't know. His own father had barely acknowledged being a parent to him. Even with Lawford, his father had been stiff and formal. It was hard to imagine Spence, whom Owen had known for over two decades, being dotty over a child—much less a daughter.

"I look forward to seeing them at some point," he said.

"I know!" Adalyn cried. "We will have a house party once the Season ends. That is in another two months or so. You will be more settled at Danfield, Owen, so you won't have to worry about being away for a week or so. I will invite a select group you will feel comfortable with, naturally including Tessa and Spencer.

That way, you will have already mingled a bit in Polite Society and be acquainted with some others by the time the next Season begins."

"I don't know," he said stubbornly, not wanting Adalyn to start planning his life as she must do with Ev.

His friend laughed. "You might as well give in now, Owen. Else Addie will wear you down with kindness. Or determination. Or browbeat you. She's actually quite good at all three. But she always gets her way."

"Who is running this household?" he demanded, put out that his friend seemed so easily swayed by his duchess.

Ev's mouth hardened. "We both do, Owen." He took his wife's hand and threaded his fingers through hers. "We are partners in every sense of the word. Addie is the intellectual equal of any man I have known. She doesn't force me to do anything—and I would never do that to her."

"It is all right, Ev," Adalyn said, her words seeming to calm him. "Owen is merely you months ago when you first saw how Spencer was with Tessa. You had no idea of the deep and abiding love that could exist between a man and woman. In fact, you scoffed at it if I recall. Let Owen find his own way to love. Then he will understand."

Ev looked appeased. Owen held in the snort he wished to issue but was wise enough not to do so in front of Adalyn, not wanting to distance himself from his old friend any more than he had.

"I know you want to dislike me," she told him, as if she was reading his mind. "I understand. I fought what was happening between Ev and me. He did the same. But we were meant to be together. I hope you can accept that, Owen. I promise never to get in the way of your friendship with him. You are his oldest and dearest friend."

Ev lifted their joined hands and kissed her fingers. "And it will stay that way. But you have to understand that I have changed, Owen. I am not the man I was. I am a better man. Because of this woman."

Owen took in both their words, still amazed at the difference he was seeing in Ev—and not certain if he liked the changes or not. Still, Ev seemed incredibly happy and Owen knew Adalyn would have been quite the catch in Polite Society. The fact that his friend had claimed her for himself spoke volumes.

"Will you come to the house party if I plan it?" Adalyn asked, tears glistening in her eyes.

If there was one thing that weakened him, it was seeing a woman in tears.

"Yes, of course," he said hastily. "It will give me a good chance to catch up with Spence and meet Tessa."

"And other members of the *ton*," Adalyn added.

"That, too. Most of my acquaintances are either still in the army or dead," he said lightly.

"Thank you, Owen," she said, rising. "I think I will give you two some time together while I start planning things."

"Such as what?" he asked, curious.

"Who to invite. What activities to prepare. The kinds of food that will be served. Quite a bit goes into planning a house party."

Adalyn said her goodbyes, leaving just the two of them together.

"She is definitely opinionated," Owen said.

"By far the most opinionated woman I know," Ev said cheerfully. "Also stubborn, strong-willed, and a bit spoiled. She was an only child and used to getting her own way."

"I can see that."

"Can you?" Ev asked.

"She certainly is a force of nature. Like a very spirited horse."

"I shall never break her," Ev said. "Instead, I will always celebrate her."

"You have changed, Ev."

"I have. I will never be comfortable claiming the center of attention but I am more comfortable in my own skin now, thanks to Addie. She is my very soul, Owen. The love between us is powerful."

"I can see it. It is palpable," he agreed.

"Spence and Tessa have the same kind of relationship. Not quite as volatile as mine and Addie's can be." He grinned. "But there is always the fun of making things right again between us."

Owen burst into laughter. "I can tell that I will want to always be on Adalyn's good side."

"You are one of us," his friend said. "Family. And Addie is fierce about family. She will defend you. Protect you." He chuckled. "Plot for you."

He frowned. "What do you mean?"

"And here I thought you to be so very clever, Lord Danbury." Ev paused. "This house party is not merely to allow you time with Spencer and Tessa. Yes, it will allow that, as well as help introduce you to some influential people of the *ton*. But the real reason Addie has decided to hold it?

"She is going to help find you a wife."

CHAPTER THREE

London—July 1814

LOUISA GOULDING SAT brooding. The Season she had looked forward to for so long had proven to be disastrous. Well, perhaps not disastrous. That was an exaggeration. Merely uneventful was closer to the truth.

It would wrap up in another three weeks but she did not think she could bear to attend another event. She glanced at her calendar and counted up the number of affairs she and her aunt and uncle, Lord and Lady Uxbridge, had committed to attend.

She couldn't do it anymore.

How would she tell her aunt and uncle of her dilemma? She had nowhere else to go since her father had left England for abroad. He worked for the War Office and with Bonaparte's recent abdication, Europe had been thrown into turmoil. There was to be a gathering of nations at a congress in the autumn and her father had gone early to help plan and prepare for this auspicious event.

At least the Season had been fun when her cousins, Adalyn and Tessa, were still in London. The three of them had been best friends since childhood. Tessa had wed Spencer, Lord Middlefield, last year and Adalyn had married Everett, the new Duke of Camden, a few months ago. Both couples had remained in

London until mid-June, when they departed for their country estates, both located in Kent.

Ever since their departure, Louisa seemed to be drifting through the Season. Not a single gentleman interested her. Though she had made her come-out five years ago, she had only attended a handful of events each year at her father's request. Instead, Louisa had served as his hostess the majority of the time. Papa held many meetings at their London townhouse, worried about spies planted within the War Office. Because of that, she had managed the household and made certain that every meeting went smoothly. She provided tea, planned meals and refreshments for late night gatherings.

Because she had spent so much of her time these past few years with older gentlemen from the War Office, the young swains of this Season—her first to attend most every affair—seemed incredibly immature to her. The only bachelor she had even liked was Everett and the two of them had determined early on that they would not suit as husband and wife. As it was, Everett and Adalyn were a perfect match and Louisa could not be happier for her cousin in her new marriage. The same held true for Tessa, who was now a mother to little Analise.

Was it so wrong to wish for what her cousins had?

She did want a husband who would give her children. She wasn't even asking for love, as Tessa and Adalyn had found, merely a man she could get along with and who treated her with kindness and a bit of respect.

If he existed in Polite Society, he had not been attending *ton* events this Season.

Louisa felt much older than her years. She had hoped by the end of the Season that she would have received an offer or two of marriage and accepted one of them. She doubted any offer would be forthcoming and if it did occur, she would not be accepting it. All she wanted to do now was leave London and lick her wounds.

Since she had been staying with her aunt and uncle, she supposed she would return to the country with them since there was no telling when her father would return to England. Louisa wouldn't mind spending several months in the country because she rarely had an opportunity to do so. As a second son, Sir Edgar Goulding had no country estate and so she and Papa lived in London year-round. Even if her father had a small country property, they never would have gone to visit it because of his work at the War Office.

She hoped Adalyn and Tessa might ask her to come and visit for a few weeks. It would be good to see her cousins away from town and have an opportunity to see what their lives were like in their new homes in the country with their husbands.

She supposed it was almost time to dress for tonight's ball and went to the wardrobe, wondering what gown Tilly had chosen for her to wear this evening.

A knock at the door sounded and she bid them to enter. It was a footman who greeted her, handing her a letter. She thanked him and sat in the chair by the window to read it. Immediately, she recognized Adalyn's handwriting and eagerly broke the seal. This would be the second letter she had received from Adalyn since her cousin's departure from town.

Dearest Louisa,

I hope this finds you well and that you are still enjoying the Season, though your last letter led me to believe otherwise. If that is the case, why don't you come to us here at Cliffside? It doesn't seem as if you have found a suitable husband and I would not want you to rush at the end and accept an offer halfheartedly.

Ev is also eager to see you. In fact, he is the one who suggested that we invite you to Cliffside for an indefinite stay.

Do what you wish. Finish out the Season and then come to us—or have Papa allow you to come to Cliffside as soon as you can. Either way, we will be delighted to host you.

All my love,
Adalyn

Tears brimmed in Louisa's eyes. She would not have to suffer through the rest of this unbearable Season. She hoped Uncle Uxbridge would agree to her leaving town quickly.

Tilly arrived and prepared Louisa for the ball, dressing her in a gown of pale yellow with mint green trimmings. Louisa joined her uncle in the foyer and he complimented her on her appearance as he always did. Her aunt arrived and the three of them went to the waiting carriage.

Inside, Louisa decided to broach the subject and said, "I have received a letter from Adalyn. She conveyed that His Grace has invited me to come and visit them."

She thought if the Uxbridges believed it was a ducal invitation being extended, they would be more amenable to allowing her to go.

As she expected, the couple beamed at her and her uncle said, "Of course, you need to go to them. Adalyn is probably missing you. His Grace is wise enough to know how to keep his wife happy."

"It would mean you missing the tail-end of the Season," her aunt remarked. "Would that be acceptable, Louisa?"

"Yes, I think I have had enough of the company of Polite Society for this year. I have missed Adalyn something terrible. I would love to go to Kent as soon as possible."

"Then we can spend tomorrow packing," her aunt said brightly. "You could leave for Cliffside the day after. Once you have finished your visit with His Grace and Adalyn, you may return to us. By then, I am certain we will be in the country ourselves. In fact, we could leave town and call at Cliffside for you so that we might journey home to Conley Park together. Would that be agreeable?"

Louisa nodded. "Yes, Aunt. That would give me a good three weeks or so with Adalyn. I don't wish to wear out my welcome."

"I will leave the planning to you ladies," her uncle said. "I will let our coachman know, however, that you are to depart the day after tomorrow."

They arrived at their destination and exited the vehicle, joining the receiving line inside the townhouse. For once, Louisa was not impatient waiting in it, knowing it was the last one she would stand in until next spring. She parted from her aunt and uncle, watching Uncle Uxbridge head toward the card room, while her aunt made a beeline for her friends.

Louisa accepted a programme from a footman and joined a group of acquaintances. She had never realized how catty many women of the *ton* could be, another reason she was eager to be back with one or both of her cousins.

A few gentlemen approached her and requested a dance. She agreed to do so with each of them though it still left more than a few empty spots on her dance card. She was afraid she had gained something of a reputation as a bluestocking among the carefree bachelors of the *ton*. None of them ever seemed interested in talking about anything of substance. Especially politics. Louisa knew as much as any member of the House of Lords—probably more so—because of her many conversations with her father and his guests. Instead of talking about the war or other newsworthy items, the eligible men she danced with seemed to have no conversation at all and were surprised when she tried to bring up matters of substance. Because of that, she danced less than other single ladies.

It did not matter. She would be escaping town soon.

Lord Smythe claimed her for a lively country reel and she was out of breath by the time it finished. He was, too, and asked if she would care for a glass of ratafia. Louisa eagerly accepted his offer and they went to a section where the refreshments were. Claiming a glass for each of them, Lord Smythe handed hers over and then said, "Would you care to get a bit of air, Miss Goulding? The ballroom in July grows rather heated and I could stand some fresh air."

"That is a good idea, my lord," and she accompanied him out a set of French doors.

A few other couples strolled along the terrace and they did

the same, walking the length of it as they sipped their drinks. As they turned and made their way back along the same route, Lord Smythe asked if she might wish to sit a moment. Since she was not engaged for the next dance and the evening air felt incredibly refreshing compared to the stifling ballroom, Louisa agreed.

They sat for a brief while in silence, which she did not mind. Making small talk was something she had come to dread and so Lord Smythe's silence was a welcomed relief.

Suddenly, he took her free hand, surprising her. She actually spilled a bit of her ratafia on his sleeve as her glass fell to the ground.

Jerking her hand from his, she apologized, "I must apologize, my lord. I hope I have not ruined your coat."

He shrugged it off. "It is dark material. The stain will not show." He paused and then swallowed hard.

Louisa stilled. She feared what would come out of his mouth next and guessed he was about to offer for her.

"Miss Goulding, I find you to be a lady of good breeding. You come from a good family. I am looking to—"

"My lord, let me stop you. I fear I am not a good match for you and because of that, I hope you will recognize that and merely let us return to the ballroom without further conversation."

He cleared his throat, her message received. Downing the remainder of his ratafia, he set down the glass on the bench. Rising, he offered his arm and she took it. He placed her hand on his sleeve.

"Shall we?" he asked and led her back into the ballroom.

He returned her to where he had approached her before and bowed stiffly.

As he walked away, she hoped his dignity was still intact. She would never breathe a word of the almost proposal and she doubted he would either.

Once the dance concluded, her next partner found her. They had danced at least on four other occasions and yet the man asked the exact same, inane questions every time they were together. She tamped down her exasperation, knowing this was the last time this Season she would be in his company or any other gentleman's, as well.

The ball concluded and she located her aunt. They joined Uncle Uxbridge and headed to their carriage.

"I hope you enjoyed the ball," her aunt commented.

Louisa didn't see the harm in a small, white lie and said, "I certainly did."

They arrived at the townhouse and she found Tilly waiting up for her.

"Tilly, this is the last *ton* event I will attend this Season," she informed the maid. "Please pack for me tomorrow, for we are departing the day after to go and visit my cousin, Her Grace, in Kent."

"Of course, Miss Goulding," the lady's maid replied. "Will you be taking all your clothing or will we return to town?"

"The plan now is for me to visit the duke and duchess for the remainder of the Season and then Lord and Lady Uxbridge will come to Cliffside. I will return with them to Conley Park. So yes, please pack all my belongings for our journey."

"Yes, Miss Goulding."

Louisa climbed into bed, pulling up the bedclothes to her chin and burrowing into the pillow. For the first time in a long time, sleep came easily.

Chapter Four

Cliffside, Kent

LOUISA WATCHED THE passing countryside, the lush green of Kent in full summer bloom. It had been far too long since she had been in the country. She used to go regularly, visiting her cousins, especially when her mother was still alive. Once Mama died, though, when Louisa was fifteen, her father had clung to her. He insisted she run the household. Give him advice. Plan meals for the many occasions when he invited colleagues from the War Office to their townhouse. Gradually, Louisa had been drawn further and further away from her cousins and Polite Society in general.

At least her aunt and uncle had come regularly to town for the Season, bringing Adalyn with them. It was convenient for her cousin to only be a few doors down. Tessa, though, had quit coming to London once her mama passed and her papa grew quite ill. Because of that, it had been years since Louisa had seen Tessa, until recently. At least Tessa had finally been able to come for a Season and gained a husband from it. Spencer was an excellent match for Tessa, just as Everett was a perfect complement to Adalyn.

If only she could be fortunate enough to find a husband as her cousins had. Perhaps one of Adalyn's neighbors might do. Louisa did not have to wed a member of the *ton*. She would be quite happy with a country doctor or gentleman. Titles meant nothing to her. Only finding happiness did.

The carriage slowed a bit and turned down a lane. They must have reached Cliffside. Anticipation filled her. She was eager to see where Adalyn now lived and knew it would be grand since Everett was a duke.

Nothing could have prepared her, though, once the vehicle came to a halt. Tilly, who had been dozing ever since they had stopped and changed horses, now became alert.

"We're here?" the servant asked, glancing out the window.

"We most certainly are," Louisa said, her eyes wide as she took in the grandest house she had ever seen.

A footman opened the door and handed her down. Immediately, Adalyn rushed toward her and the two women embraced.

"Oh, I have been anxiously awaiting your arrival," her cousin said. "I am so glad you came, Louisa. Ev wanted to be here to meet you but he had some business to attend to. He'll join us this afternoon for tea."

"I appreciate your invitation," she said, gazing at the house. "I do believe you now live in a palace!"

"Oh, I cannot wait to show you around Cliffside," Adalyn said. She turned. "Bridget, come help Tilly and the footmen."

Adalyn's maid hurried to meet Tilly and the group of footmen who were busy unloading Louisa's trunks.

"I know it looks as if I have brought everything I own. I almost have. Do not think I am moving in permanently, though."

"I would be happy if you did," Adalyn told her, linking an arm through Louisa's and bringing her inside.

"Your mama suggested that once the Season ends, she and Uncle Uxbridge will come here to Cliffside for me and we will return to Conley Park from here. So I brought everything from London with me that was at their house. Only a few of things remained behind at Papa's townhouse."

"I was going to write to Mama and ask her and Papa to come

to Cliffside so they might see it. But you—and they—will need to stay for a while. You see, I am going to hold a house party."

Adalyn led her up the stairs as she spoke. Immediately, dread filled Louisa.

"Are you doing this because I did not land a husband?" she asked warily.

"No. I am doing this so my friends can see Cliffside and enjoy a respite after a very long Season. Of course, I will invite some eligible bachelors to attend. All hostesses do." Adalyn paused on the landing. "A house party is a wonderful way to get to know people, Louisa. The Season is not. Why, women become betrothed after dancing a handful of times with a gentleman—and they don't even know the first thing about him. A house party, on the other hand, allows people to gather in small groups. True conversations can take place."

"I have never attended one," Louisa admitted. "I have been curious about what goes on at them."

Adalyn tugged and they continued up the stairs. "I didn't think you had. It will be so much fun. Why don't I show you your bedchamber and allow you to freshen up? Then we can have some tea and discuss the guest list and activities. You will have to help me plan everything because you have such a good eye for detail."

They arrived at a lovely bedchamber, far larger than hers in London. Adalyn introduced Mrs. Arthur, the housekeeper, who told Louisa hot water would be up soon. Her trunks began arriving and Bridget offered to assist Tilly with the unpacking. Once the hot water came, Louisa had Tilly remove her gown so she could wash up. The carriage had grown hot and dusty and it felt good to change from her traveling clothes into another gown.

Mrs. Arthur returned and escorted Louisa downstairs to a lovely sitting room done in shades of peach and mint green. Adalyn explained this was her retreat, one of her favorite rooms in the house, as she poured Louisa a cup of tea.

"Naturally, Tessa and Spencer will be invited," her cousin

said, handing over the saucer. "I have already written to them to let them know. Let's talk about activities."

She chuckled. "Since I have never been to a country house party, I haven't the faintest clue what it involves."

"Then it is a good thing I have been to a few in my time," Adalyn joked. "Walking and riding are two activities both the men and women will participate in."

Louisa bit her lip. "I haven't ridden in quite a while. The only time I ever have was visiting you or Tessa in the country and it has been many years since I did that. I have not been on a horse in all that time."

"Then we will definitely get you on one during the next three weeks before our guests arrive. By that time, you should be comfortable in the saddle again."

She laughed nervously. "I don't know if I was ever comfortable in the saddle. Your groom always made certain I had a horse with a good temperament and a tough mouth. Even then, I have never felt at ease atop one."

Adalyn thought a moment and then said, "I believe I know the perfect person to help you. But as to other activities, the men can shoot and ride. We ladies will visit and write our usual letters. As a group, we can also picnic and play lawn games."

"Lawn games? Oh, I will probably be dreadful at those."

Her cousin smiled. "Then the gentlemen present will have to help you."

A queasiness filled her at the thought of Adalyn trying to force a match. "Just because you are happy with Everett does not mean I will find the same."

"There is no reason you shouldn't find a good match, Louisa. Remember, I am good at putting people together," Adalyn reminded her. "I already have a couple of gentlemen in mind. But back to the house party. The evenings will be full of entertainment. Singing and dancing. Card games. Parlor games. I think I will also hold a ball at the end of things. I will open that up to the entire neighborhood. It will allow me to meet our neighbors."

"It sounds as if we will be quite busy."

"Only as busy as you wish to be. I want this time to be relaxing for you. I know the whirl of the Season can exhaust even the most energetic."

Adalyn squeezed Louisa's hand. "Oh, I am so glad you came."

"I will admit I had tired of the activities—and the company—in town. Coming to Cliffside will be the perfect respite."

"You know you are welcome to stay after the house party ends."

"Oh, I think not, Adalyn. You and Ev are newlyweds. You deserve time to yourselves. I will go home with your parents. I believe I will be with them a good year, based upon what Papa has written to me. The conference won't start until late autumn. He believes it will be months of hammering out agreements and trying to settle the map of Europe to all the delegates' satisfaction. That means I will return with your parents to town next spring and start the Season anew. Hopefully, Papa will make his way back to England before it is over."

"I still would rather have you with me than having you go to Conley Park with my parents." Adalyn's eyes sparkled with mischief. "Besides, I have a greater need for you." She beamed. "We are going to have a baby."

"A baby? Oh, Adalyn, that is wonderful news." Louisa hugged her cousin tightly. "When might this little bundle of joy be expected?"

Adalyn's palm touched her belly. "Most likely the middle of next February. I believe I am about eight weeks along now."

"Are you ill as Tessa was in her early months?"

Her cousin laughed. "Not a bit. I know the nausea could possibly come but I am hoping to hold it at bay."

"Everett must be ecstatic."

"Oh, he is. I remember watching him the first time he held Analise. Spencer thrust the babe at Ev and the look of panic on his face was priceless. Ev took to her, though, and I believe he will make for an excellent father."

"You will both be wonderful parents," Louisa said, tamping down the slight bit of jealousy, knowing both Tessa and now Adalyn would have children while she remained a spinster.

Or perhaps Adalyn was correct and this house party might make a difference. The events during the Season were chaotic, with so many in attendance. Conversations were all too brief and usually of no consequence. With a smaller group at a house party, however, the same people would be in contact with one another for many days in a row. She would be able to have time to speak to gentlemen invited at length.

Hope filled Louisa that Adalyn's plan might actually bring about a betrothal. Louisa had heard talk of how many house parties ended with more than one engagement announced. She would anticipate a happy ending but prepare herself in case no offers were extended. Even if no gentleman found her worthy, Louisa hoped to make a friend or two with the females in attendance.

The cousins talked for another hour and then Arthur slipped into the room.

"His Grace has returned, Your Grace. He is waiting in the library for you and Miss Goulding."

"Thank you, Arthur. Please have tea brought at once," Adalyn said.

They left the sitting room and went to the library, an imposing room with books lining three of the four walls from floor to ceiling and a giant ladder that could be used to retrieve those on the highest shelves.

Everett strode toward them, first greeting his wife and then taking Louisa's hands in his.

"It is good to see you again, Louisa." He kissed her cheek. "I hope Addie has told you that you are to stay as long as you wish. Even if it is until next Season." He paused, his eyes gleaming. "Has she shared the good news?"

"She has. Congratulations, Everett."

"I am hoping for a girl," he revealed as they sat. "One with

Addie's azure eyes and honeyed hair. One I can spoil almost as much as her mother."

She thought that unusual, believing a duke would naturally be thinking of an heir. But Louisa saw Everett glance at his wife and realized he truly did want a daughter.

"I just want a healthy child," Adalyn said as her husband took her hand and threaded her fingers with his. "Ev wants at least six children. Hopefully, not all of them will be girls. He does need an heir."

Everett smiled. "An heir will come when the time is right. I am eager to fill Cliffside with the sounds of children squealing and running through the halls."

Louisa had known of Everett's desire for many children and couldn't help but smile. He and Adalyn were such a wonderful match.

"Addie would appreciate having your company," Everett said. "You are as sisters. It would only be right for you to be together at such a happy time."

"I will be available to stay as long as Adalyn wishes," she promised.

Tea arrived and as Adalyn poured out for them, Everett suggested various sandwiches and cakes for Louisa to try.

"Louisa hasn't ridden in a good many years, Ev," Addie said. "During the house party, it is likely people will go out riding every day. She could use someone to help refresh her riding skills and give her confidence on a horse."

A look passed between the couple, something conveyed without words that Louisa couldn't begin to guess at. Everett nodded and smiled pleasantly. He turned back to Louisa.

"I have the perfect person to reacquaint you with horses. Owen is our closest neighbor and will be attending the house party. He is also my oldest friend."

"But I thought he was in the army. With Bonaparte's abdication, has he been granted leave for a short while?"

Everett shook his head. "No. Owen is now the Earl of Danbury. In fact, I am spending all day tomorrow with him. I think I will invite him for dinner so that you might become better acquainted."

Chapter Five

Danfield, Kent

OWEN WAS FINISHING his breakfast when Ev showed up, two men accompanying him.

"Lord Danbury, you have met my steward, Painter," his friend said. "This is his cousin, Mr. White."

"Have a seat," he invited. Looking to his butler, he added, "Coffee all around if you would, Croft."

"Yes, my lord."

As more cups and coffee were fetched, the three guests were seated. Owen had spent several days with Ev and Painter at Cliffside, learning the intricacies of property management since he lacked a steward. Painter had mentioned that his cousin, whom he had grown up with, was currently an assistant steward on a large estate and looking to better his position. Tossing the dice of life, Owen had told Painter to have White put in his notice so he could report to Danfield and be in charge of the entire estate.

Apparently, today was the day that new employment would begin.

"Tell me about yourself, White," he encouraged.

"I lost my parents when I was but three years of age," White began. "I can't say I remember either of them. My aunt and uncle brought me up. George here was only six months older than I was and we were raised as brothers. My uncle's farm was productive and the two of us worked it from the time we were small. My aunt, though, believed an education was important and taught us to read and write and do sums. Later, we took lessons with the local vicar."

WHITE PAUSED TO take a sip of his coffee and continued. "I have worked for two previous employers, my lord, in management positions. The latter was for a viscount in East Essex. While I liked the property, the estate's steward was only eight years my senior—and the viscount's younger brother."

Owen nodded. "So, no chance of advancement."

"Exactly, my lord. I did a majority of the work while the gentleman received the better title and pay."

"I have spoken to His Grace regarding salary terms," he told White and named an annual figure.

White nodded. "That is more than generous, my lord. I promise you that I know my way about an estate. I won't let you down."

"Shall the four of us tour Danfield now?" he suggested. "His Grace and your cousin have already given me a few ideas but I would be interested in what you think could be done with the estate."

"I would be happy to do so," White said.

"Can you and Painter stay, Ev?" Owen asked.

"We would be happy to do so," his friend said, grinning. "In fact, I had planned on it."

They went to the stables and, once horses were saddled, took a tour about the property. He liked that White didn't shy away from difficult questions nor did the new steward hesitate when asked for his opinion. Quite a bit of back and forth occurred between the two stewards, with input from Ev. Owen had discovered by this point that it was best to keep silent and learn as much as he could in these situations.

They remained out and about until mid-afternoon, when they returned to the house. He showed White the room designated as his office and White and Painter remained there to look over the ledgers, with Owen agreeing to meet with White tomorrow morning to discuss the estate's profits and losses at length.

He and Ev retired outside, where they sat in the shade and drank lemonade, which tasted refreshing on this warm summer day.

"I think White will be a wise hire," Ev said. "I thought he would be since I have come to depend upon Painter. The two are very much alike. Knowledgeable. Steady. Willing to try new ideas."

"I am already pleased with White. I will have to thank Painter again for recommending his cousin to me."

"And you can thank *me* by having dinner with us tonight," Ev told him.

"Oh, I don't know. I fear I should study up on the ledgers myself before I meet with White in the morning."

"I won't take no for an answer, Owen." Ev chuckled. "Actually, it's Addie who wouldn't accept no from you."

"She is going to get plenty of my company during the house party," he said cheerfully. "Although I may stay here at Danfield for the duration."

Ev shook his head. "That won't do at all. I know my Addie. She'll want you under our roof the entire time, along with our other guests."

He snorted. "Because she thinks she is going to find me a wife at this house party. No, Ev. I am not ready to settle down. You should know that better than most. You might recall I have a roving eye when it comes to the ladies."

"I seem to remember a good many of them have claimed your attention over the years."

"I plan to keep it that way for some time. Yes, I will go and partake of the Season next year. I will need to take my seat in the

House of Lords and I do want to get to know my fellow peers. As for women? The Season will give me the perfect opportunity to find willing widows I can service." He grinned. "Or bored wives who have provided an heir and now look for more adventure than their husbands can give them."

He placed the glass of lemonade on the table between them. "No, I will enjoy myself for a good five years or more. By then, I should be ready to plant roots and shackle myself to some eager bride and get my heir and, hopefully, a spare."

"I hope you are wrong, Owen. I am not one to meddle in your affairs—"

"But you think Adalyn is?" he interrupted.

Ev laughed. "She might wish to. She will introduce you to any woman you wish to know. Addie is acquainted with simply everyone in Polite Society. It wouldn't hurt for you to listen to her advice regarding a wife."

"As I said, that is several years down the road. For now, I am going to enjoy having a title and no worries about money. I will attend your little house party and be kind to and flirt with all the ladies Adalyn invites. But I have no desire to become betrothed any time soon."

Ev set down his glass and stood. "I will take my leave—but come for dinner tonight. Drinks in the drawing room at half-past six. I insist."

He rose. "Thank Adalyn for the invitation. I will see the two of you this evening."

"Actually, there will be three of us. Addie's cousin, Louisa, has come for a visit," Ev explained.

Dread filled Owen. A scheming Adalyn—and now her cousin conveniently comes to visit?

"Isn't the Season still going?" he asked lightly.

"It is. Louisa had tired of it, though, and Addie longed for a visit from her cousin. The two of them and Tessa are extremely close."

"This cousin is unmarried, I assume."

"She is. And she is a lovely woman. A year younger than Addie and Tessa."

That meant this cousin was a spinster. Owen recalled that Adalyn was five and twenty. So Cousin Louisa was unwed and bored with the Season. Most likely, it meant she was receiving no offers at her advanced age and wished to escape town and the flurry of the end of the Season engagements. As much as he liked both Adalyn and Tessa, Owen was not eager to meet their cousin.

Much less be paired with her by the matchmaking Adalyn.

"I don't know, Ev," he began.

His friend glowered at him. "You will come to dinner because my duchess wants you to do so. You will be nice to Louisa because she is a lovely young woman. For goodness' sake, Owen, I'm not asking you to wed Louisa. Merely come and have dinner with us. Yes, she will be at the house party, along with several other unattached ladies and gentlemen. You should be so fortunate as to have a woman of Louisa's charms be interested in you."

"That's quite a speech, Ev. All right, I will come for dinner this evening. I will even be nice to this spinster cousin. But tell Adalyn in private before I arrive that she is not to push Louisa and me together. My plans are to enjoy life after years at war. And that includes making love to a good number of women for quite an extended time."

Ev looked at him with disgust. "You always have done as you wished, selfish as it might be. I hope you don't realize what a gem Louisa is—and that she has no regard for you. Because she deserves better than you."

Owen's jaw dropped as Ev stormed off.

They had disagreed in the past over things but never really fought before. Seeing Ev leave after such harsh words made Owen's stomach sink.

This is what marriage did to a man. It changed him. Ev was already different from the friend he remembered, thanks to wedding a strong-willed woman. It was apparent Ev thought every man should be married and as besotted with their wives as he was. As Spence was.

He had visited Spence and Tessa for a long weekend a month ago. It had been wonderful reuniting with his old friend and meeting Spence's countess. Spence had welcomed Owen with open arms and Tessa had been friendly and encouraging. Yet the bond between the pair was obvious, just as it was with Ev and Adalyn. They were still his friends—with limits, it seemed.

It made Owen all the more certain that he did not want a wife, especially one that he loved. He didn't want to invest that much of himself in a woman. His motto had always been to enjoy female company when he could before moving on. A wife was the last thing he wanted in his life. Already, so much upheaval had occurred in these last several months. He didn't want or need a woman in his life. Though he might at one point have experienced a bit of jealousy at the closeness Ev had with Adalyn, he could see now it was actually detrimental.

Marriage was the last thing on his mind. He would make that perfectly clear to Adalyn and anyone else who tried to steer him toward matrimony.

Owen would go to dinner at Cliffside tonight and tolerate this cousin. He would do the same with the other females at this silly house party that Adalyn was planning.

He would remain true to himself—and hope the distance between Ev and him would eventually close.

LOUISA DID NOT want to go down to the drawing room. Her sweating palms and roiling belly told her this was a mistake.

Meeting Lord Danbury would be a mistake.

Oh, eventually, she knew she would have to meet him. After all, he was Everett's closest friend and his nearest neighbor. What she didn't want was to meet him with . . . expectations. At least on the part of Adalyn and Everett.

Her cousin had spent most of yesterday singing Lord Danbury's praises. Owen, she called him. That was Adalyn for you. Already on a first-name basis with the man since he had arrived back from war. Louisa didn't begrudge Adalyn for being that way. Her cousin was so open and friendly. And Lord Danbury was Everett's lifelong friend. But she resented Adalyn thinking she could simply match Louisa to this man without even asking her if it was acceptable to her or not.

In this case, it certainly was a resounding no.

She didn't see herself with a military man, one hardened by war. This Owen was also supposedly a bit of a rogue if she read comments that Everett had made correctly. That was two strikes against the man and she was certain to come up with more. If Louisa ever did find a husband, it would be a gentle kind of man. More scholarly and humble. Lord Danbury did not fit this description in the slightest.

Tilly finished dressing Louisa's hair. "There you go, Miss Goulding. What do you think?"

She had asked for something simple yet elegant and her lady's maid had come through. The image in the mirror spoke well of Louisa. It emphasized her swanlike neck, with a few wisps of hair framing her face. Her gown was the palest shade of blue, emphasizing her sapphire eyes. At least she was garbed appropriately. The gown and new hairstyle gave her confidence. She would look this earl in the eyes and then smile politely, letting him know that she had no interest in him at all. He would be one of several gentlemen who attended the upcoming house party. This way, she would claim an acquaintance with him and move on, hoping that others would be more to her liking.

"Thank you, Tilly. It is exactly what I wished for."

Louisa rose and dismissed the maid, pacing the large bedchamber for a few minutes, trying to calm her nerves. She told herself Lord Danbury was not the husband she sought. She would get through this evening and then make her feelings known to

Adalyn. Discreetly, of course. She would never tell her cousin she had already taken a disliking to the man when she had yet to even meet him. But Louisa knew Lord Danbury was not the one for her.

Making her way downstairs, she entered the drawing room and paused.

Lord Danbury had already arrived.

"Louisa!" cried Adalyn. "Come and meet Lord Danbury."

She took a calming breath and moved across the room, feeling the earl's eyes upon her the entire time. She finally looked at him as she arrived.

And almost had the breath knocked from her.

He looked to be an even six feet and was lean yet muscular, based upon the way he filled out his clothes, which lacked in style, looking to be several years old. His hair was a medium brown and his eyes were the color of melted chocolate. He smiled at her, a smile so winning and charming that she found herself tongue-tied.

Lord Danbury had to be the most devastatingly handsome man she had ever seen.

Louisa steeled herself. Her resolve strengthened. This was the kind of man who never gave her a second glance in the ballrooms of London. He had an energy brimming about him, a vitality that fairly hummed. A man this good-looking would want nothing to do with her. Oh, he would be polite because it was what was expected.

But she doubted he would speak two words to her at the house party.

Knowing that, she relaxed. Her years of entertaining her father's guests took over and confidence filled her.

"How do you do, my lord?" she asked, her voice low and modulated.

He took her hand, which she wished was gloved, because his warm fingers sent tingles up and down her spine.

"I am very well, Miss Goulding. Ev and Adalyn have spoken

so fondly of you."

"They would, wouldn't they?" she asked, tugging gently so that he released her hand. She kept her gaze even and added, "They have also said many kind things about you, my lord."

He chuckled. "Kind might be stretching it. Ev knows all my sins. He is simply being tactful in not revealing them to you. And I have been on my best behavior around Adalyn so she doesn't know any better."

"Then you are telling me you are a rogue," she said, not surprised at his candor.

"I will admit to being mischievous as a boy and enjoying the company of females as an adult," he said lightly.

"Owen, quit trying to scare off Louisa," Adalyn admonished. "He is much better behaved usually."

"Or showing his true colors," Louisa said.

Arthur appeared with a tray of drinks and they each took one. Adalyn ushered them to a grouping of chairs and Louisa found herself seated next to Lord Danbury on a small settee. She could feel the heat radiating from him and swallowed, maintaining her poise. It wouldn't do for him to realize his effect on her. She had no plans to be one of his conquests. That is, if he attempted to make her one. She doubted he would.

"Owen was a major in the war," Ev said.

"How did you attain your rank, Lord Danbury?" she asked. "Did you come up the ranks through displaying leadership skills?"

He chuckled. "Sometimes, I think it was because too many officers above me were killed and they had no one else to promote."

His honesty struck a nerve with her but she did her best to ignore it.

"Don't let him fool you. Owen is one of the bravest men I have known. Although he was quite the daredevil while we were growing up."

"You knew each other from boyhood?" Louisa asked politely, already knowing the answer to her question.

"We did. Our older brothers were the same age and good friends. Ev and I came as afterthoughts. Second sons. We bonded over the fact our fathers ignored us and our brothers despised us."

Ev nodded. "That is true. But Owen did more for me. He helped draw me from my shell. He did the same for Spence when we met at school. Owen has always pushed us to be more outgoing and friendly."

She looked at the earl coldly. "Sometimes, a shy person does not wish to be pushed. I know. I am one."

Adalyn frowned. "Louisa can be a bit shy but she is quite the hostess. She has entertained for her father, my uncle, ever since my aunt's death. Uncle works in the War Office."

Lord Danbury cocked his head. "Does he now? Who might your father be?"

"Sir Edgar Goulding," Louisa replied. "You would not know him. He is not really known outside of his colleagues but he has had a hand in many decisions regarding the war. In fact, he has gone ahead of the English delegation to help plan the congress being held at Vienna. It should be called into session very soon."

Arthur announced dinner and the four of them rose. Lord Danbury offered her his arm and she placed her hand upon his sleeve. The contact caused those tingles to race through her again. Louisa had never experienced them and was upset that they now appeared. She fought to maintain control of her emotions as the earl led her into dinner.

Once seated, she contributed little to the conversation. Lord Danbury dominated it in a friendly way, telling stories both of his time at war and growing up at Danfield with Everett as a frequent visitor. She found herself growing resentful by how at ease he was, as if he lived here at Cliffside. She disliked men who were so smooth and comfortable and could see how women easily fell under his charm.

Well, she would not be one of those women.

They adjourned to the library, the men bringing their glasses of port instead of staying in the dining room. Everett poured

Adalyn and her a sherry. Louisa sipped it carefully, wanting to keep her wits about her.

"Louisa used to come visit me at Conley Park," Adalyn said. "As did Tessa before her mother passed and her father grew so ill. We enjoyed riding together but Louisa has not ridden in almost a decade now." She glanced to her husband.

"Yes. We were thinking that it might be a good idea for Louisa to grow comfortable in the saddle again. We'll probably ride daily during the house party," Everett said. "You are the most skilled rider I know, Owen. Would you mind taking her under your wing and help familiarize her with horses again?"

"Just because I ride extremely well does not mean I am a good teacher," Lord Danbury said.

Louisa felt her cheeks heat in embarrassment. "You do not need to concern yourself with it, my lord," she said quickly. "I will get some practice in before the house party starts so that I will not embarrass myself."

She glanced away but could feel his gaze on her. Reluctantly, she turned and met it.

"On the contrary, Miss Goulding, I would be delighted to reintroduce you to riding again. Might we start tomorrow morning?'

"If you insist," she said, sounding churlish and not caring that she did.

Lord Danbury gave her a winning smile. "Then perhaps I could call for you at ten o'clock tomorrow morning?"

"That is awfully late. You have an estate to run, my lord. Shall we say eight o'clock instead? That way, we could ride for an hour and you could still return home at a decent hour."

He nodded thoughtfully. "Then eight o'clock it is."

"I shall meet you at the stables," she told him.

The earl rose. "Since we are getting such an early start, I will bid you all good evening."

"I will walk out with you," Everett said and the pair left together.

Adalyn turned to Louisa, an odd look on her face. Before her cousin could question her, Louisa said, "I think I shall also say goodnight. I will see you in the morning, Adalyn."

She quickly left the library and hurried upstairs to her bedchamber. Tilly helped ready her for bed and Louisa pulled the bedclothes up.

Her heart was still racing. She tried to slow her breathing.

And eliminate Lord Danbury from her thoughts.

It proved impossible.

He was so cocky. So polished and suave. He made her feel as a gawky as a schoolgirl. She dreaded going riding with him tomorrow but knew she had no way to get out of the commitment. Fine. She would ride with him once and then tell Adalyn that her confidence had returned. Because riding with the extremely handsome Lord Danbury was a terrible idea. She feared she would concentrate more on him than her horse and that was never a good thing with an inexperienced rider.

Louisa tossed and turned, finding it hard to get comfortable.

And when she did finally fall asleep, she dreamed of the rogue.

CHAPTER SIX

OWEN WAS DAMNED intrigued by Miss Louisa Goulding.

She hadn't said much at dinner last night but he had felt her presence, nonetheless. When Spence suggested that Owen help her become reacquainted with horses, he had expressed that he didn't have the patience to teach, even though Adalyn had mentioned that her cousin already knew how to ride.

It was the blush that had stained Miss Goulding's cheeks after his comment that made him change his mind. He had thought her pretty before. Not a raving beauty as Adalyn and Tessa were, but a very pretty woman with her white-blond hair and large, sapphire eyes in an elfin face. Her bosom was ample and her bottom nicely rounded. She also smelled of lavender.

Owen couldn't resist that scent. Especially on a pretty woman.

Suddenly, her embarrassment made him want to help her. It was obvious to him that with Miss Goulding being unwed that this house party Adalyn was giving was to help her cousin find a husband. He wondered why she didn't already have one. Physically, she was attractive. The little conversation they'd had let him know she was no simpering miss. If being a competent rider would increase her chances of finding a suitable spouse, he decided it was the least he could do for Ev and Adalyn.

As long as they remembered he was not in the market for a

wife himself.

He remembered to ring for Strunk, who helped him dress, and then Owen went downstairs and informed Croft that he would be breakfasting with his neighbor. He also looked in on Ronald White, his new steward, whom Croft informed him had already eaten and was in his office. Owen informed the steward that they would meet at eleven. That would give him two hours with Miss Goulding and plenty of time to return to examine the ledgers and get White's opinions on them.

In the stables, a groom saddled Galahad for him. The horse had become his favorite in the small stable and he'd taken to riding him regularly. He set out for Cliffside at a trot and arrived a quarter-hour later, handing the mount to a groom.

"I will be taking Miss Goulding out riding after breakfast," he told the man. "Has she ridden since she's been in the country?"

"No, my lord."

"She hasn't been on horseback in a good while. She'll need a horse with a calm temperament."

The groom grinned. "That would be Fancy, my lord. Sweet as the day is long."

"Good. Then have Fancy ready when we return."

"Yes, my lord."

Owen headed to the house, cutting through the kitchens and causing a bit of a stir by doing so. He greeted Cook, who had sneaked sweets to Ev and him when they were boys, and then made for the breakfast room.

"Good morning, Ev," he said brightly as he entered. "Room for another at your table?"

His friend smiled. "You are always welcome, Owen."

As he went to the buffet and began perusing it, he heard Ev say, "Good morning, my love. Louisa."

They greeted Ev and joined Owen at the buffet. Adalyn welcomed him warmly. Miss Goulding's hello was lukewarm at best. He wondered what he had done to make her dislike him because he now felt she certainly did. And here he was, trying to do his part and help her!

The three returned with their plates to the table and footmen brought coffee and tea for them. Owen mentioned his upcoming meeting with White.

"Isn't he Painter's cousin?" asked Adalyn.

"Yes. White was looking for a new position. The timing could not have been more perfect. Already, I am very pleased with him. He has experience at large country estates but this will be his first time to be totally in charge at one."

Trying to be polite, he looked to Miss Goulding so that she could also be included in their conversation.

"It seems as if you have not been in the country in a while, Miss Goulding. Are you enjoying your respite from town?"

She gazed at him evenly. "I grew up in town and have lived there all my life but, yes, I do enjoy time spent in the country. I am grateful Everett and Adalyn invited me to visit a few weeks at Cliffside before I return with my aunt and uncle to Conley Park."

She returned her attention to her plate and Adalyn said, "Louisa came to stay with my parents in London when her father left for Vienna. I am trying to change her mind and have her remain at Cliffside, though."

Adalyn looked intently at Ev, who said, "We aren't revealing this to everyone right away but Addie is with child."

Owen smiled. "My congratulations to you both. Little Analise will have a playmate."

"I am hoping Louisa will be with me until after the baby is born," Adalyn revealed. "Having her here would make me happy."

"And it is all about keeping my Addie happy," proclaimed Ev, who took his wife's hand and laced his fingers through hers.

"Then if you are extending your stay, Miss Goulding, it is imperative that you are comfortable in the saddle," Owen stressed. "It is the easiest way to get about in the country."

They finished their meal and he said, "I see that you already came to breakfast in your riding habit. Shall we go straight to the stables?"

"Of course, my lord."

They bid Ev and Adalyn goodbye and struck out for the stables. He offered her his arm but she waved him off.

"I asked for a horse to be saddled for you when I arrived. The groom knows it has been some time since you have ridden. I specified a gentle mount."

"That was thoughtful of you, my lord."

He stopped in his tracks. "I'd like it if you would call me Owen. It seems silly of you to be so formal, especially since we will see each other frequently during your stay at Cliffside."

"I would prefer to maintain that formality, my lord. I assume you will be attending the house party Adalyn is planning. It would not be appropriate for me to address you informally with all the guests present."

"You could call me Owen until the house party," he suggested.

She appraised him coolly. "I don't think so, my lord."

Miss Goulding continued on and Owen hurried to catch up to her.

"You don't have to be so prickly," he told her.

Her level gaze met his. "You haven't the faintest idea what prickly is, my lord. Don't tempt me to behave that way toward you else you would be stung."

She started up again. He wondered exactly just how prickly this woman could be and decided it was one of the reasons she had yet to wed.

"Are you always so hardheaded, Miss Goulding?" he asked.

"No. My cousins would say I am even-tempered. Mature for my years. Kind to a fault. I don't think of myself as stubborn at all, my lord," she said airily.

He grasped her elbow and felt the racing of electricity at the contact. Swallowing, he said, "Why mature?"

Her lips twitched in amusement. "Besides the fact that I am already on the shelf?"

He fought the urge to kiss her as he forced his eyes from those lips to her eyes. "A woman on the shelf is usually there by her own making."

Anger sparked in her sapphire eyes. "You are blaming the woman because she cannot find a husband? Why not the myriad of bachelors who are rakes—or worse—and pay not the slightest attention to a woman of substance?"

Jerking away, she stormed toward the stables.

She had been hurt. By a rake.

Or worse.

Sympathy filled Owen. Miss Goulding seemed to be a kind person. Except to him. He supposed because she sorted people into categories and he had fallen into the one she labelled *rake*.

It was true. He loved the company of women and worked his way through them at an alarming rate, even when at war. He also planned to move through the women of the *ton*, enjoying himself for several years before settling into marriage. But it bothered him that she knew what he was. That she cared so little to get to know him, despite his friendship with Ev and Adalyn. That she was judging him—and finding him lacking.

He caught up to her as she reached the stables and signaled the groom to bring their horses.

"Miss Goulding, I am sorry you took offense at my remark. I did not mean to indicate that you . . . well, that you . . . did not have a husband because of your age."

"Four and twenty is not so old in my book," she replied. "But Polite Society finds it ancient for a woman who has yet to wed. Frankly, I have enjoyed a large degree of independence, my lord, by not being wed. I act as my father's hostess. I attend several meetings he holds at our house with various members of the War Department and take notes for him and others. I have spent the last several years doing so and find those mature men to be far more interesting than the bachelors that attend *ton* events."

She sniffed. "Try holding a conversation with one of them. They think women can talk about nothing but the weather and bonnets. I tried this Season, I truly did. It was the first that I went to almost every event held. The men introduced to me were less interesting than that tree stump over there. They didn't care a whit about talking of anything of consequence."

Understanding filled him. "Perhaps they were threatened by not only your beauty but your intelligence, Miss Goulding."

She snorted. "Please, my lord, no false flattery. I am no great beauty like my two cousins and many of the women in Polite Society. I never was and never shall be. I do, however, refuse to hide the fact that I know a great deal about a good number of topics and am not afraid to hold opinions of my own. If that makes a man feel threatened, then what need have I of him anyway? Not that I expect to be friends with my husband. Or even be in love with him. I merely want a man who will treat me with kindness and respect and give me the children I desire. It seems as if that is too much to ask."

Before Owen could reply, the groom appeared with their horses. He thanked and dismissed him.

"A horse is sensitive to its rider's mood, Miss Goulding," he said gently. "You are full of fire and brimstone now. I would advise that you take a few breaths and calm yourself before we begin."

Fire flashed in her eyes at being told to do so and then she nodded, seeing the truth of the matter. She did as he suggested, taking three long, deep breaths and expelling them slowly.

"I am quite better, my lord. Thank you."

"That is good. I want to say this, Miss Goulding. I am not judging you in any way. In fact, I can see why you would prefer the company of the men planning and executing England's war strategy than a group of randy bachelors who only commit to marriage when forced to by their nagging mamas or forceful papas. I am sorry we seemed to have gotten off to a bad start. If I did anything to cause this rift, I apologize."

She studied him a long moment and then said, "I still believe you to be a rake, my lord, but somewhere in there is a good man.

Else you wouldn't be such a close friend to Everett. I suppose you were also an excellent officer, as well. I apologize for being waspish with you. I feared that Everett and Adalyn might try to force us together, especially with this upcoming house party. Despite what Adalyn says, I know she is holding it to find me a husband."

"Or me a wife," he countered. "That's what Ev thinks."

The color rose on her cheeks, making her very appealing.

"I had not thought of that. It does make sense, though. Both Everett and Spencer are besotted with my cousins. They would want the same for you, as do Adalyn and Tessa for me."

She laughed. "I am sorry that I have made this all about me. They are conspiring on both our behalves, I daresay."

He grinned. "Then perhaps we should unite, Miss Goulding. It is true that I have no desire to enter a state of matrimony at this point. Why, I never thought to claim a title, much less the estate and the immense wealth that came with it. I already have my hands full as I try to figure out how to become a good landlord and peer. I have decided that a wife can wait until later down the road.

"Perhaps we can stick together during this house party."

"How so?" she asked, her brow furrowed, making her very attractive.

"You can help shepherd away any young lady that might try to make a claim on me, while I will steer away any rogues that show an interest in you. As a man, I will be party to various conversations with those men invited to the house party. I will pass along to you if any of these guests are suitable husband material."

Owen smiled charmingly. "And, of course, I will sing your praises to any that you find interesting."

"Hmm." She considered his proposition. "That might not be such a bad idea, my lord."

"Owen. If we are to conspire together in this endeavor, I would like you to call me Owen."

"Owen," she tried out.

He found he very much liked the way she said his name.

"So, we would protect each other and our interests?" she asked.

"Yes, indeed. I do plan to flirt because that is what I do when women are around. I can't seem to help myself. However, you could tell me who has set their cap for me and help me avoid being found in any kind of compromising position. I, on the other hand, will keep the rogues from you and only encourage those you might have an interest in."

"Your proposal is intriguing, Owen."

"It's bloody smart if you ask me," he quipped. "It could help protect us both. What do you say, Miss Goulding?"

She smiled brilliantly. "I say that you should call me Louisa."

Chapter Seven

LOUISA WATCHED AN appealing smile cross Owen's face. Her heart skipped a beat.

At least they had cleared the air. She had known him to be a rake the moment they met, even if he hadn't participated in Polite Society yet. He was extremely attractive and knew it. Confident. Sophisticated. Comfortable in any situation. Because of his looks, she was certain women had fallen at his feet from the time he had become aware of females. But he knew that she knew what he was—and she would use it to her advantage.

As a man's man, other males would speak openly to Owen. Possibly even confide in him. If he could get to know the house party guests and only steer steadfast, kind men her way, then her qualms about this party might be calmed.

It didn't hurt that he had been frank with her and let her know he wasn't interested in wedding her or any other female Adalyn had invited to Cliffside. That he was willing to work with her spoke well for him. Perhaps they might even form a friendship, as she had with Everett to a large degree and Spencer to a smaller one, simply because she had not been around him as much.

She also wouldn't have to worry about being attracted to him. He had said he would flirt with the other female guests in attendance. Naturally, he would do the same with her. She would take it in stride, knowing exactly who and what he was and knowing he was not one to be considered husband material.

Besides, it might actually be fun to flirt with him.

If she knew how to flirt.

Boldly, she said, "Besides teaching me to ride, would you consider also giving me a few pointers on how to flirt?"

His eyes lit with interest. "You don't know how to flirt?"

"Not a bit," she admitted cheerfully, beginning to relax in his company since he would never be a man she would consider as her future husband. "I made my come-out five years ago but only attended a handful of events that year. It's been the same for subsequent Seasons. Papa had a greater need of me and so I have never experienced all that the other girls did. I think perhaps I should become acquainted with flirting. If you are willing to help me do so, Owen."

He laughed, the sound rich and deep. "I would be happy to give you a few lessons in flirting, Louisa. For now, however, we need to concentrate on riding."

"Very well."

She turned to look at the horse the groom had brought out for her. A bit hesitantly, she reached out a hand and stroked the velvet nose.

"Ah, that's nice."

"A good first move," Owen praised. "Horses are observant creatures. Always looking around at their surroundings. They especially are interested in those who climb upon their backs. Many believe a horse can read a person's mood, which is why I wanted you to calm your anger before you got on Fancy's back."

"Fancy? Is that her name?"

"It is."

"Hello, Fancy," she cooed to the horse, stroking it again. "My, aren't you a lovely thing?"

"Go ahead," he encouraged. "Keep talking to her. Petting her."

Louisa did as he suggested. "I am going to ride you in a few minutes, Fancy. Lord Danbury, who lives on the neighboring estate, will be riding the other horse." She looked to Owen.

"Galahad," he provided.

"This is Galahad," she said, introducing the other mount. "And I am Louisa. My papa and I live in London, which is a great city. He is a very important man and I help him some in his work. Because of that, I haven't ridden in years, not since I used to go to the country and visit my cousins, Adalyn and Tessa."

"Tell her what you like to do. Any kind of conversation to put Fancy at ease," Owen suggested.

Louisa stroked the horse's side. "Well, I am quite fond of fruit tarts. I also enjoy reading and music. I play the pianoforte and sing a bit. Perhaps I will sing to you."

"That's good," he encouraged. "Why don't you sit atop Fancy now. Keep talking to her. Nice and easy."

She nodded and, suddenly, his hands captured her waist. All the air seemed to go out of Louisa as her heart slammed against her ribcage. She grasped the saddle horn and hooked her leg about it, swallowing hard.

"Don't tense your body," Owen said. "You want to always stay relaxed. Horses sense anxiety. When we do start out, we're going to go slowly. You'll want to move with the horse. You need to project an easy air of confidence so that Fancy will also have confidence in you."

"I hope I can remember all of this."

"It will come back to you since you rode as a girl and young lady. The important thing is not to overthink things. Relax and the horse will relax with you. Fancy wants to be safe with you atop her, just as you wish to feel safe while riding her."

He moved to Galahad and swung up into the saddle.

"We're going to walk our horses now. Follow my lead. Hold your reins in both hands. Don't yank back on them. You wouldn't want your head jerked back and neither does Fancy. Gently nudge her with your thigh."

Louisa did as instructed and Fancy began to move. She tried

to calm her beating heart, though she didn't know if it was pounding so because it had been so long since she had been on a horse—or if she was still reacting to Owen touching her as he lifted her onto Fancy's back.

He guided Galahad next to her so they could speak as the horses moved at a leisurely pace.

"Hold your reins firmly in your hands but leave a little slack so you can steer Fancy where you want to go. Remember, you are in charge. She isn't. Never let her get the idea that she is."

"All right," she said, making sure that she breathed in and out slowly while keeping her body relaxed.

They moved first toward the house and then down the lane that led up to the house. Owen let her concentrate on what she was doing but remained by her side. She asked him a few questions and he responded.

"You seem to know what you are doing," he said.

"So far. Picking up the pace might challenge me a bit but I know I need to trot."

"Did you ever have an accident on a horse? Ever fall from one?"

"No. I simply lack recent experience in riding. I would go to visit Adalyn and Tessa in the summers when Mama was alive. We would ride a couple of times a week but there were always other things to do. That meant I was on a horse perhaps eight or ten times at the most until the next year. I always understood the basics but I didn't get to practice my skills once we returned to town."

"Your father does not have stables?"

"Papa is a second son. While he is Sir Edgar, having been knighted for his work for the crown, he makes but a decent wage. We have no mews. No carriage or horses. We hire a hackney cab when we want to go somewhere. In town, Adalyn's parents live only a few doors away and I walk to see her. Living with Lord and Lady Uxbridge this past Season, I rode in their carriage to *ton* events."

"Practice is important in anything, especially when learning to ride. Hopefully, we can go out every day until the house party begins and allow you to gain that valuable experience. Once you return to town, you might see if your uncle will allow you to ride a mount from his stables and keep your skills fresh."

"I will go to the country first with my aunt and uncle. Or at least, that is what I had planned until I learned Adalyn was with child."

"Will you stay with her?"

Louisa shrugged. "She wishes me to remain after the house party. I hate doing so because she and Everett are still newlyweds. I don't want to encroach on their privacy."

He chuckled. "When they want their privacy, they will retreat to their bedchambers."

She sensed her cheeks heating. "Yes, they have already done so."

"Then you should stay. You can find ways to entertain yourself while they do . . . other things." He cleared his throat. "Besides, you might even find a husband at the house party and leave to make a home somewhere for yourself."

"I hadn't really thought of that. Actually, I haven't thought too terribly much about marriage. I suppose you think that's foolish, someone my age not having considered it, but I have always been too busy either running our household or helping Papa with his work." She hesitated.

"Go on," he encouraged.

"I was actually disappointed during this Season. With Papa in Austria, it was the first time I had attended the full slate of events. I went to balls. Routs. Tea parties. The theatre. I just supposed I would find an interesting, kind man and that things would work out between us."

"And that didn't happen. Instead, you found yourself bored."

She nodded. "Frankly, I did. It makes me question if I truly do want to seek a marriage or find something else to do with my life. Papa would be more than happy if I stayed with him."

"But he won't always be here, Louisa. You must look to your future."

"You're right. I truly want children and that certainly means finding a spouse. We'll see what this house party brings."

Louisa could feel his gaze upon her but she kept her eyes focused on the road ahead.

"Shall we try and pick up the pace?" he asked. "If we venture down the main road half a mile, there is an entrance to the meadow. Remaining in a confined space while we trot is a good idea."

"I will bow to your wishes," she told him.

"First, take a moment and scratch Fancy on her neck."

"Why?"

"It is a bit of a reward for her behaving so beautifully."

She did as he requested and sensed the horse's enjoyment. "There, little love. That's nice, isn't it?"

"We'll trot down the main thoroughfare until we reach the gate. Are you comfortable with that?"

"Yes, I believe I am."

"Nudge her again. She's a quiet, steady creature. When I pick up the pace with Galahad, Fancy will follow."

It was as Owen said. When he increased their speed, Fancy joined in. Instead of being afraid, Louisa felt happy. She kept beside Owen until they reached the gate and he dismounted, opening it and having her ride through before he pulled Galahad through and closed the gate before remounting.

"Still feel comfortable trotting?"

"Yes."

They went around the pasture for a few minutes until he said he was going to canter. Dread filled her but she nodded. Again, Galahad began to move faster and Fancy followed suit. This time, though, Louisa made certain to keep her body loose and banished her anxiety. The reward was a feeling of exhilaration as she cantered.

After several minutes, Owen reined in Galahad and she did

the same with Fancy.

"How was that?"

"Marvelous," she exclaimed. "I don't believe I have ever been so comfortable atop a horse."

"Then let's cut across the meadow and return to Cliffside. It will be shorter than returning to the main road."

Louisa nodded and spurred on Fancy. They were moving at a fast clip, not galloping, but making good time.

Then without warning, a deer bolted in front of them, emerging from the nearby wood. The creature almost collided with Fancy, causing Louisa to panic. She jerked on the reins and Fancy stopped abruptly. Because she wasn't ready for such a sudden halt, Louisa found herself off-balance and fell from the saddle, landing on the ground.

"Louisa!" Owen cried, leaping from Galahad and racing toward her.

He knelt beside her, his large hands framing her face. "Are you hurt?"

"I don't think so. Well, my ankle stings a bit."

"Let me see. Which one?"

"The right."

She stretched her legs in front of her and felt a slight twinge, her nose wrinkling. She watched Owen take her right foot in hand. Rotating it slightly, she sucked in a quick breath. His fingers unlaced her boot and he gently removed it from her foot. He held her ankle in both hands, causing a delicious ripple within her. Her breathing was quick and shallow. As he rotated her ankle, she sucked in a quick breath.

His eyes, the color of melted chocolate, focused on her. "It's not broken but you do have a sprain. It will swell some. It needs to be elevated and a cold compress put upon it." He frowned. "I am so sorry, Louisa. Here I had thought our first lesson went so well."

"It did," she assured him. "No one could have predicted a deer darting in front of Fancy, startling both her and me."

"Then . . . you aren't upset? Or frightened to ride again?"

She laughed. "Not in the least. If anything, I felt more comfortable than I ever have on a horse. You have given me a confidence I never had, Owen."

He gazed at her steadily. "You have always possessed it, Louisa. Your perspective has merely changed. You believe in yourself now whereas you didn't before. You're certain you'll be ready to get back on a horse then after this incident?"

"Absolutely," she told him.

"Then we need to get you back to the house and see to your injury, slight as it may be." He glanced up at the horses. "I think it best if I tie Fancy to Galahad and have you ride with me."

She bit her lip. "If you think it best."

Louisa didn't think it was a good idea at all. Already, being this near to him had her heart palpitating and her palms sweating. If only he weren't quite so good-looking.

Owen stood and secured Fancy to his horse and then returned for her. With an ease that surprised her, he lifted her as if she weighed next to nothing and carried her to Galahad.

"Hang on to him while I mount then I'll lift you up."

She did as told and he mounted, reaching down and lifting her into his lap. Oh, this wouldn't do at all. He smelled absolutely divine, a mix of sandalwood soap and a bit of sweat from exerting himself during the ride. The lethal combination was utterly male and had her mouth going dry.

Then he shifted her and his arm went around her waist, drawing her into his chest.

"Lean into me," he said. "I don't want you bouncing about and having your ankle jarred more than necessary."

She tried to use the lessons he had issued when she was atop her horse. Relax. Breathe. Show confidence.

As they returned to Cliffside, Louisa's insides were aflutter. Her body came alive as never before. She dared not speak else she'd stammer like a schoolgirl in the presence of the king.

Once they rode into the yard, a groom met them.

"Bit of a mishap?" he asked worriedly.

"A pesky deer practically collided with Fancy," Owen said. "It jarred Miss Goulding from her saddle. She's slightly twisted her ankle. Rub the horses down and have someone fetch the doctor."

"No!" she cried. "My lord, that is not necessary."

"Are you certain?" he asked, leaning close, his lips almost grazing her ear.

"Quite," she managed to squeak.

"All right. I will trust you in this matter."

Owen swung from the saddle and then lifted her to the ground. Or at least that's where she thought she was going. Instead, he somehow twisted her about and began carrying her.

"Put me down," she hissed as he moved away from the stables.

"Why?"

"I am not truly injured."

"You need to give it a day or so, Louisa, before you try to walk on it. Make sure no tendons were stretched. I will deliver you safely to the house."

He carried her through the kitchens, where the scullery maids tittered, and told Cook that a poultice would be needed, along with some hot water, even instructing Cook what he wished to see in the poultice.

Leaving the kitchens, he asked, "Where is your bedchamber?"

She told him, her face now flaming as he carried her past servants. They passed Arthur and Owen informed the butler of her mishap and asked that the servant find Her Grace and have her come to attend Miss Goulding.

"At once, my lord," Arthur said.

They reached her bedchamber and he carried her inside, placing her gently on the bed.

"Besides the ankle, you are going to be sore tomorrow from all the riding," he reminded.

Louisa groaned. "I had forgotten that part."

Adalyn arrived. "What's this about you being hurt?" she

asked as she rushed into the room.

Quickly, Owen explained what had happened, assuring Adalyn that Louisa was fine. Then the hot water and poultice arrived, courtesy of Mrs. Arthur, who said she would take over the ministrations. Still, Owen stayed, even supervising the housekeeper on what to do.

"I will be back to see you in the morning, Louisa," Owen promised. "I'll see myself out, Adalyn."

He left with Mrs. Arthur.

As the door closed, Adalyn said with a gleam in her eye, "I see you are now on a first-name basis with Owen."

CHAPTER EIGHT

OWEN LEANED BACK in his chair, deciding it was time to make his way over to see Louisa. He had deliberately put off going until now, not wanting to appear keen on seeing her.

But he was eager. Probably too eager, which was why he had delayed going to Cliffside.

He had spent the morning out on Danfield, along with his new steward, and they had met with a small group of tenants who were leaders on the estate. They discussed the upcoming harvest and also made a few plans for once the harvest had been completed. Owen had then returned to his study, sitting for a good hour, doing absolutely nothing.

No, that wasn't exactly true. He had been thinking.

Of Louisa.

He could not understand why thoughts of her kept occurring. Yes, she was uncommonly pretty. Yes, she was interesting. Intelligent. A bit fiery, flashes of her temper coming out despite her reserved nature. He shouldn't be enamored with her.

But he was.

That spelled danger for him. First of all, she was Adalyn's and Tessa's cousin and he would do nothing to alienate his friends' wives. Even if he had numerous thoughts of kissing Louisa. No, Miss Louisa Goulding was not to be dallied with. If she were anyone else, he would consider a brief affair with her. Because of her relationship with his fellow Second Sons, however—and the fact that despite her age, Louisa still had to be a virgin—it definitely put her off-limits.

But he still yearned to kiss her all the same.

Owen shook his head, trying to clear such thoughts from his mind. He liked Louisa and that was it. Period. He had never been friends with a woman before, though he suspected both Adalyn and Tessa would claim that honor in the future. He would behave toward Louisa as he did those two. No untoward behavior. He would be the perfect gentleman with her. Her friend. He would discern whether any of the male houseguests were worthy of her and encourage their suit of her.

If he deemed them worthy.

The problem was that Owen already knew he wouldn't like any of them.

Because he wanted her for himself.

This was madness. He needed to live up to his end of their bargain. He would keep his lips to himself. His hands to himself. His wicked thoughts to himself. He would be an ideal gentleman and help Louisa find a spouse.

Even if it killed him in the process.

He tossed the paper he had been holding back onto the desk, not having bothered to examine it. He would leave now for Cliffside and make a short visit to Louisa in order to see how her ankle fared. They could spend a bit of time together and, by then, it would be teatime. He could either stay at Adalyn's urging or make some excuse and leave. He would see how he felt and how his time with Louisa went before making a decision.

He went to the stables and had Galahad readied for him and rode to Cliffside. On his way there, Owen counted his blessings. He was a second son who had never assumed he would receive anything from his father, much less the title and Danfield. In an odd twist of fate, both Ev and Spence had also achieved the same status. He knew he was fortunate, first not having been killed in battle and second, receiving all that he now possessed.

A restlessness filled him and he wondered if it truly was time to find an anchor and settle down into his new responsibilities fully as Ev and Spence had done. His friends were good men and Owen was lucky that Ev lived next door to him and Spence was only a few hours' ride away. They would see each other frequently over the years—and that would include their wives and children.

Again, Owen thought of how much in love Ev and Spence were with their wives and if there might actually be something to that. Oh, he didn't truly believe in love or that it was for him but he saw the stability and happiness that Adalyn and Tessa had brought into his friends' lives and, for a moment, felt envious. Perhaps he did need a wife, one that he could share things with. Owen didn't know if he had it in him to be faithful to one woman for the rest of his life but the prospect was actually interesting for the first time.

If that was the case, he could get a preview at this house party and see what a small handful of women in the *ton* were like. If he enjoyed their company during this house party, it might bode well for next Season and him actually looking and finding his countess. He would have to go beyond physical beauty, though. If he was going to try and make a true go of things, unlike his parents had, and truly share things with a wife, he would need to find someone both intelligent and interesting. Owen bored quickly and he would need someone who challenged him, keeping him on his toes.

Someone like Louisa Goulding.

No, he would not consider her. If they did wed and he found himself bored, looking to other women and leading separate lives as most couples in the *ton* did, it would definitely cause a rift between him and his close friends. Best to help Louisa find a husband and for Owen to look for a wife somewhere else.

He arrived at the Cliffside stables and handed off Galahad to a groom before making his way to the main house. As usual, he cut through the kitchens and spent a moment visiting with Cook.

"How is Miss Goulding?" he asked. "Have you been sending invalid food to her?"

Cook shook her head. "No, my lord. Miss Goulding has not wanted any special treatment, other than taking her dinner on a tray in her room last night in order to keep her ankle elevated."

"Well, I suppose that is good news."

Owen departed the kitchens and passed Mrs. Arthur. He greeted the housekeeper and asked, "Where might I find Miss Goulding?"

"She is in the library, my lord."

"Thank you," he replied, making his way directly there.

Entering the room, he spied her on a settee, engrossed in a book she held in her lap. Owen took the opportunity to study her for a moment. The white-blond hair was pulled away from her face, settled in a simple chignon, allowing a good glimpse of her elfin face. He watched a smile play about her lips, figuring that some passage amused her.

Then she chuckled softly and bit that full, bottom lip, causing a rush of desire to flood him.

He cleared his throat and made his way toward her, tamping down the deep yearning within him.

A genuine smile lit her face. Louisa was a woman who would never play games or make a pretense of her emotions. She deserved a good man. The love of a good man.

Owen knew he could never be that man.

"How is the invalid?" he asked, smiling down at her.

Her brows arched. "I am not an invalid. I told you yesterday it wasn't even a true sprain. Just a few twinges of discomfort."

"I'll be the judge of that," he said, boldly raising her legs and sitting on the settee before lowering her legs into his lap. Glancing at her, he saw her face flood with color and bit back a grin.

"Isn't this a bit too . . . intimate?" she asked. "Even for friends?"

"Concerned friends want to make certain you are absolutely

fine, especially since you refused having the doctor come and call," he told her.

Owen raised the hem of her gown and forced his gaze from her face to the ankle in question. Gently, he probed it with his fingers, made easier because she wore no slippers.

"I don't see any swelling," he noted, his gaze returning to hers—even as his fingers remained on her ankle.

The color was high on her cheeks as she said, "It was only slightly swollen yesterday and only for a very short while. The poultice and then cold compresses made a difference. I kept to my bedchamber and made certain it stayed elevated. I even dined in my room last night. I did the same this morning for breakfast, requesting a tray, but I knew I must get up and move on it some," she told him. "That is why I came downstairs to the library."

"You walked all the way?" he asked sharply, wishing he had been here to carry her.

"I did," she proclaimed, satisfaction in her voice. "I will practice a little more on it today and then by tomorrow, I will be fine. In fact, I am going to resume riding tomorrow. On Fancy. I think she and I suit each other quite well."

"What time do you wish to ride tomorrow?"

Louisa shook her head and said, "No, Owen, you do not need to come. I can take a groom out with me."

"Nonsense," he said, stroking her ankle lightly, enjoying the intimacy of the gesture. "I had told you I would come daily to ride with you. I intend to keep that promise."

Stubbornness set in both her mouth and chin. "You have far too much to do, Owen. I know that you are like Everett and Spencer, second sons, and not trained to the roles you now hold. It hasn't been that long since your brother passed and I know you must concentrate on your estate and tenants, not squiring me about."

Stroking her ankle, he said, "That is why I hired Painter's cousin, Ronald White, as my steward. I met with him at length both yesterday and today. In fact, today we were out on the estate all morning, discussing the autumn harvest and beyond. You seem to forget, Louisa, that I was not only a soldier—but an officer—in His Majesty's army. I am perfectly capable of handling several things in a single day, especially since it no longer involves being shot at on a regular basis."

She chuckled at his words and a frisson of desire rippled through him.

By God, he still wanted to kiss her.

"Oh, all right," she said. "We can ride for an hour each day. By the time the house party begins, I will be more comfortable in the saddle than ever before. On another note," she added, "I did ask for Adalyn to share a list of the guests she has invited with us. I thought you and I could become familiar with their names. Perhaps Adalyn and Tessa could tell us a little bit about each of the guests before they arrive. Tessa and Spencer, along with Analise, are coming a few days before the house party begins so that we can all have a nice visit before the place is flooded with people."

"That's an excellent idea. Since we don't have this list now, perhaps we could do something else. Something sedentary. Perhaps you could read to me from your book."

"Actually, I am a bit tired of reading. I spent most of yesterday afternoon and evening doing so and the same today. Might I suggest we play a game of chess instead?"

"You play chess? I know Adalyn mentioned wanting to learn how and I told her I would help her do so."

Louisa laughed aloud. "Adalyn is always full of ideas such as that but she does not have the patience. Chess is a complicated game and while Adalyn is quite bright, she is not one to stare at the playing pieces and map out the strategy necessary for victory."

"And you are?" he asked, almost seductively.

Owen couldn't help it.

Louisa laughed heartily. "Why, Owen, I do believe you are flirting with me," she declared. "That reminds me that you were going to help me learn how to flirt."

Teaching this woman to flirt was the last thing he wanted to do. If he did, she would use the lessons well. For some reason, Owen did not want her flirting with anyone but him.

"Let's save that for another time," he suggested. "I haven't played chess in a good while and would like to do so. As long as you don't mind being severely trounced, that is. I'll tell you now, Louisa, I won't go easy on you."

Her brows arched again. "You think you will actually beat me?" A devilish smile appeared and she added, "Bring forth your best effort, Lord Danforth."

"You seem quite sure of yourself," he said.

"Oh, I am. I daresay I have played more matches of chess than you have. I know it is not a typical woman's game but, then again, I am not your typical woman."

No, you aren't, Owen thought to himself.

He raised her legs and slipped from under them, freeing himself in order to cross the room. Retrieving the chessboard from the table where it usually sat, he returned with it.

"Where should we put it?" she asked, looking about.

"Hold it," he ordered, handing her the board. Returning to the end of the settee, he lifted her legs again and settled them into his lap. "Put the board in your lap. We can both reach it if it is rests there and you won't have to turn awkwardly since it is right in front of you."

Color bloomed on her cheeks again, making her practically irresistible. Owen decided that he would kiss her. Just once. Perhaps when he was teaching her a bit about flirting. In fact, he might need to teach her something about kissing, as well. And whom not to kiss. There were plenty of rogues out there who might take advantage of her. At least they wouldn't on his watch.

She held the chessboard high and wriggled a bit, settling herself, which made his heart pound, wishing she sat in his lap and that wriggling, rounded bottom –

"Owen?"

"Hmm?" he asked, glancing up.

"I asked if you would care to go first."

He smiled. "No, ladies first."

"But when I win, you will say it is because I was allowed the opening move."

He chuckled. "You are almost as cocky as I am, Louisa."

Mischief filled her eyes. "Is that a good thing?"

"We shall see. Go ahead. You may start."

She lifted her piece and did so.

"Who do you play chess with?" he asked as he answered her move.

"Practically every man from the War Department that comes to our townhouse." She moved another piece.

"Why do they come to see your father at home? I assume he has an office provided to him." Owen moved a second time.

"Oh, he does. Papa is very conscious about spies, however. More than one was planted in the offices during the war. While Papa likes to believe the best of everyone, he is very hesitant to speak of sensitive information. Oftentimes, he would hold meetings at our home or even meet one-on-one with various colleagues, wanting to ensure privacy. At any given time, our house would be filled with workers from the War Office, busy completing reports, waiting to discuss strategies, or assembling in order to hear dispatches."

She considered the board before moving another piece.

"Because of that, I wound up entertaining all sorts of gentlemen while they waited to meet with Papa or if they had arrived for one meeting or another. Sometimes, several meetings would be held and workers and diplomats would remain in order to wait for the next one. I would feed them. Give them tea. Listen to them. Talk with them. And yes, even play chess with them sometimes."

Louisa smiled. "So you see, I have quite a lot of experience at chess, challenging some of the best players in England."

He paused to study the board before making another move—

and caught a smile which she quickly hid. Owen studied the board, trying to see what he might have done wrong and could find nothing amiss with his move.

Yet eleven moves later, she had not only checked him, but she had uttered, "Checkmate." Not in a gloating manner.

But she did have a smile on her face when she claimed victory.

"I suppose you will want a rematch," she said. "Most men do when they lose to me the first time."

"How did you know you would win? Or rather, when?"

She told him and he shook his head. "I don't see how you knew that early."

"You were concentrating more on our conversation than the playing board, Owen. Chess really requires a player's full attention."

"You were speaking with me and didn't seem to have any trouble at all in winning," he pointed out.

"I was listening to you, I'll admit, but I also was thinking ahead. Papa taught me to play chess at a young age and his lasting words were to always think in advance. Two moves. Five. Ten or more. I try to play out various scenarios in my head. If Owen moves his knight, how might I counter the move? If he chooses his pawn instead, what should I do?"

Louisa shrugged. "I can see it clearly in my head. Actually, I prefer not conversing when I play."

He began returning the pieces to their starting points. "Then we shall go at it again. No discussion allowed this time."

She brightened. "Very well. I haven't played since Papa left for Vienna so I'm happy to do so again."

Owen liked the not talking part because it allowed him to watch Louisa as she focused on the board, her brow sometimes furrowed as she concentrated. She was growing prettier by the minute. He could understand in part now why she hadn't wed. All the randy bachelors of the *ton* would not have taken the time to get to know her. Louisa Goulding had depths to be mined and most men, even those looking for a bride, would not have taken the time to unravel the layers of this remarkable woman.

He finally quit looking at her so much and began concentrating on his own game. He had been the chess champion of his school three years running and even played on a team at university. Winning came handily to him. Yes, he usually did what Louisa did and mapped out several moves in advance.

She, however, did it far better than he.

The match lasted close to an hour but she took the game in the end.

"Checkmate," she announced, giving him a sympathetic smile.

By now, Ev and Adalyn had slipped into the room. Owen had been aware of their presence but did not attribute that to his second loss. Instead, he knew it was because Louisa was the superior player.

"You have a fine mind, Louisa," he praised.

"I had thought you could teach me chess, Owen," Adalyn said. "Seeing you lose makes me reconsider that."

Ev chuckled. "You would not like it, my love." He brought her hand to his lips and kissed it. "There is not enough activity for you. People stare at the board for minutes at a time before they make a move."

Adalyn snorted. "Then it definitely is not for me. Are you two finished? If so, it is almost teatime. Owen, would you care to stay for tea?"

"I would be delighted," he told her, happy to stay. "Will we take it in the drawing room?"

"It is such a pleasant day. I wish we could do so outside," Louisa said. "I have been cooped up all day and would appreciate some fresh air."

"I'll let Arthur know," Ev said, rising and bringing his wife to her feet with him. "We shall see you outside on the terrace."

The couple left and Owen slipped from under Louisa's legs and lifted the chessboard from her lap, returning it to its former place.

She swung her legs to the ground and said, "If you will help me to stand, I am a bit stiff after sitting for so long."

"That won't be necessary," he told her, slipping his arms about her and scooping her into them.

"Owen! Please, put me down," Louisa protested. "I can walk to tea. It would be good to test out my ankle."

Reluctantly, he set her on her feet but kept one arm about her waist. Their bodies were close. The scent of lavender hung in the air, tempting him.

Temptation won—and he lowered his mouth to hers.

CHAPTER NINE

LOUISA SAW THE look in Owen's eyes—and knew he was going to kiss her. She should have stopped him. He wasn't for her. She surely wasn't for him, rake that he was.

And yet, curiosity won out.

She quickly inhaled as his lips touched hers, brushing them ever so slowly, hypnotizing her, enthralling her, heating her blood. One hand came up and cradled her face tenderly, the other possessively curled around her, drawing her to him until her breasts brushed against his chest.

She had been kissed twice before and wondered how Owen would kiss her. This was the only reason she let him do so. She wanted to see if his might be different than the other times. Part of her wanted it to be no better than the other two so that she might stop thinking about him constantly.

The other part wanted his kiss to be wild and wicked and wonderful.

His thumb stroked her cheek as he nibbled on her bottom lip. The gesture caused sparks to shoot through her. She gasped and heard him chuckle. Slowly, he coaxed her mouth open and she opened for him, knowing he wanted to use his tongue. That's what had occurred with her other two kisses. One had been fairly pleasant. The other had been revolting and Louisa had forcefully kneed the man in his groin, a move she had taught to both Tessa and Adalyn.

No kneeing would be necessary this time.

Owen's tongue swept inside her mouth, stroking hers sensually. A delicious chill raced along her spine and she made a noise she had never heard herself utter before. She could feel his mouth smiling against hers as he pulled her closer, crushing her to him. His hand moved from her cheek to her nape, cradling it possessively, his thumb moving up and down it, bringing delicious tingles. Suddenly, the place between her legs sprang to life, throbbing strongly. She wanted to press it against him and thought that to be horribly wicked. In fact, she wanted him to touch it. The thought of his hand there made her face flame.

His fingers moved up into her hair and he tugged, pulling her head back, deepening the kiss. She moaned. He groaned. Again, he brought her even closer. Louisa felt she was practically inside his coat. She couldn't possibly get any closer.

Unless there were no clothes between them and bare skin touched bare skin.

That thought caused her breath to hitch.

Owen broke the kiss, his lips moving to her throat, licking where her pulse pounded. She whimpered, clinging to him.

What was she doing?

Louisa pushed him back, trying to create some distance between them.

Her lips throbbed as much as the place between her legs. She saw those gorgeous chocolate eyes hot with desire.

For her.

She had never been confident in her appearance. While she thought her image pleasantly pleasing when she looked into the mirror, she knew she was no great beauty as Tessa and Adalyn were. Yet knowing this handsome earl desired her made Louisa feel empowered.

Swallowing hard, she again pushed against him. He didn't budge.

"I thought we were to be friends," she accused quietly.

"I thought so, too," he said, looking a bit sheepish. "I don't know, Louisa."

"Well, I do. You have admitted to me that you are a rogue. I still feel you fairly honorable but you cannot go around kissing me like that."

He smiled lazily at her. "It was nice, though, wasn't it?"

"It was," she said begrudgingly. "But you didn't mean it. You aren't interested in me. You know I want a husband. I am not one to play games, Owen. We shouldn't be kissing."

"Have you been kissed before?" he asked suddenly, throwing her off-guard.

"Yes. Why?"

"I just wondered. How did my kiss compare to the other? Or others?"

"It was . . . better than the other two. One I fairly enjoyed. One, I did not."

"But mine?"

She shook her head, losing the battle to hide her smile. "Oh, it was very good, Owen, but you already knew that, didn't you?"

A smug look crossed his face. "It was good. Very good." He paused. "I would like to kiss you again, Louisa."

"No," she said firmly. "You may flirt with me. Even teach me something about flirting back. But there is to be no more kissing. We cannot stay friends and do so."

"You would rather be friends than kiss me?" he asked, his gaze dropping to her mouth.

More than anything, she would like to kiss him again. Repeatedly. But the scoundrel didn't need to know that.

"Yes. Definitely friends. You are close to Spencer and Everett. I am close to my cousins. It would be too awkward being around one another if we continued . . . doing . . . well, kissing. Besides, I am looking for a husband. Not a kisser."

"A husband should be a good kisser," Owen pointed out matter-of-factly.

She arched one eyebrow. "While I would prefer that he be skilled in that area, it is not one of my requirements."

"It should be," he told her. "Kissing is important in a marriage."

She sniffed. "You know nothing about marriage," she accused.

"I see how Ev and Adalyn are. How Spence and Tessa behave. They seem to think kissing is quite important. I know—because I catch them at it all the time."

"They are also in love," she said, a bit wistfully. "I am not looking for love, Owen. I am looking for a good man who will be a good father."

He frowned. "You deserve to find love as much as your cousins, Louisa."

"What I deserve is a chance to live my own life," she told him. "For too long, I have helped Papa live his. I am ready to be on my own. Run my own household. I know what marriage in the *ton* consists of, Owen. It is not what my cousins have found with their remarkable husbands. They are definitely exceptions to the rule."

His frown deepened. "Then you won't care if your husband has a mistress? Or takes lovers?"

Louisa shrugged, feigning indifference. "That is the way of Polite Society. As long as he practices discretion, I won't complain. If he provides for me and the children—and especially if he spends time with our children—then I won't begrudge him finding someone else. If that's what makes him happy."

His hands tightened on her waist. "Do you hold yourself in such little regard, Louisa? You deserve more than a husband with a roving eye."

"I am four and twenty, Owen. I cannot make too many demands or I won't find a husband at all. I have already just gone through a very unsuccessful Season and I'm not getting any younger. I can't be as choosy as fresh young girls making their come-outs."

She ignored how it felt to have his hands on her and pleaded with him. "Please, let us go outside. Adalyn and Everett will be wondering where we are."

Owen swept her off her feet. "No arguments. If we are to get there quickly, you will allow me to carry you."

Louisa merely nodded, looping her arms about his neck, inhaling the sandalwood soap clinging to his skin.

They stepped out into the sunshine of the late July afternoon and she saw the teacart already there. Adalyn and Everett were seated.

"There you are," her cousin said. "Let me pour a cup of tea for you. What took you so long?"

"Louisa thought she could walk the entire way here, stairs and all. It was taking forever and so I finally scooped her up and brought her outside," Owen lied smoothly.

"Is your ankle troubling you that much?" Everett asked, looking concerned.

"I am afraid I was babying it too much," she said. "I will practice putting more weight on it after tea. It really doesn't hurt at all and there is no swelling today. I will be right as rain tomorrow."

"In fact, Louisa wants to ride again tomorrow," Owen interjected. "We are going to do so every morning at eight o'clock. That way, I will have the bulk of the day to do what needs to be done on my estate and she will be free to help Adalyn in planning the house party."

His announcement was a surprise to her but she doubted she would be able to get rid of him. Louisa knew she did need practice in riding in order to feel comfortable. If Owen was willing to take her out for an hour each morning, that would be pleasant. She could then send him on his way and not have to worry about him the rest of the day. She would put him out of her mind.

Or so she told herself.

OWEN ENTERED THE Cliffside breakfast room. His habit of the last week had been to start his day with Ev, Adalyn, and Louisa at breakfast and then take Louisa riding. Nothing untoward had occurred between them since he had kissed her. If anything, Owen had bent over backward to show absolutely everything was right between them.

When it was far from the truth.

Somehow, Louisa had gotten under his skin. He didn't understand it. He thought of her at odd moments, wondering if she would enjoy the roasted carrots Cook put on his table or how she might approach a particularly prickly tenant. He would be reading at night and pause, wishing he could discuss a passage with her. In bed, he would close his eyes and see her image, causing him to lose countless hours of sleep.

He greeted Adalyn, the only one present, and asked where the others were as he filled his plate with dishes from the sideboard.

"They both have already come and gone," she informed him as she looked at Arthur and nodded brusquely.

Owen watched the butler signal the two footmen and all three men left the breakfast room. He seated himself on Adalyn's right.

"You must want to scold me since you've dismissed the servants but for the life of me, I cannot fathom what I have done to land on your bad side."

She studied him a moment and then said, "Have you done something I would be displeased with?"

"On the contrary, I have behaved like a perfect gentleman in recent days. Exemplary behavior is not my strong suit. I suppose I am settling into the earldom."

"And what about Louisa?"

He frowned. "What about her? Is there something wrong with her? What has she said?" He realized his words sounded a bit too eager and added, "I hope she still wants to ride today else I would have stayed at Danfield."

"Do you have feelings for her?"

"What? What did she say?" He groaned. "Don't tell me she

told you about the kissing."

Adalyn gasped. "You *kissed* her?"

"You didn't know?"

"I did not." She glared at him. "How could you do that, Owen? Ev has already told me how you plan to cut a swath through the women of the *ton* next Season. That is your business and I will not lecture you on it. But Louisa is my cousin and dearest friend. I will not have you dallying with her, do you hear me?"

He raked both hands through his hair. "I didn't mean to. That is, I didn't set out to dally with her, Adalyn. I know Louisa is beloved by you and I wouldn't hurt her for the world. Not simply because of her but because I value my friendship with Ev and you."

She gazed at him steadily. "Then why did you do it? Kiss her."

"Because I couldn't help myself," he admitted.

She sniffed. "Tell me everything, Owen."

He pushed away his plate and sat back in his chair. "It happened over a week ago. That is all I am going to say. I am not one to kiss and tell. I know other men enjoy giving blow-by-blow accounts of their conquests, often exaggerating the incidents, but that has always left a bad taste in my mouth. Suffice it to say that I kissed Louisa. I succumbed to temptation. She is a very beautiful woman. And I apologized. We talked about things and we decided to remain friends. In fact, I am going to help her during the house party. I will get to know the gentlemen you have invited and if I believe any of them worthy of Louisa, I will encourage them to pursue her. But they damned well better be honorable men. Else I will make certain she is protected from any scoundrels."

"Hmm."

Owen frowned. "What?"

Adalyn shrugged. "You sound quite vehement."

"Well, I am taking this seriously. I like Louisa. Quite a bit. She has lived in her father's shadow far too long. It is time she stepped from it and lived her own life with a man who cares about her."

"You like her."

"Yes."

"And you kissed her."

He waved a hand. "That is all behind us. We are happy in one another's company now. We trust one another. She's come a long way in the past week as far as riding is concerned. Louisa will have no problems at all when the house party commences. We do, however, want access to your guest list. She wants you and Tessa to sit with us and discuss those who have been invited so we know what we are getting into."

Adalyn nodded. "I am happy to share the list with the both of you. Tessa will know several of the guests upon it. Once she and Spencer arrive at Cliffside, we will be more than happy to speak to the both of you." She paused. "Have you changed your mind, Owen? Might you look for a wife while Louisa seeks a husband?"

A hot feeling washed through him. No, it couldn't be jealousy. But thinking of someone else kissing Louisa bothered him a great deal. Owen knew if a suitable spouse attended the house party, Louisa would need to kiss the man.

And that didn't sit well with him. At all.

He rose. "If you will excuse me, Adalyn, I need to find Louisa and go for our morning ride."

"She is already at the stables."

"Then I will see you later," Owen said curtly and left the breakfast room.

He wanted to think it was none of Adalyn's business if he had kissed Louisa but he knew how much she loved her cousin. It was interesting, though, that Louisa hadn't shared with Adalyn that the two of them had kissed. He wondered why Louisa had withheld that information and then decided that it might have embarrassed her to admit it, especially since nothing would come of it.

Owen would refrain from thinking about those kisses. Today was about riding.

And flirting.

He had put off Louisa long enough. It was time she learned to flirt a bit before the houseguests arrived at Cliffside.

CHAPTER TEN

LOUISA HAD NOT slept well and got up early, pacing about her bedchamber. She hadn't bothered ringing for Tilly. Instead, she had dressed in her riding habit on her own and plaited her hair in a single braid before heading downstairs to breakfast.

Everett had been finishing his meal, saying that he was expecting his solicitor soon and they would be closeted for most of the day. She wished him well with his business and finished her tea and toast just as Adalyn arrived. She told her cousin she was going down to the stables to help curry Fancy and to tell Owen to meet her there.

Stopping in the kitchens, she snagged an apple for her horse. She had begun to think of Fancy as hers. When it was time to leave Cliffside, Louisa would be sad to leave the horse behind. At least she had been offered an extended invitation, which she was still considering. While she was thrilled of the possibility of spending the next several months with Adalyn as she increased, Louisa didn't know if she should stay.

Because of Owen.

He had not kissed her during the past week, for which she waffled between being terribly grateful and horribly annoyed. He had respected the boundaries she had set and kept his lips and hands to himself, taking her out every day for a ride and a pleasant bit of conversation. While she liked being friends with him, especially because he was quick-witted and fun to be around, she had constant thoughts of his kiss in her head. They had begun to dominate her every waking thought.

It wouldn't do.

Owen was not meant for her. She sensed the wildness in him. The sensuality. He would have a fine time moving through Polite Society, sampling the wares of willing women, before eventually settling down.

That was not the kind of husband she wanted. Louisa needed a gentle soul who would be patient at her lack of experience in the bedroom. One who would enjoy being around their children. If he did stray from his marital vows after giving her a few children, it would cut her to the quick. She expected it, though. Most men of the *ton* did so.

Especially men such as Owen.

He would seek out worldly widows and bored wives and give them pleasurable experiences. He would have to teach nothing to these women. Unlike her, who didn't even know how to flirt. She had not brought up the flirting lessons since their kiss because she didn't want to practice the art of flirtation on him or with him. Thank goodness he seemed to have forgotten all about the promised lessons.

Arriving at the stables, she asked a groom for a curry comb and went to Fancy's stall. The horse nickered and came toward Louisa.

"You know I have something for you, my sweet girl, don't you?" she asked, presenting the apple in her palm to the horse.

Fancy took it daintily, her lips grazing Louisa's palm in a tickling fashion, and the horse ate her treat.

"There, my wonderful girl. That's right." She stroked the velvet nose. "Apples are good for you. So is brushing."

Louisa had one of the grooms show her how to curry Fancy a few days ago. She now entered the stall and began to move the comb in a circular motion. The horse chuffed, making her smile. She continued, softly humming, her thoughts only on the steadying motion and nothing else.

"Someone has been hanging about the stables," a familiar voice said.

Louisa leaned around and saw Owen standing in front of the stall, wondering how long he had been watching her.

"I had one of the grooms show me what to do the other day. I find it rather soothing to curry Fancy. Mama used to brush my hair for me when I was small. It was calming. Just as this is."

A look crossed his face. One she couldn't read.

"Are you at a stopping point?"

"I can stop at any time," she assured him.

"I'll fetch a groom to saddle Fancy."

He left and Louisa wrapped her arms about the horse's neck, giving her a kiss before exiting the stall. She returned outside and found Owen waiting for her.

"Where would you like to ride today?" she asked.

"How about Danfield? We have been all over Cliffside. It's about time I was able to show off my own property. Mind you now, it belongs to a mere earl and not a lofty duke. It isn't quite as grand." He paused. "But it's mine and I do take pride in it."

"I would love to see your estate," she told him.

A groom appeared with both their horses in hand and Owen placed her into the saddle. As always, when he touched her, a ripple of anticipation flared through her, wanting more from him. She ignored it and took up her reins.

"Lead the way," she said.

He urged Galahad on and Fancy followed suit. Instead of taking the main road, they rode across an open field and then into a wooded area.

"Slowly here," he cautioned. "It's a bit dense but a nice shortcut between our properties."

They came out the other side of the thick woods and Owen galloped away. With her newfound confidence, Louisa followed at the same pace.

He took her around the entire estate and they even stopped

to speak to a few of his tenants. She noticed that Owen called everyone by name. Despite the fact he was not brought up to be an earl, she knew he would be a good one. His capacity for leadership, either innate or taught to him by the army, would make him excel in his earldom.

Finally, they came to the house. It was not as enormous as Cliffside but all the same, it was most impressive in size and looks.

"Would you like to go inside?"

Louisa hesitated. "We have already ridden for longer than usual this morning and still need to return to Cliffside. Don't you have things to do?"

He laughed and the sound fluttered on the breeze, making her chest grow tight. "I am the earl, you know. I make my own schedule—and today, I have made time for you."

She sensed her cheeks heating and glanced away, staring at the house again.

"Yes, I would love to see your house," she told him. "A quick tour would be nice."

"Let's go to the stables then and leave the horses there."

He led her around the side of the house and to the stables, where he told a groom to water the horses and give them a bit to eat.

"Not too much because Miss Goulding and I will be riding them back to Cliffside in an hour or so."

"Yes, my lord," said the groom, leading the mounts away.

Owen slipped her hand through his arm and said, "I am famished. We'll cut through the kitchens and let Cook know we need some tea and cakes to fortify us before our tour."

They entered and the scullery maids went about their jobs as usual, leading Louisa to believe that the master of the house often cut through the kitchens on his way to and from the stables.

He came to stand in front of a stout woman with a kind face and graying hair.

"Cook, this is Miss Goulding. We've been out riding and

could use a spot of tea and something to eat. Is there anything available?"

"There are some of those raspberry scones, my lord. Would you like those with a bit of clotted cream?"

"That would be perfect, Cook. With tea, please."

Guiding her toward a small table in the corner of the room, he pulled out a chair. Louisa realized he meant for them to sit in the kitchens.

And liked him all the better for it.

After they were seated, Owen said, "This was my favorite room at Danfield. I didn't see much of my parents. Being a spare and not the heir, my father had little use for me. Ev and I were close in proximity and age and we would roam between Danfield and Cliffside. Cook always made us feel welcomed here. Ev and I would eat cakes and biscuits and sample dishes that were being prepared."

He smiled and she said, "You have many happy memories here."

"I do. My brother was six years my senior and spent all his time with Ev's brother, who was the same age. Both Lawford and Mervyn, Ev's brother, were together from the time they were boys until they were attacked."

Briefly, he told her about what had happened. How Mervyn had quickly died, his injuries severe, while Lawford lingered for months until his recent death.

By then, Cook had brought over steaming cups of tea and two plates of the promised scones, along with a jar of clotted cream. They ate as Owen told a few stories about his and Ev's boyhood adventures and how they met Spencer when they first went away to school.

"We were a trio as thick as thieves until university. The Second Sons expanded our number to five with two cousins, Percival Perry and Winston Cutler, officers in His Majesty's army."

A shadow crossed his face. "Do you miss those friends terribly?"

Owen nodded. "It's not just missing them. It's worrying about them. Having been at war for years, I know exactly what they face every day. The perils. The pitfalls. The law of averages has some men return home and others fall. I would hate in our group of five to lose one of them, especially after so many years at war."

"But England is no longer at war with Bonaparte," she protested. "That ended this past April. Surely, they are safe now."

"What of the war in America?" he countered. "Yes, negotiations to end that conflict have begun in Ghent." He frowned. "Politicians talk too much, though. It could take a good while for peace to come. It doesn't mean that war is letting up and men aren't still dying daily. The Americans recently captured Fort Erie, a supply depot for British troops. Percy and Win could be sent from Europe to North America."

Owen raked his fingers through his hair. "There always seems to be trouble somewhere in the world."

Louisa ached seeing the frustration on his face. She placed a hand on his arm. "I know it hurts to leave good friends behind, especially when you are now part of a world that, for the most part, doesn't understand war or its sacrifices."

He covered her hand with his. "It is only one of the reasons I am reluctant to belong to the *ton*. My heart and gut tells me I may never truly belong."

She squeezed his forearm. "You will. You have your battlefield experience and a keen intelligence. You will make for a fine member in the House of Lords. You will eventually wed, aligning your family name and title to another established one in England. You will have children and see them go on to wed others of their class, as well. Give it time, Owen."

Nodding brusquely, he looked about. "Are you ready for your tour?"

"I would be delighted to see Danfield."

He helped her from her seat, tucking her hand possessively through the crook of his arm. Louisa liked that he was solicitous and took care of her. She liked being near him and inhaling his wonderful, masculine scent and feeling the heat from his body.

If only she could forget about how his kiss made her knees weak and her bones melt.

"I'll only take you to a few of the rooms. Just to give you a general sense of the house," he told her.

They saw the library and drawing room, along with his study and the wine cellar. She was grateful that he did not take her to his bedchamber. Or any bedchamber. The thought of being alone with him in a room with a bed caused her to grow lightheaded.

Owen led her to a final room, tossing open the doors and pulling her inside.

"The ballroom," she said, gazing about at the vast room, wondering what it would be like when it was full of dancers as an orchestra played.

"I never entered this room," he said. "My parents never used it once. They did hold balls at the London townhouse but this one has stood empty for all these years."

"What a shame," she said, sadness filling her. "A room this beautiful should be used. Why, you could hold a country ball."

He frowned. "What is that? I have never heard of this."

"One in which you invite all your neighbors. Titled peers. Villagers. Your tenants. You could meet your neighbors that way. I would suggest that you hold a harvest ball to celebrate the crops that have been gathered and stored."

Louisa smiled. "I can picture it now. Couples dancing and twirling, the music lively and loud."

She turned to look at him and found his gaze intense.

"Do you enjoy dancing, Louisa?"

Her smile faltered. "Not really. I suppose if I had more practice at it—like riding—that I might."

"I don't understand," he said, his confusion obvious. "You told me you attended most all of the events of the Season this year. I know there are a plethora of balls held."

She swallowed and lightly said, "Well, you have to be asked

to dance, Owen. That didn't happen very often."

"Why not?"

She felt tears sting her eyes. "I suppose I have gained the reputation of being a bit of a bluestocking. Dashing rakes of the *ton* don't waste their time dancing with women like me, you see."

Louisa glanced down, trying to keep her tears at bay, embarrassed at becoming so emotional around him.

His fingers captured her chin, raising it slowly until her gaze met his.

"Miss Goulding, may I have this dance?"

Stunned, she only looked at him.

Then Owen took her in his arms and began twirling her about the ballroom.

CHAPTER ELEVEN

As Owen moved about the empty ballroom with Louisa in his arms, he was shocked at her earlier words.

It infuriated him that men of the *ton* did not recognize what a jewel Louisa Goulding was. He had seen the tears well in her eyes and knew the immense hurt she must feel being left out, pushed to the side to sit with wallflowers who received little to no attention from roguish bachelors.

As he began humming, he searched his mind, trying to think of a worthy, eligible husband for her. He had been gone far too long from society to know what his various schoolmates were up to and, frankly, he didn't know if he could recommend any of them as a husband to her. The *ton's* reaction to such a gem as Louisa only reaffirmed his poor opinion of Polite Society in general and made him not only wary but reluctant to join its ranks.

The only men he thought might be worthy of her were Win and Percy, though that would be a disservice to Louisa. While his two remaining single friends were of extremely good character and possessed both intelligence and dashing looks, the fact was they were, as second sons, committed to a lifetime in the military. As officers, both men would rarely be in London—or even England. While some officers actually brought their wives to war with them, Owen thought the practice incredibly self-serving on the man's part. The battlefield and a life roaming during war was no life for any woman, much less one of Louisa's worth. He hoped again that whomever Adalyn had invited to her house party would include men of character who would recognize Louisa's value.

He continued humming, concentrating on their dance steps, a waltz. He had chosen it subconsciously but was glad that he now held her close in his arms. He enjoyed the feel of her, as well as that wonderful scent of lavender that wafted from her skin toward him.

"Might I take over the music?" she asked, mirth dancing in her eyes.

"If you wish," he told her. "Am I truly that bad?"

She chuckled, low and throaty, causing him to tighten his hold on her.

"Much worse than you think you are," she said. "You are perfectly awful. I know you think you are carrying a tune but I cannot discern one."

A giggle escaped, endearing her to him even further.

"Then be my guest, Miss Goulding. Only let it continue to be a waltz."

"Certainly, my lord."

After only a few bars, Owen decided Louisa was infinitely better than he was. She more than kept a tune. She made humming incredibly sensual. He continued guiding her about the large space, wishing that other men could see what he saw in this woman. More than anything, she deserved to find the rich happiness her cousins had found.

She also deserved love.

She had downplayed the idea, telling him she merely wanted a good man who would be a decent father and spend time with their children. Owen now knew she needed much more than that.

And wished he could give it to her.

Granted, he was attracted to her. There was no getting

around that anymore. But love? He didn't know if he had such an emotion inside him, especially after all he had given of himself in the war. At times, he believed himself to be a dried husk, empty, devoid of all emotion. No, it wouldn't be fair to either of them if he tried to pursue her. Delightful as she was, he knew he had a roving eye and no urge to became a father anytime soon. In the foreseeable future, he wanted to lose himself in drink and beautiful women without promising any kind of commitment. Louisa warranted more than what he had to give.

But he vowed he would help her find a decent, honorable man. If not at this upcoming house party, then next Season.

The music came to an end and she wet her lips, tempting him even further. The gesture reminded him of what they needed to do next.

"Come with me," he said, releasing her but claiming her hand as he led her from the room.

Owen took her to the library again and had them sit on a small settee. Louisa frowned.

"We already saw your library. Did you forget that?"

"No. But I did remember we were going to have a few lessons in flirting. I have neglected those."

"Oh!" Color bloomed on her cheeks.

"There are all kinds of way to flirt with your fan. I am certain Adalyn knows all about those and can show you. We will work on other things."

She swallowed. "If you insist."

"If you find yourself interested in a gentleman and he comes to call, invite him to sit with you a bit on a settee of this size. It is smaller than usual. Notice how close our bodies are. Not quite touching—but I can still feel your body heat. I can smell the lavender you used in your bathwater."

Her face flamed. "Owen, this isn't an appropriate conversation."

He laughed. "Most of flirting isn't. Here, stand again."

He helped her to rise and they sat again, this time with him sitting so that their thighs brushed.

"You're too close," she complained.

"Not if you are interested in a man." He almost had said interested in him and corrected himself. "One way to let a man know if you find him attractive is to sit close."

"All right," she said reluctantly.

"Another way? Pick a piece of lint from my sleeve."

Louisa glanced down at his arm and frowned. "But there isn't one."

"There doesn't have to be. You pretend. It is merely an excuse to brush your fingers along a man's forearm. Try it."

She did and he praised her. "Now, I want you to glance down. Look at your hands in your lap. Good. Turn your head slightly toward me. Eyes still downcast. Now, glance up slightly at me and then lower your lashes. That's a girl."

Owen had her practice the accidental art of fingers brushing each other. He had Louisa cock her head a touch and work on her sideways glance some more. When he thought she had mastered those, he cleared his throat.

"Lick your lips," he instructed. "Slowly. As you look at me."

Her face flamed. "This is all too much," she said.

"Just do it."

She did, her gaze locked on his, causing a frisson of desire to ripple through him.

"Very good," he said softly. "That is your ace. Save that move for when you are most interested in a gentleman. Preferably after you have been in close contact. I would do so if you were strolling on a terrace after a dance. Suggesting to go outside for fresh air is a way a man will usually let a woman know he is attracted to her."

"That is why they kissed me," Louisa said thoughtfully.

"Who?" he barked, immediately regretting his tone.

"The two men I kissed—before you. It was during my come-out Season. Both led me outside. We strolled to the far end of the terrace. That is when each kissed me."

"Did you enjoy it?" he asked, his curiosity overriding his good judgment.

"The first time I did. It was nice. He used his tongue, though, and I didn't know kissing involved tongues."

Oh, she was such an innocent.

"The second time I didn't like it at all. It was . . . slobbery. And he wouldn't stop."

Anger surged within Owen. He wanted to demand the man's name so he could bash his nose in.

Calmly, he asked, "What did you do?"

"I kneed him in the groin as Papa had told me to do."

Owen burst out laughing.

"Oh, it wasn't funny at all. I think I quite injured him. He made an awful noise and doubled over in pain. I did not see him the rest of the evening."

"And you say your father taught you this move?"

She nodded. "Mama passed when I was fifteen. Papa told me he had no idea what she would have taught me about men. He said a good many men only want one thing—a lady's virtue—and that if I ever felt threatened, that is what I should do. I also taught Tessa and Adalyn the same move in case they might need to use it on an unscrupulous suitor."

Louisa sighed. "I don't know if he told any of his friends. I only went to a few more events that Season. It has been the same every year until this past year, when I attended the majority of events."

"Did you ever see this man again?" Owen asked.

"I did this spring. He and a young woman were in the receiving line a few people ahead of me and my aunt and uncle. When he caught sight of me, he glowered and turned in the other direction, his hand on the woman's back." She chuckled. "I don't even recall his name. He must have wed, though, because I saw a ring on her finger."

"We will hope you don't have to resort to that move in the future," he told her. "But I would only go out for a breath of fresh air with men you are truly interested in."

"Should I kiss them?" she asked. "Both Adalyn and Tessa have told me that kissing is very important. They urged me to kiss anyone I might be considering for a husband." Her gaze fell. "I really didn't find anyone this Season that I liked enough to pursue a kiss. I also worried about scandal. If you are caught kissing a gentleman, marriage is expected."

She rubbed her hands along her arms. "I wouldn't want to force anyone to wed me."

"Then make certain you aren't caught kissing anyone," he suggested.

Louisa expelled a long breath. "Something tells me that I won't have to worry about it. Not only did I find all of my partners to be dull this Season, not a single one of them took me away from a ball for a moonlight stroll or asked me to walk through the gardens during a tea party." She swallowed. "I told you, Owen. No one is interested enough in me to even suggest a kiss."

He framed her face with his hands. "Then they don't know what they are missing. If you wait, the right man will come along, Louisa. And when he does, you will know it from his kiss."

"But I barely know how to kiss. At least, I didn't know anything about it before you kissed me." A blush spilled across her cheeks. "I know I am supposed to like it but I'm not even good at it," she complained.

"You are better than you think," he said. Against his better judgment, he added, "Perhaps we should practice it a bit. Like we have riding."

"Do you think so?" she asked, her eyes hopeful.

It was the absolutely wrong thing to do. Owen knew it. Yet he heard himself say, "We should. Follow my lead. What I do, do the same. Imitate me the best you can."

He lowered his lips to hers, his hands still cradling her face. He could sense her trembling, whether with nerves or anticipation, he didn't know. Pressing his mouth to hers, he began kissing her. Her lips were divine. Soft. Pliable. Smooth. His thumbs stroked her cheeks.

Then her palms framed his face. He let his drop to give her better access. He let her take charge of the kiss now and she did so, pressing soft kisses against his mouth and then allowing them to grow firmer. Longer.

Owen's hand cradled her nape as his tongue swept along the seam of her mouth, back and forth, urging her to open. She didn't, which surprised him. Then she imitated the move and he allowed himself to open to her. With no hesitation, Louisa's tongue plunged into his mouth, causing heat to roar through him. Her hands settled on his shoulders as she ran her tongue against his.

He took control of the kiss, his free hand going to her waist. He anchored her and deepened the kiss, his tongue exploring her. She responded, doing the same, her tongue leisurely stroking his. His heart raced and he stood, bringing her with him. He tugged on her hair, tilting her head back, allowing him better access. She didn't yield. Rather, she linked her arms about his neck and pulled him close, her breasts teasing him as he crushed her to him.

An all-out war occurred, with both seeking to dominate the other. One kiss became a dozen, blending until he lost count. And still they kissed one another. At this rate, they would both have bleeding lips.

Owen broke the kiss, moving his lips along the line of her jaw, tugging on her hair again until her beautiful neck was exposed. He found her pulse point and licked it, hearing her moan. He bit her neck softly and heard her groan. Her fingers thrust into his hair and kneaded his scalp. He nibbled along her throat, working his way back to her mouth, another soft bite capturing her full, bottom lip and teasing it. She whimpered and lust shot through him. He had to force himself not to sweep her up and march her straight to his bed.

Then she bit into his lip, holding it captive with her teeth, and he heard his own groan of pleasure. What was it about this woman?

He tried to clear his mind as they continued to kiss. She was an innocent—though she certainly had caught on fast to the art of kissing. He had to remember she was a virgin who didn't know she was playing with fire.

That allowed him to break the kiss and end this foolish session.

They both panted, their breath quick and rapid. Owen looked at her, seeing her bosom heaving, those sapphire eyes dark and longing.

"That is more than enough kissing," he told her, easing her onto the settee as he took a step back.

Her cheeks were pink, her lips bruised with their kisses. She was the most desirable woman he had ever beheld. She was forbidden fruit, though.

"You are an excellent student," he said. "But I would not kiss a man that much. Else he might want other favors from you."

Her brows knit. "What kind of favors?"

She truly did not know what he meant.

Owen took the seat next to her and took her hands in his. "That kind of kissing leads to dangerous actions, Louisa. Ones that once a man starts, it is hard for him to regain control again."

"I d-don't understand," she stammered.

"I will be blunt. Kissing like that makes a man want to kiss you everywhere. He would want to lick the curve of your breast as it peeks from your gown. Push that gown down and capture your nipple in his mouth. Suck on your breast as hard as he can. Even bite your nipple."

Her eyes grew round but he continued.

"He would want to raise your hem. Skim his hand along your leg. Move to your core. Push his fingers inside you."

She looked utterly confused. Shaking her head back and forth, she asked, "What?"

His blood heated.

"I'll show you," he growled.

He dropped to the settee, his mouth slamming against hers, kissing her hard and deep. He kissed her until she had to be senseless and then he let his lips trail down her throat to the sweet, tempting curve he had longed to taste. Owen allowed his tongue to travel along the curve of her breast, hearing her sharp intake of breath. Then his fingers pushed down her gown and slipped inside her corset, cupping her breast and freeing it. He licked the nipple and then blew on it, feeling her shiver. His mouth went to her, sucking hard, drawing as much of her breast into his mouth as he could.

Her fingers pushed into his hair, holding him against her as he sucked and laved. She began to squirm beneath him and he flicked his tongue back and forth over her nipple before softly capturing its tip between his teeth.

"Owen!" she cried.

He lifted his head and slipped her breast back into the prison of her corset. His gaze held hers as his fingers reached the bottom of her hem and slid up her stockinged leg. They went higher and higher until they brushed against the seam of her sex.

Louisa gasped, her eyes widening.

"This is where a man desires to put his fingers," he said, his eyes steady on hers as he moved his hand back and forth. She was already wet and he knew she wanted him without even knowing it.

He parted her folds and gradually pushed a finger inside her. Her eyes loomed large as she bit her bottom lip and whimpered as he began to intimately stroke her.

"If you were seen with a man doing this, you would be ruined," he said softly.

She nodded, trembling, and he slipped a second finger inside her. She began to move her hips, meeting him, her eyes still captive to his. Owen increased the speed and pushed deeper, stroking her as she began to whimper.

"You feel a pressure building now, don't you" he asked.

She nodded, her eyes now glassy.

"Soon, it will crest and spill over. You will let it, do you hear me?"

She nodded again, words apparently beyond her.

Owen continued to touch her intimately, enjoying the catch in her throat, the little noises of submission, the frantic look in her eyes. Then he sensed her on the brink of orgasm and stroked her a final time.

Suddenly, a cry erupted from her and she moved violently against his fingers, spasming and bucking, tears streaming down her face.

"Ride it, Louisa," he ordered. "Wring all the pleasure you can from it."

She did as he said and finally calmed, collapsing, gulping air. He slipped his fingers from her and licked them, watching the surprise in her eyes.

He took hold of her shoulders and pulled her close. "That is what too much kissing can lead to."

"What was that?" she asked in wonder.

"It is called an orgasm. The French call it *la petite mort*—the little death."

"It is incredible," she exclaimed.

"It can also occur when you couple with a man," he explained. "When he uses his cock to thrust in and out of you. Or his tongue."

"His tongue?" she squeaked.

Owen stroked her cheek. "There are many mysteries between a man and a woman. You will discover these when you wed. But take care, Louisa. You don't want to kiss a man the way you kissed me before you are wed because it can lead to you losing your virginity before your vows are spoken."

Panic filled her face. "Am I no longer a virgin? Because we did that?"

He laughed. "You still are, my sweet. But you never want anyone to catch you doing that or it will certainly mean a ring on your finger and marriage to the man you are doing it with."

He brushed a tender kiss to her brow. "I think we have had enough lessons, whether it be riding or flirting or kissing. You are ready for this house party, Louisa. Do not compromise on what you want. If no man in attendance captures your fancy, you wait until one does, is that understood?"

She nodded, still looking slightly befuddled.

"Come, let us get you back to Cliffside."

He helped her to her feet and took her to the stables. They rode to Cliffside in silence and when they arrived at the stables, he helped her from Fancy's back.

"I won't come calling again until Spence and Tessa arrive. I'm sure you have a lot to think about. Learn what you can from Adalyn regarding the gentlemen invited."

Louisa nodded. "I will." She searched his face a moment and then placed a hand on his forearm. "Thank you, Owen."

"For what?"

"For making me feel like a woman. For making me feel I can be desirable. For helping me to understand that I shouldn't compromise when it comes to choosing a husband."

"You're welcome," he said softly.

She squeezed his arm and let her hand drop. He mounted Galahad and gave her a wave as he galloped from the yard.

Owen wondered if he would be able to watch another man court Louisa—without beating him to a bloody pulp.

Chapter Twelve

"I do hope Tessa will find the nursery adequate," Adalyn fretted.

"It is perfectly fine," Louisa assured her cousin. "I am certain you have thought of everything. And if there is some addition needed, it can be provided quickly. Analise is only a baby. She won't need that much."

"It is a good thing Tessa had the first babe," Adalyn said. "I know so little about them. Other than I want Ev's desperately." Her hands came to her belly and she stroked it lovingly.

"You have already been around Analise some," she reminded. "Tessa will be generous and let you hold her babe and learn."

"You are always so calm and logical, Louisa. I daresay when you become a mother, it will be as if water is merely rolling off your back."

She wondered if she would have that opportunity. It would involve acquiring a husband.

And doing things like she and Owen had done a week ago.

He had not made an appearance for the last seven days, begging off their riding lessons. He had sent word around to Everett that he had things to do on the estate and some quick business to attend to in London. Louisa had done her best to go on with some kind of routine while Owen was gone but it seemed she was sleepwalking as she did so. She found herself absentminded and she thought far too much of his kisses.

And those other things.

Oh, those other things . . .

Knowing he had put his fingers inside her brought a wave of heat through her. She understood that what they had done would not make a baby. But oh, dear Lord in Heaven, how wonderful it had felt. She had no idea that was something a couple could do. She had a vague idea about a man needing to slip his cock inside a woman to get her with child but had no idea of the particulars. And Owen had said something about a tongue going the same place his fingers had. That brought heat to her cheeks.

"Are you overwarm, Louisa?" Adalyn asked.

"It is a bit warm in here," she said, quickly heading to the French doors and opening them. "Perhaps this will let in a bit of a breeze."

They were in Adalyn's sitting room, a place she loved to retreat to with her cousin. No doubt when Tessa arrived, the three of them would be closeted in here talking about the upcoming house party.

Where she hoped she might find a husband among the guests.

She pushed into the far recesses of her mind the desire for Owen to be that husband. He was a rogue. An honorable one, in her opinion, for he could have taken greater advantage of her than he did. While she knew they never should have done the things they had in private, she guessed other men would not have shown as much restraint as Owen had.

He had done her a favor, though. Louisa had come to look upon herself as an ugly duckling. Her heart now told her that she was as desirable as any woman in the *ton*. She would just have to discover the right man who would see something in her that no other gentleman did.

No one except for Owen, that is.

A knock sounded at the door and Arthur entered. "Your Grace, Lord and Lady Middlefield's carriage has been sighted."

"Oh, thank you, Arthur. Please let His Grace know. He is in his study. We will go out to greet our guests."

Louisa and Adalyn exited the room and went to the foyer, where Mrs. Arthur waited.

"Is everything ready for Lord and Lady Middlefield's visit?" Adalyn asked.

"Yes, Your Grace," the housekeeper assured her mistress.

Everett joined them. "Shall we go outside?" he asked, escorting them through the front door, where a warm summer day greeted them.

Two carriages came up the drive. Louisa knew the first would hold Tessa and Spencer, along with Analise and her nurse. The other would be for their servants and luggage. Then she saw a rider alongside the first carriage and her heart skipped a beat.

Owen . . .

She took a deep breath, trying to tamp down the excitement she felt at seeing him again. It was foolish on her part. He was not for her and never would be.

The first carriage came to a halt and Owen rode up beside it, handing Galahad's reins to a footman and opening the vehicle's door himself as another footman placed stairs down so that the vehicle's occupants might descend with ease.

Spencer appeared in the doorway, Analise in his arms. Louisa couldn't help but chuckle. The earl constantly wagged around his daughter to the point of Tessa sometimes complaining that she needed a turn holding Analise.

Bounding down the steps, Spencer thrust Analise at Owen. "Hold her," he commanded and turned, reaching out his hand to Tessa and assisting her down the stairs. Adalyn and Everett went to greet the couple.

Louisa's eyes were fastened on Owen, who wore a perplexed look as he cradled Analise in his arms. He looked down at the infant—and smiled. Louisa heard Analise coo at him.

"She likes me," Owen said to no one in particular.

"She's only seven months. She likes everyone," Spencer

pointed out, releasing his wife's hand and reclaiming his daughter from his friend.

"Louisa!" Tessa cried and stepped forward so they could embrace. "I am delighted you are already here."

"I came a bit early. The Season seemed to drag once you and Adalyn left for the country."

Tessa linked her arm through Louisa's. "Well, a house party is always something exciting." She glanced over her shoulder. "You are coming to it, aren't you, Owen?"

He joined them as everyone moved toward the house. "I have been invited but will most likely remain at Danfield and ride over each day."

"No, that won't do," Tessa scolded. "I insist you pack up and come to Cliffside."

"You are sounding as bossy as Adalyn," Owen observed.

"No one is as bossy as Adalyn," Tessa said, chuckling.

They entered the foyer and Adalyn said she and Ev would escort the couple to their bedchamber, as well as look over the nursery with their nursemaid.

"Would you keep Owen entertained while I do so?" she asked Louisa. "We'll have tea once they get settled."

"Of course. Come along, my lord," she said jauntily, trying to quell the nerves that rose within her as Owen came to her side and she got a whiff of him.

They went to the drawing room. Louisa took a seat in a chair and Owen went to stand in front of the fireplace, leaning his arm against the mantel. He cut a picture of the perfect gentleman, with tight fawn breeches, a snow-white shirt, and a coat of deep brown, making his hair and eyes look even darker than usual.

"How have you been?" she asked brightly, hoping that she didn't sound too eager for his reply.

"I have been busy. Spending time with White, my steward. I also went to London to visit with my tailor. I had several things made up since I had been neglecting to do so. Ev urged me to update my wardrobe. I came home with nothing but my uniform and had scrounged and found a few things at Danfield and purchased a few more from the local tailor. With the house party approaching, however, Ev said that I looked like a ragamuffin and needed the proper attire so as not to embarrass myself."

It was funny but Louisa had never noticed what Owen had worn in the past. Only him.

"Well, your tailor did a fine job. You look fashionable and dashing."

A silence fell between them. She had no idea what to say. They had never been awkward in one another's company and she could only think of that day in his library. The feel of his mouth on her breast. The taste of his kiss. His fingers driving her wild.

"Have you been riding?" he asked suddenly.

She thought that a safe topic and elaborated for a few minutes on where she had been riding over the last week, a groom escorting her.

"And have you played any chess?" Owen asked as the others joined them.

"Did I hear chess?" Spencer asked.

"If you decide to play against Louisa, be forewarned," Owen cautioned. "I have lost to her twice."

"You lost?" Spencer said, astounded. "Why, Owen, you were a champion chess master back in school."

"I know—which tells you just how good Louisa is," Owen praised. "Don't think it is a case of me being gallant and allowing her to win. I'm afraid our Louisa is quite cutthroat and most competitive."

Spencer laughed. "Still, I would like a go at you, Louisa. I haven't played in a good while but always enjoyed it. I will make certain Analise is on my lap when we play. It is never too soon to start children at games."

Tessa shook her head. "She won't understand a thing about it, Spencer. The most she will do is swipe a piece off the playing board and jam it into her mouth."

"She does that with everything," the proud papa bragged.

"Dogs sniff their way about the world. Our Analise sees it by holding and tasting everything."

The teacarts appeared, rolled in by two maids as Mrs. Arthur supervised them. Soon, Adalyn was pouring out and everyone was talking fast and furiously as they caught up with one another. Louisa was so happy to have Tessa and Spencer there, realizing how much she had missed the couple.

"Will you stay for dinner, Owen?" Adalyn asked.

"I suppose I could," he said slowly, his eyes focused on his hostess.

"Excellent. I will tell Arthur to inform Cook that we will be an even six for dinner. For now, why don't you men remain here and talk about manly things? We women will retreat to my sitting room and discuss the house party."

"And the guest list?" Owen asked with interest.

"Yes, I suppose we can," Adalyn replied.

"Then I will head off with the ladies," he informed the other males. "I am curious to learn who will be attending and want to hear a little bit about each of the guests before I meet them."

Adalyn rose. "Come along, then."

Louisa and Tessa rose and followed Adalyn and Owen from the drawing room. She dreaded being in his company as they talked about the eligible men.

"Are you seeking a bride among the guests, Owen?" asked Tessa.

"Not at all," he said breezily. "I do know that I have a role to play during the week others are here, though."

"And what might that be?" Tessa asked.

"I am to get to know the eligible bachelors in attendance and see if they are worthy of our Louisa," Owen replied.

"Is that so?" Tessa pursed her lips. "I thought that would be a task for Louisa to accomplish."

They reached the sitting room and entered, as Owen said, "Of course, it is for Louisa to decide if she is interested in anyone. Unfortunately, men do not always reveal their true nature to women, especially those they are courting. I will get to know my peers through the various activities Adalyn has planned and pass along my opinions to Louisa."

"I see," Tessa said, taking a seat next to Adalyn.

That left a settee available and Louisa perched upon it, Owen sitting beside her. She remembered the last time they had sat on one together, as he gave her lessons in flirting. She had not shared that with Adalyn, nor asked her cousin how to flirt with a fan. Instead, she had kept what occurred between her and Owen private. It was unlike her to hide things from either Adalyn or Tessa. The three cousins were the closest of friends and told one another everything.

She doubted telling them that Owen had kissed her senseless and given her an orgasm was something they needed to hear, however.

"All right," Owen said, rubbing his hands briskly together. "Share with us the names of the gentlemen invited to your country house party."

"Why don't we talk about the ladies first?" suggested Tessa. "I am much more interested in hearing about them and I know Louisa will also want to know who will be in attendance. She may or may not know them."

Adalyn lifted a page from the writing desk next to her. "The ladies it shall be."

Louisa could tell Owen was irritated but he held his tongue. In a way, she thought it comical that he would have to wait and hear about the female guests.

"Perhaps one of these women will appeal to you, Owen," Tessa said sweetly. "That would save you from having to peruse the Marriage Mart next Season."

"I have no desire to peruse anything having to do with marriage," he said testily.

Adalyn cleared her throat. "I limited those invited so the group wouldn't become too large. There will be five unattached females, including Louisa, and five bachelors, including you,

Owen."

Her cousin smiled. "You'll like the first one, Louisa. Her name is Miss Peterson. I considered her as a candidate for Ev, which tells you how much I like her."

"I have heard the name," she said. "I have never been introduced to her, though."

"She is a bit of a bluestocking. Quite thin with lively blue eyes and brown hair. Then there is Ev's distant cousin, Lady Sara. She is blond with blue eyes and quite sweet. She only made her come-out this year."

"I didn't get to know any of the younger girls," Louisa admitted. "Actually, they wanted nothing to do with someone as old as I am."

"Lady Sara is nice. And her good friend, Miss Oxford, will be accompanying her. They made their come-outs together. From what I understand, they do simply everything together. Miss Oxford has brown hair and brown eyes and according to Lady Sara, she giggles a lot."

"Oh, great. A giggler. Just what we need," said Owen sourly.

Adalyn ignored his comment. "The final guest is Miss Rexford."

"Oh, I know who she is," Louisa said. "We have never met but she has a bit of a reputation as a rule-breaker."

Owen sniffed. "At least she sounds interesting compared to the others."

Adalyn shot him a look. "She is also quite beautiful. Dark-haired with light blue eyes. I think you will enjoy getting to know her, Owen."

He waved a hand in front of him. "We're not here for me. Despite what Ev said."

Adalyn's brows arched. "And what did my husband say?"

"That you are a matchmaker and you will try to pair me up with someone."

Adalyn shrugged. "I am merely bringing interesting people together. Make of it what you will."

Owen leaned his forearms on his thighs. "Get on with it. You've told us about the female guests. Let's hear about the men."

Adalyn consulted her list. "Viscount Hurley is someone Ev knew in the army. He has recently returned from the war. Ev says that Hurley is lanky. Just over six feet. Blond and very intelligent."

"Hmm," Owen murmured. "I don't know him. Go on."

"Then there is the Earl of Marksbury, a school chum of Ev's."

"I know him," Owen said. "A couple of inches under six feet. Stocky. Smart. Quiet."

"Ev said he doesn't go to many *ton* events," Adalyn added.

"Who else?" Tessa asked.

"Viscount Boxling," Adalyn said.

Louisa thought a moment. "The name sounds familiar but I do not remember a Boxling from this past Season."

"We know him," Tessa said. "He is most likely six feet, with dark hair and eyes. Very funny and smart. I heard his father, the previous viscount, passed away last Christmas and Boxling skipped the Season because he was settling into his duties. Spencer knew him at university."

"As did Ev and I," Owen said cryptically.

"The last of the eligible men is a gentleman from our neighborhood. A Mr. Hampton. He is close to six feet and quite muscular. Lovely brown hair and eyes. He is the third of three boys. Once he graduated from university, he returned home and helped care for his father, who was very ill."

"Was his father Viscount Loving?" Owen asked. When Adalyn confirmed that, he said, "He doesn't have a title. The rest do."

Louisa snorted. "If you think I am interested in a man solely because he holds a title, you are mistaken. Character is what is most important."

"But Louisa, you need someone who will care for you. That includes a roof over your head and material goods." He glanced at Adalyn. "What does Hampton do now that his father is gone?"

"I am not certain," she revealed. "But he was available to come to the house party while his brother is not. The new Viscount Loving recently wed and is on his honeymoon."

"I don't know if any of these prospects will do for Louisa," Owen said flatly.

"Why not?" Tessa asked.

"Call it gut instinct," he said gruffly. "None of them sound good enough in my opinion."

"I think it should be up to Louisa to decide if any of these men interest her or not," Adalyn said. "I have told you a bit about them, knowing you'll keep an open mind."

"Yes, it will be up to me to see for myself," she said. "I will not prejudge anyone. Rather, I hope to have time to get to know each of them."

Owen stood. "I've heard enough. I think I will rejoin Ev and Spence."

"We will see you at dinner," Adalyn called out as Owen sailed through the doors.

The moment he had closed the door, Tessa turned to her. "Louisa, I think Owen is interested in you—and that is why he believes none of these invited guests will suit you."

She only wished it were true. "No, you are wrong, Tessa. We have gotten to know each other and I think it is a case of Owen seeing himself as a protective big brother. I doubt anyone I become interested in will pass muster with him. Besides, he has made it quite clear that he has no interest in marriage anytime soon."

"I believe Owen is interested in you, Louisa," Adalyn said. "After all, he kissed you. Men don't kiss a woman unless they are interested in her."

Panic flooded Louisa and her cheeks burned. Even now, she could feel Owen's mouth on her breast. His fingers intimately caressing her. The raging orgasm that had erupted, sending her to the heavens and beyond.

Why had Owen told Adalyn what had passed between the two of them?

Embarrassment filled her as she looked at Adalyn, who wore a puzzled expression. "Is there something you are not telling us, Louisa? Your face is flaming. Owen told me he had succumbed to temptation. He even called you beautiful. Did Owen do *more* than kiss you?" her cousin demanded.

Relief swept through her. Owen had been a gentleman. He had not revealed to Adalyn the intimacies that had occurred between them.

But the fact he had thought her beautiful made her heart sing.

"Of course not," she said quickly. "I am merely upset that he shared knowledge of the kiss with you. I thought it was a . . . private matter."

"How was his kiss?" Tessa asked eagerly. "I have sensed his interest in you, Louisa. And we have both told you how important kissing is." Her cousin paused. "Do you have feelings for the earl? Of course, he does seem to be a bit of a rogue. Then again, you are a clever, mature woman and would certainly know how to handle any challenge he presented. If anyone could tame a man such as Danbury, it would be you."

Louisa fought for a way to answer her cousin without outright lying to her. She refused to admit that Owen stirred things within her. That he made her feel things she had never experienced and how she wished he were the marrying kind.

Because she would accept an offer of marriage from him in an instant.

"I am interested in that answer as well, Louisa," Adalyn said. "Did the kiss you and Owen exchanged make you believe there could be a future between you?"

"The kiss was pleasant but no," she said firmly. "We are merely friends."

"I don't think so," Adalyn said. "I have seen something in his eyes when he speaks of you, not to mention you have gone beet red as we have discussed him."

Oh, dear. Adalyn could be worse than a dog guarding a bone. Louisa had to bring a halt to this conversation for good and make certain the topic would not be brought up again.

"I will not be marrying Lord Danbury," she said with conviction. "I am looking forward to meeting the gentlemen who will attend the house party."

Tessa shook her head, doubt reflected in her eyes. "We'll see."

It didn't matter what her two cousins thought. Louisa knew she was right. She would never receive an offer of marriage from Owen because he had no plans to settle down. With anyone.

Especially not her.

Chapter Thirteen

Owen climbed into his carriage and tapped on the ceiling. The driver started the vehicle and he settled back against the cushions. As they made their way toward Cliffside, he contemplated the four men Adalyn had announced were her upcoming houseguests. That one was a former military man was a good thing, even if Owen did not know Hurley. The military instilled leadership and discipline within a man, honing his character. Of the four candidates, Owen already had a favorable opinion of Viscount Hurley.

As far as the Earl of Marksbury was concerned, he had been a classmate of theirs at school, a few years behind them. Owen had neither a favorable nor unfavorable impression of Marksbury. To the contrary, he had no impression at all. He vaguely recalled a solemn, sturdy lad who spoke little. It would be interesting to see the man Marksbury had become.

He did remember Viscount Boxling from university days and hoped that Louisa would immediately dismiss the man once she met him. From what Owen recalled, Boxling had been a wild one, charming his professors and fellow classmates while he made his way through every woman in Cambridge, single or married. Hopefully, Boxling would show his stripes quickly so that Louisa might eliminate him from her pool of potential suitors.

He wondered about this Mr. Hampton, the neighbor. Owen

had known Viscount Loving, Hampton's older brother, and thought him bland. He had no recollection of this younger Hampton brother. He supposed it did speak good of the man for having tended to his dying father, the old viscount. But at the same time, Owen wanted more for Louisa. She might not consider a title important or necessary but he certainly did. It was funny how his thinking had changed since he himself had gained a title but he wanted that for Louisa.

He wanted the world for Louisa.

He wanted Louisa . . . for himself.

Owen shoved that thought into the far recesses of his mind. No, he did not want Louisa Goulding. He didn't want a wife, period. He was merely acting on her behalf, as a concerned friend, and hoped that she would be able to find her future husband among the house party guests. He still found it hard to believe that a woman of Louisa's distinctive qualities had not been snapped up by an eligible bachelor of the *ton* but he did know what insensitive oafs most men could be. Even if a diamond of the first water were placed in their paths, they rarely recognized her. Louisa was the brightest of diamonds as far as Owen was concerned and he would make certain that she had the best husband possible. If she was happy, he would be happy.

He ignored the fact that he was lying to himself.

When had he changed? He had returned from the war depleted, so many years spent in battle and surrounded by death all his adult life. Though he had been reluctant to leave the military, wanting to see the conclusion of the fighting and Bonaparte knocked off the pedestal he had placed himself upon, Owen now found that he liked a life away from the army. He had thought he would be bored in the country and hadn't been. The many challenges on his estate kept him busy and thriving. Yes, he would go to town eventually, taking his seat in the House of Lords, and enjoying the finer things London had to offer. But he now understood the value of a quiet life in the country. He was fortunate to have Ev next door and Spence less than twenty miles from Danfield.

What he did need was to find a husband for Louisa and make certain that she was happy with him—and that they did not live anywhere in this area. Jealousy already seeped through his bones and he would not want to watch her on a regular basis, seeing her happiness in her marriage or the times she would be increasing, glowing with the prospect of being a mother. Anger filled him thinking of another man's child growing in her belly. That alone made Owen know Mr. Hampton would not be a suitable candidate for her hand, especially if he remained in the area with his brother, Viscount Loving.

His carriage rolled up the drive and stopped in front of the house. Owen climbed down and looked up as his valet did the same from where he had ridden next to the driver.

"See to my trunk, Strunk."

"Yes, my lord."

Owen then turned to the groom who had followed them over on Galahad. "Take my horse to the stables and you may return in the carriage."

The groom nodded and turned Galahad toward the stables. Owen then made his way to the front door. He had brought the carriage as much for his trunk as himself, not wanting to be ruffled and mussed. Though it was but a short ride from Danfield to Cliffside, he did not want to smell of the sweat of a horse as the other guests arrived. He wouldn't need the carriage, however, which was why he was sending it home. This also allowed him use of Galahad during the house party.

Arthur greeted him at the door. "Good morning, Lord Danbury. We were not expecting you quite this early."

Owen grinned. "Is that your way of saying that I am too early, Arthur?"

"Never, my lord," the butler said smoothly. "Your bedchamber is ready and His Grace is breakfasting if you wish to join him."

"What a splendid idea," he said and strode toward the breakfast room.

Entering, he looked about and was surprised to find only Ev dining there.

"What the devil are you doing here?" his friend asked. "I thought our invited guests would be arriving from mid-morning on. Addie and Louisa both had a tray sent to their rooms since they thought it would be quicker. Spence and Tessa have already eaten and are out taking a walk with Analise."

Owen took a seat as a footman poured coffee for him.

"I thought I would come a bit early and help you greet your guests," he said, taking a sip from his cup.

Ev studied him a moment. "You came early so that you would be able to see every guest who arrived," his friend surmised. "Might you actually be looking for your countess among them?" Ev paused. "Or are you playing scout and looking over the men for Louisa?"

"The latter, of course. You know of my intentions to wait on marriage. I have a good five years or more before I will even consider leg shackles."

Ev shook his head. "Keep saying that. One day, you might actually believe it."

"What do you mean?" Owen asked, not bothering to hide his irritation.

"I think—whether you know it or not—that you will be wed sooner than later. And to Louisa."

Owen shook his head, vehemently denying it. "No, Ev, you are wrong. I merely feel solicitous toward her. She has no father or brother here to look after her interests."

"So, you have taken that upon yourself?" Ev asked. "To be a protector to her."

"Yes, that is it exactly. I want to get to know these gentlemen and what makes them tick. Once I do, I will know if any of them are good enough for Louisa."

Owen watched Ev bite back a smile.

"You say that now, Owen, but I can tell you in advance that you will find none of these men to your liking."

"Then why were they invited?" he asked, aghast. "I thought Adalyn, matchmaker that she is, wanted the best for her cousin."

"Oh, Addie does want the best for Louisa. I am merely stating that you are going to find something wrong with every single suitor here. Face it, Owen. You have feelings for Louisa. This arbitrary idea of waiting years to wed needs to be shoved to the side. The perfect woman for you—the one who would be an ideal Countess of Danbury—is right before you. You won't be able to do better than Louisa, so why wait?"

Owen regarded his friend solemnly. "You think you know everything simply because you are in love with your wife and will be a father soon. You have been back in England longer than I have, Ev. I need to get a better grasp on being the Earl of Danbury. I need to learn more about my responsibilities and place in a society I never thought I would join."

"I am telling you that Louisa would be the best partner to help you in those endeavors, Owen. After years of managing her father's household and entertaining a slew of people from diplomats to war office workers, she would be an excellent countess. You are already friends, good friends if I'm not mistaken, and friendship can lead to love." Ev gave him a sly look. "Unless you already are in love with her. In that case, you don't want to lose her to another man because of some stubborn idea you are clinging to about marriage."

He felt his face flush, whether in anger or embarrassment he didn't know. "I'll have you keep such thoughts to yourself, Ev. I am here as a favor to Adalyn—and Louisa, of course—and I will be a proper guest as I help Louisa navigate the society about her. No further discussions on this topic will be tolerated, else I will return to Danbury and leave you with uneven numbers."

"And sulk, I suppose." Ev regarded him and finally said, "All right, Owen. You can have it your way. But if you lose out and lose Louisa because you're a bloody fool, don't come crying to me afterward. End of discussion."

Owen sipped on his coffee, an uneasy silence between the

men.

Finally, Ev said, "I have a new colt which was born yesterday. Would you like to go to the stables and see it?"

"I would be delighted to, Your Grace."

The pair rose from the table and made their way down to the stables, Owen fighting thoughts of Louisa flirting with the guests yet to arrive.

LOUISA SMILED AT her image and said, "Tilly, you have done wonders with my hair."

"Thank you, Miss Goulding," the maid replied. "I hope you'll enjoy this house party."

Tilly quietly left the room and Louisa sighed heavily. So far, all the guests had arrived and their rather large group had taken tea together in the drawing room this afternoon. It was a mishmash, with half a dozen conversations going on at once.

Louisa had immediately been drawn to Miss Peterson, a bright woman with lively blue eyes who was easy to talk with. After only a few minutes in Miss Peterson's company, she knew they would become friends, probably good ones. She also enjoyed meeting Miss Rexford, a true beauty with coal-black hair and sparkling blue eyes and an air of mischief about her. Louisa believed Miss Rexford would draw—and keep—the attention of the males attending the house party.

She thought Lady Sara, one of Ev's cousins, and her friend, Miss Oxford, were sweet girls but didn't believe any true friendship would spark between them. The pair was young and Louisa felt a hundred years older as she listened to their conversation about which color of bow should be placed upon Lady Sara's shoe for dinner that evening.

She had spoken to each of the male guests briefly, so briefly that she hadn't formed any solid opinions about any of them.

Lord Marksbury seemed witty for a man who shunned *ton* events. Lord Hurley appeared a bit withdrawn. She wondered if it was because he had only recently returned from serving in His Majesty's army and hadn't had time to adjust to claiming a title and being in polite company again. Mr. Hampton was gracious and complimented her on the color of her gown. He mentioned his brother, who had been recently wed and now honeymooned in Scotland with his bride.

The only one she had previously been introduced to had been Lord Boxling. She had met him during her come-out Season and they had danced once, before he held his title. He did not mention it and Louisa doubted he remembered a dance from five years ago. She did express her sympathy for the passing of his father, which he thanked her for.

She wondered if it was possible that she might form an attachment with any of the four. Tessa said that house parties were known for blossoming romances. Even Adalyn had mentioned that it would be much easier to get to know both the men and the women because they would be around each other for an extended amount of time. Frankly, Louisa didn't believe in ten days she would know someone well enough to commit to them for the rest of her life. Then again, most engaged couples at the end of the Season had usually only spoken to one another a handful of times.

She had a small dowry, which was thanks to her mother. Her father's salary in the War Office was merely adequate. Mama had been an earl's daughter, though, and what she had brought into the marriage had been put aside. That settlement was to be used for future daughters' dowries. Since Louisa was their only child, she claimed all of it. She wondered if the small dowry influenced men's opinions of her. And granted, she was older than the other unattached females but she thought her looks held up. Rising from the dressing table, she smoothed her gown, trying to calm her nerves. Either she would come to find a husband or she wouldn't. She might form a few new friendships or not. The possibilities were open as she left her bedchamber and descended the stairs.

Going to the drawing room, she joined the others already gathered, declining a drink offered by a footman. Tessa waved at her and she joined a group with Tessa, Miss Peterson, Mr. Hampton, and Lord Boxling.

Mr. Hampton finished a story he was telling and then Lord Boxling turned to her.

"I believe I have seen you at a few *ton* events, Miss Goulding. Not often, though."

"Up until this Season, I only attended a limited number each year. I was more useful serving as my father's hostess."

"Sir Edgar Goulding?" the viscount asked, interest lighting his face.

"Yes. Do you know my father?"

"We have met previously. I hear he is part of the delegation England has sent to Vienna."

Louisa nodded. "Papa has already been there several months and will remain until the map of Europe is redrawn. During his absence, I went to stay with my aunt and uncle, Lord and Lady Uxbridge, Her Grace's parents. I accompanied them to most of the affairs this past Season so it was a very different spring for me."

"I am sorry to have missed you," he said. "Normally, I am at most events but after my father's death, I found the estate and our financial affairs in disarray. My time was better spent at Boxwell Hall."

"Is that your country estate, my lord?"

"Yes, it is in Sussex. The property is quite lovely. Fortunately, after several months, I have made sense of the ledgers and feel I have a good handle on the estate, which is why I was eager to accept Her Grace's invitation for this house party. It is nice to be in the company of others again." He paused. "Especially one as lovely as you, Miss Goulding."

Louisa sensed the blush tinging her cheeks. "Thank you, my

lord," she said graciously.

The viscount glanced up. "I see the butler has arrived so it must be time to go in to dinner. Might I escort you to the dining room, Miss Goulding?"

Before she could reply, Owen appeared at her side. "I am afraid Miss Goulding has already promised me that honor," he said smoothly. "Perhaps another time, Boxling." He offered her his arm.

Louisa was dismayed at the interruption and the fact that Owen had lied. Though she took his arm, she looked at Lord Boxling and said, "I would be happy to continue our conversation after dinner, my lord."

The viscount brightened. "That would be delightful, Miss Goulding. We might even take a stroll through His Grace's gardens. I have heard they are lovely."

"Excuse us," Owen said brusquely and led her away as Arthur announced dinner.

"What was that all about?" she demanded.

"I wanted to warn you about Viscount Boxling."

"Warn me? What has he done? Stolen the silverware? His lordship seemed to be quite nice."

"I knew him at university," Owen said.

"That was years ago. If he acted immaturely then, I am certain he has changed. I found him to be quite charming."

"Oh, he is always charming. The ladies flock to him."

Louisa frowned. "You seem jealous of him."

Owen snorted. "Not in the least. I merely wanted to confirm he was the same man I remembered from university. Boxling was a womanizer then and I doubt he has changed. You don't need to be strolling through any gardens with him, Louisa."

They entered the dining room and she said, "I found Lord Boxling most agreeable. Remember, Owen, this is my time. If I choose to walk in the gardens with one of the guests, it is my business. Not yours."

He led her to a chair, where a card displayed her name, and

seated her. Leaning down, he said, "You said you would listen to me. My advice is to stay away from Boxling."

"I will take your opinion under consideration. But for now, I plan to get to know Lord Boxling—and the other guests, of course. Go find your seat, Owen, and leave me be."

He frowned at her and strode away to the far end of the table.

Mr. Hampton took a seat next to her. "It's Miss Goulding, isn't it? I'm trying to keep everyone's name straight."

Louisa smiled. "It is, indeed."

As the rest of the company took their seats, she reined in her temper.

And hoped she wouldn't have any more problems with Owen trying to ride roughshod over her.

CHAPTER FOURTEEN

OWEN WATCHED LOUISA surreptitiously throughout dinner, upset that she had waved away his advice about Viscount Boxling. He made certain that he spoke with the man once Boxling arrived at Cliffside, hoping that he might have changed from their university days. Though the viscount hadn't mentioned his womanizing in the past, he did fondly recall carousing with other young Cambridge men. Owen had asked if Boxling still enjoyed making merry and the viscount merely smiled enigmatically.

That was proof enough to Owen that Boxling was not good enough for Louisa.

Unfortunately, she was proving hardheaded. He would try again to get her alone and explain to her, without giving too many details, why he believed she should eliminate the handsome viscount from her list.

"You live nearby, my lord?" asked the woman on his right.

What was her name? She was distantly related to Ev. He hadn't bothered to remember any of the female guests' names since he didn't plan on interacting with them. This one was a perfect example of why he had no plans to be trapped in marriage anytime soon. She was blond, blue-eyed, bubbly, and didn't seem to have a brain in her pretty head. The little conversation he'd tried to have with her during the soup course bored him beyond tears.

"Yes, my lady," he said, hoping since she was related to a duke that she was the one who was a lady. The other three claimed the title of miss.

"What is your estate like?"

"Large," he said, seeing that Louisa was glancing down the table at him. Deliberately, he gave his dinner companion a lazy smile. "It's called Danfield."

She blinked. "You are Lord Danbury. Your home is Danfield. Oh, that's very clever," she noted.

He smiled again, hoping Louisa was still watching. "I had nothing to do with the naming of it, my lady. Some long ago Lord Danbury came up with the name, I suppose."

"Have you been friends with His Grace for very long?"

"Only from the cradle," he said and she giggled at his wit.

Owen took a chance and looked Louisa's way. She only had eyes for the man next to her and was smiling at something Mr. Hampton said. The man was handsome. In fact, all four of the male guests Adalyn had invited had looks, charm, and other than Hampton, a title. Owen didn't want Louisa to be amused by Mr. Hampton. He certainly didn't want her strolling through the gardens with Boxling.

"Since that was the final course," Ev said, "I believe the ladies will retire to the drawing room while we gentlemen sip our port."

"No cigars," Adalyn said. "I might as well tell everyone now. The smell of a cigar nauseates me to no end. I hated them before but now that I am with child, I cannot bear the scent of a cigar."

Congratulations were swiftly offered to Ev and Adalyn, with people asking when the babe would arrive and if they had decided upon any names.

"We should become parents sometime in February," Ev said. "As for names, we really haven't discussed any yet." He smiled down the table at his wife. "I suppose since Her Grace will be doing all the work carrying and delivering our child, I should let her decide on his or her name."

Owen noticed that Lord Marksbury frowned at that remark. That was a black mark against him, Owen decided. Marksbury was probably one of those men who dominated women and expected his wife to defer to his every whim. If that was the case, then he certainly wouldn't appreciate Louisa.

Adalyn rose and said, "If the ladies will accompany me to the drawing room, I will ask His Grace to shepherd the men our way once they have finished their port. We'll allow the ladies to entertain us once we're back together as a group. I know my cousin, Louisa, will want to sing for you."

His eyes flew to Louisa, who pinkened slightly as she nodded. That was good. If Louisa were to sing for everyone, she couldn't be strolling in the gardens with Boxling.

The women excused themselves and port was poured for the men. They gossiped idly about politics until it was time to rejoin the others. Owen tried to join Boxling so that he might detain him long enough to keep him from sitting with Louisa. Instead, Viscount Hurley ambled over to Owen and struck up a conversation as they left the dining room.

"You were in the army, His Grace tells me," Hurley said. "I am surprised our paths did not cross."

"Yes. I sold out as a major. My brother had been severely injured and had fallen into a coma. I was summoned home to manage the estate since it was unknown if or when he might rouse from it."

"I assume since you were introduced to me as Lord Danbury that he did not and succumbed to his injuries."

"He did," Owen said, leaving it at that.

"I was among those who marched into Paris," Hurley revealed. "A day that I never thought would happen. Then I received a letter informing me that my brother had passed unexpectedly, which left me as the new viscount."

"It's hard, isn't it?" he said. "Having never trained for such a position. Thinking you would be in the army your entire life."

Hurley nodded. "It has taken some getting used to. I love my country estate, however. Always did as a boy growing up there. I look forward to raising my own boys on it and teaching them to swim, hunt, and fish."

"Then you want children?" Owen asked.

"The sooner, the better," Hurley confided. "I never thought I would have the opportunity to be a family man. Now that I am a viscount, I can dedicate myself to my wife and children." He chuckled. "Of course, I will need to get said wife first."

As they entered the drawing room, the viscount said, "I know Their Graces didn't ask me to this house party merely for my sparkling company. There are five unattached females here. I plan to leave this gathering engaged to one of them."

His bluntness surprised Owen. "You do?"

"I have no qualms about offering for a woman. Her Grace seems to be a good judge of character. She has brought us here for a reason." Hurley gazed about the room. "They all seem nice but I find myself drawn to Miss Goulding, in particular. She has a grace and maturity about her that the others do not possess."

Of all the bachelors present, Owen knew Hurley would be the best choice for Louisa. With a heavy heart, he said, "Miss Goulding is a wonderful woman. Charming and intelligent. I wish you luck with your endeavor."

Owen excused himself and retreated to a corner of the room. Unfortunately, Miss Rexford motioned for him to come closer. He did, claiming the empty seat next to her.

"No need for you to hide in the corner, Lord Danbury," she said, her eyes sparkling with interest. "This will give us a chance to visit."

"I thought it was polite to keep silent while others performed," he said lightly.

Miss Rexford grinned. "I am afraid I am terrible at obeying conventional rules, my lord. If there is an atrocious singer, I will whisper so in your ear. I will wager that I might possibly even make you laugh."

This one was a spitfire. He would need to stay as far away

from her as possible.

He gazed about the room and saw that Louisa was sitting with Miss Peterson. Both Hurley and Boxling stood behind the two women. A flare of jealousy rushed through him as Boxling placed his hand on Louisa's shoulder for a moment, leaning down to say something to her.

Adalyn claimed everyone's attention, saying, "I know many of you traveled a good distance to be here and so we won't make this first night a late one. I have a full slate of activities for us tomorrow. I thought, though, that it would be nice to hear a little music this evening to calm us before we adjourned for the night."

She smiled at Lady Sara. "Would you grace us with a song? I have heard that you have a lovely voice and that Miss Oxford often accompanies you."

The young woman rose. "I would be happy to, Your Grace." Looking to her friend, she said, "Come on, you."

Miss Oxford stood, her hand covering her mouth as she tried—and failed—to stifle a giggle.

"This is going to be a long night," Miss Rexford murmured behind her fan. "Even if Her Grace promised it would be short."

Owen grunted in agreement.

Fortunately, Miss Oxford played quite well and Lady Sara had a sweet soprano voice. She sang two numbers and then thanked everyone for their attention before returning to her seat.

"I think one more pair should perform and then we might retire," Adalyn said. "Cousins? Would you mind?"

Owen had heard Tessa play when he visited her and Spence. Even as a mother and countess, Tessa practiced a good hour a day. She had remarked to Owen that playing kept her happy. When Spence had given his wife a lascivious look and said that he thought he kept her happy, Tessa smugly told her husband, "You kept me satisfied."

Owen thought the room might go up in flames as the married pair exchanged a heated glance and they soon excused themselves to attend to household business.

He knew exactly what that business had entailed.

Tessa rose, as did Louisa, and they met at the pianoforte. Tessa seated herself and they spoke briefly. He assumed they discussed what song they would use to entertain the group. He wondered if Louisa's voice was as high and clear as Lady Sara's had been.

From the first note that came from her mouth, it was apparent it was the complete opposite. Louisa's voice was low, rich, and sultry. It made Owen think of the many decadent things he wanted to do with her. The ways he would touch her. The little cries she would make. He relived the memory of having intimately touched her, his fingers feeling her juices as her orgasm spilled from her. He had deliberately avoided recalling any part of that moment.

Until now.

By God, he wanted her. All of her. For those kinds of moments and so many others he wished to create between them.

The last note sounded and a hush filled the room. Then enthusiastic applause broke out.

Miss Rexford leaned close and said in his ear, "Remind me never to follow Miss Goulding in song."

"She is quite gifted," he said neutrally. "And the countess plays beautifully."

"Please, Miss Goulding, you must sing something else for us," Lord Marksbury enthused. "Your voice is simply breathtaking."

Owen watched Louisa flush at the compliment. "One more and then we should bring an end to this night," she said.

After conferring with Tessa again, Louisa began to sing. Once more, her voice brought stirrings to Owen that he should not be feeling. While he thought Hampton and Marksbury not quite good enough for her and Boxling wildly inappropriate, he decided that Hurley would be the best for Louisa. He vowed to help the younger man press his suit.

Louisa ended the song, the last note rich and tender. His gaze met hers and he nodded at her in approval. She returned his nod and then smiled at the room.

"I suppose most men here just fell in love with Miss Goulding," Miss Rexford observed. She casually placed a hand on his arm. "Would that include you, my lord?"

"I don't believe in love," Owen told her. "Besides, Miss Goulding is like family to me. I am not one to lust after a little sister."

Miss Rexford's eyes lit with interest. "That is good to know, Lord Danbury. Very good to know."

Owen realized he now had a tiger by the tail—and hoped it wouldn't be his undoing.

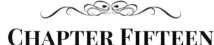

CHAPTER FIFTEEN

LOUISA HAD TILLY dress her in her riding habit since Adalyn had mentioned to the group last night that riding was planned immediately after breakfast. Breakfast would not be served in the breakfast room. It was simply too small to accommodate such a large party. Instead, the meal would be held in the dining room.

She went downstairs and found Viscount Boxling lingering in the foyer.

He brightened when he saw her and said, "Good morning, Miss Goulding. It seems to be a fine day for those of us in the country. You are looking splendid this morning. It was clever of you to show up for breakfast in your riding habit."

She figured she had already made a mistake and that none of the other female guests would be wearing their habits to the morning meal.

"I have been riding after breakfast every morning since I arrived at Cliffside," she told the handsome lord. "I have found it more convenient to simply dress in my riding habit and go straight to the stables. I hope you are not offended by my faux pas."

He offered his arm and began guiding her toward the dining room.

"On the contrary, it shows you have good sense. I appreciate that in a man—or a woman." He smiled and she felt a slight tingle at both the attention and his compliment.

They entered the dining room and she saw about half the party was already assembled, including Tessa and Spencer. She and Lord Boxling went through the large buffet and then they joined her cousin and Spencer. She noticed how easy Lord Boxling seemed in their company and how the conversation flowed effortlessly.

"Are you going riding this morning, Tessa?" she asked.

"No, I think Spencer and I are taking Analise for a walk instead," Tessa replied.

"Do you think your husband will allow you to hold your daughter?" she teased and then saw Lord Boxling's confused expression. She added, looking at him, "Lord Middlefield is quite taken with his daughter and wags her about."

Louisa watched the viscount's face carefully, wondering what his reaction would be to that bit of information.

"I have a fondness for children myself," he revealed. "My sister has two children, a boy and a girl. They both enjoy riding about atop my shoulder, where they can see the world a little better."

Tessa laughed. "Don't give my husband any ideas, my lord. Analise is only six months."

Spencer's eyes lit up. "But it won't be long before I can place her up there, my love. Good idea, Boxling. Thank you for the suggestion."

As for Louisa, it thrilled her to know that one of her prospective suitors enjoyed his niece and nephew enough to carry them about that way.

Lord Boxling added, "Once your daughter is old enough, she will also like for you to play horsey with her. I spend quite a bit of time down on all fours with my niece on my back, her hands fisted in my hair as she commands me to go faster."

They all laughed and Louisa felt warmth rush through her at the idea of seeing the viscount act as a horse with a child on his back.

Viscount Hurley and Miss Rexford joined them and the conversation was lively. Still, Louisa could feel Owen's gaze upon her the entire time. He sat at the opposite end of the table with Lady Sara and Miss Oxford and seemed most interested in the pair, though his eyes seemed to land in her direction more often than not. She remembered his warning about Lord Boxling and could find no fault in the man so far. The viscount was amiable, charming, and comfortable with himself and others. If he chose to pursue her, she would be excited at the prospect.

Viscount Hurley asked her, "How long have you been at Cliffside, Miss Goulding?"

"I came to the country with about three weeks of the Season yet to go," she told him. "I am very close with Her Grace and Lady Middlefield. My cousins have also been my closest friends my entire life and once they left town, I found that I missed them terribly. I believe you recently left the military, my lord?" she asked, wanting to purse a conversation with this viscount, as well.

"I was in the army a good while, Miss Goulding. That is how I know His Grace. In an unusual set of circumstances, I claimed the title and am finding my way through my duties—and looking to my future." He regarded her carefully and added, "I am most eager to wed and start a family. I was delighted to accept Her Grace's invitation to this house party."

Louisa nervously licked her lips and caught herself doing so. Oh, dear, would Lord Hurley think she was flirting with him? Then she decided perhaps she should. There was no reason to put all her eggs into one basket with Lord Boxling, especially if that did not work out. Viscount Hurley was a most impressive man in looks, with that ramrod posture that the army must drill into its officers. The fact that he was openly declaring he was interested in finding a wife and having children fascinated her.

"It doesn't seem as if you are here to play games, my lord," she noted.

His eyes gleamed at her. "I am not, Miss Goulding. I have

always had my own mind—and gone after what I wanted."

"Single-mindedness can be a good thing, or bad," Lord Boxling said. "So, you are here to find a wife at this house party, Hurley?"

"That is a distinct possibility," Hurley said brusquely, glancing to Louisa and back to Boxling.

Lord Boxling smiled, a steely resolve reflected in his gaze as he said, "That is also something I am most interested in, as well. I inherited my father's title at Christmastime. I will admit I have sown my share of wild oats but family has always been important to me. I hope to find a bride myself soon. If it happens at this house party, so much the better."

Louisa felt her face flush and met Tessa's gaze. Her cousin gave her a slight nod, whether in approval Louisa did not know. What she did know was that two very attractive bachelors present were actively pursuing women and they both seemed most interested in children. That she had learned all of this before the first breakfast was completed astonished—and pleased—her.

Adalyn and Everett entered the dining room and went around greeting each of their guests individually. When they reached her, Adalyn said, "My parents should be arriving by noon today. Papa had some business to finish up in town, which is why they are arriving a bit later than everyone else."

"Oh, I look forward to seeing them," Louisa said. To those sitting around her, she added, "I have been staying with Lord and Lady Uxbridge while my father has been at the congress in Vienna."

Adalyn and Everett moved on and those gathered near her began talking about the end of the long war with Bonaparte and England's hopes for how this conference would turn out. Viscount Hurley had definite opinions, having been in the army and fighting against Bonaparte, while Lord Boxling seemed to know quite a bit as well from his time in the House of Lords. Both men asked several questions of Louisa and she answered openly and honestly, wanting to see their reactions to the fact that a woman had not only an opinion but an informed one.

To her delight, neither gentleman seemed a bit judgmental and both asked several follow-up questions of her. By the time the conversation wound down, she looked about and realized they were the last ones remaining in the dining room.

"Will you be riding this morning, Miss Goulding?" asked Lord Hurley.

Lord Boxling quickly answered for her, saying, "Yes, Miss Goulding has promised to ride with me this morning. Are you also coming along, Hurley?"

Louisa sensed the sudden tension in the air between the two men and almost laughed aloud, realizing she was the source of it. Nothing of the sort had ever happened to her. Once again, she had to thank Owen for helping her to blossom and empowering her with a confidence she had previously lacked. She had always been self-assured when dealing with her father and the many men who came through their townhouse but this new social confidence surprised her. It felt good to possess it. To be a woman that not one—but two—men were interested in.

"Shall we head to the stables then?" she asked.

Both men rose quickly and Lord Boxling was the first to help her from her chair. He tucked her hand possessively into the crook of his arm and guided her from the dining room. Lord Hurley followed fast on their heels.

When they reached the stables, it was a flurry of activity, as grooms were bringing out various horses for so many riders.

Her favorite groom, Georgie, approached and said, "Don't worry, Miss Goulding. I have made sure to save Fancy for you. I'll bring her out now if you are ready for her."

"Thank you, Georgie, please do so."

Lord Boxling chuckled. "It seems you have charmed both servants and guests at Cliffside alike, Miss Goulding."

Louisa could not hide the blush that rose high on her cheeks.

Viscount Hurley claimed her attention with a question and they continued to converse until Fancy was brought out for her, as well as a mount for each viscount.

"Here, let me assist you into the saddle," Lord Boxling said, his hands clasping her waist and placing her into the saddle.

Lord Boxling's touch was pleasant but it did not bring about the tingles that Owen's did. Louisa rid herself of the thought. Owen was not for her. She must look to her future and not the brief past she had shared with him. As she waited for her escort to mount, she glanced about the yard and saw Owen already mounted upon Galahad. He was in conversation with Miss Peterson. Louisa liked Miss Peterson very much. The woman was pretty and well-spoken. It would be lovely if Owen would consider Miss Peterson to be his countess. He would have to wed at some point and it might as well be with a woman Louisa enjoyed being around. Because of her closeness to her cousins, no matter the man she married, she would always be visiting back and forth with Adalyn and Tessa. That would mean seeing Owen over the decades to come. She hoped she could be friendly with the wife he selected and that they, too, could continue the friendship they had struck up. She hadn't really known that men and women could be friends but she hoped she could with Owen.

As the last rider mounted, Louisa quickly counted heads and determined that only Adalyn, Tessa, and Spencer were not among their group. She knew Adalyn had given up riding because of the child she carried and also thought her cousin would be making last-minute preparations for her parents' arrival, especially since this would be their first time to visit Cliffside since their daughter had wed Everett.

"I thought I would take us on a tour of Cliffside," Everett told the group. "We should be gone a couple of hours. Her Grace will have refreshments waiting for us when we return."

Everett led the way and others began to fall in line behind him, including Lord Hurley. As Louisa started to move Fancy forward, Lord Boxling turned to her.

"You have probably ridden every inch of Cliffside during the past month," he commented.

"Yes. Georgie, the groom, took me to all four corners and everywhere in-between."

She neglected to mention the week Owen had first spent with her as they rode the estate and surrounding area.

Lord Boxling's penetrating gaze caused her heart to skip a beat. "The group is so large. Why don't you show me some of your favorite places at Cliffside, Miss Goulding?"

Before Owen had made her believe in herself, Louisa would have shied from such a request. Instead, she boldly met the viscount's gaze.

"I would be most happy to, my lord."

With that, she nudged Fancy and settled into a canter, Lord Boxling quickly at her side.

CHAPTER SIXTEEN

LOUISA STAYED WITH the group for almost five minutes before catching Lord Boxling's eyes and tilting her head to the left. They peeled away from the others, who continued on, and headed to the east. She kept Fancy at a steady canter for several minutes, the viscount keeping pace with her by her side. Occasionally, she would point at something and say a few words about it.

They rode to the top of a ridge which overlooked a majority of the estate. Lord Boxling swung from the saddle and then helped her down. He did smell very nice, a combination of bergamot and orange spice. He also cut a dashing figure, with his dark, wavy hair and dark eyes and tall frame. He dressed immaculately, as well, the best dressed of all the guests at the house party. She remembered he mentioned sowing many wild oats and wondered if his taste in clothing might be a holdover from days when he chased after the opposite sex.

"Come look over here," she told him, moving to the tip of the ridge. "You can see most of Cliffside from here. There are the main house and stables. The gardens are over there. The tenant farmers have their cottages that way. The fields for growing crops are next to them." She paused. "And over there you can see the sea."

The viscount stood next to her, gazing out. She glanced at his profile for a moment and found him very appealing.

"I think this view is magnificent," she said.

Lord Boxling turned and faced her. "And I believe you are magnificent," he said softly.

She heard her breath catch. "Oh! I am afraid I don't know how to reply to that, my lord. I know it is a compliment. One I never thought to receive."

His hands sought and found hers. Even through her gloves, she could feel the heat.

"I don't know why not," he said. "You are a remarkable woman, Miss Goulding. As knowledgeable as you are beautiful."

She shook her head. "Now I know you are flattering me, my lord."

"Why so?"

"My cousins are beautiful women. In the right gown and light, I can be pretty at best."

He smiled. "Then this is certainly the right light and most definitely the right gown."

"Riding habit," she corrected, feeling her cheeks heat.

"Riding habit," he agreed, his hands squeezing hers.

They stared at each other and he finally said, "I would like to kiss you, Miss Goulding. Might you be agreeable to that suggestion?"

Her cheek now burned. "I . . . suppose so, my lord." She swallowed hard. "If you want to."

His eyes gleamed. "Oh, I most certainly want to, Miss Goulding." He paused. "Might you share with me your Christian name?"

"Louisa," she said breathlessly, her heart racing.

"Louisa," he repeated as he clasped her shoulders and lowered his lips to hers.

The kiss was gentle. Unrushed. Sweet.

But it wasn't Owen.

She placed a palm against Lord Boxling's chest to steady herself as she flung thoughts of Owen as far as she could.

He broke the kiss, his lips hovering just above hers. "That was nice."

"Yes, it was," she said, swallowing.

It had been nice. Better than her first two kisses had been. Much better, in fact. If she had not kissed Owen, then she would now be perfectly happy.

She was happy, she told herself. A handsome viscount who was thinking about getting married and liked children had kissed her. What woman wouldn't be happy in these circumstances?

"Louisa, may I kiss you again?" he asked.

"Please," she whispered, hoping, praying that this man might be the one for her.

Lord Boxling's lips pressed against hers again, firmer this time. His hands tightened on her shoulders. Both her hands went to his waistcoat, gripping it tightly. She sensed that he was holding back. Part of her appreciated that he respected her and did so. The other half wished he would use his tongue so that she could compare his kiss to Owen's.

How did one ask a man to kiss that way?

Louisa thought back to what Owen had taught her. If she used her tongue, the viscount might be shocked beyond words. But she could open to him—and see what he did.

She relaxed her jaw slightly, her lips parting. She felt him stiffen slightly and worried he would think her loose.

His teeth sank softly into her bottom lip. And yes, a little tingle did surface quickly before fading. He eased the pressure and swiped at the place with his tongue. But then he kissed her again. No tongue involved. It was very pleasurable.

Breaking the kiss, he smiled down at her. "I hope you don't think me too forward, Louisa."

"No, I don't think that at all, my lord. I believe you are very respectful of me."

He framed her face with his hands. "I hope we can get to know each other better over the next few days."

"I would like that very much, my lord."

And she meant it. This nice, attractive, intelligent man was certainly worth getting to know.

"Shall we continue our ride?" he asked.

"Yes, I have a few other places I would like to show you."

"Good." He bent and quickly pressed a soft kiss against her lips and then straightened.

They returned to their horses and he stepped to her, his hands fastening about her waist.

"Thank you for allowing me to kiss you."

"I should be thanking you, my lord." She smiled. "It was very nice."

He lifted her into the saddle and they continued their ride. When they started back to the house, they came across the large group and fell in behind them. Louisa wondered if anyone would even realize that two of their party had gone off on their own during Everett's tour.

Georgie met her as they returned to the stables. "How was Fancy today, Miss Goulding?"

"She was in good spirits." Glancing at Lord Boxling, she added, "It was a most pleasant time."

The viscount helped her from the saddle and Georgie took their horses, leading them away. Everett was telling everyone to gather on the terrace for refreshments.

"I think the ladies need a few minutes to freshen up and change our gowns, Your Grace," Miss Peterson said and all the females murmured in agreement.

"I will see you in a few minutes, my lord," Louisa promised Lord Boxling and then joined the group of women heading toward the house.

She went to her bedchamber and rang for Tilly. The maid already had a fresh gown placed upon the bed and brought water with her.

"Let's get you out of that habit, Miss, and you can wash some before stepping into your morning gown," Tilly told her.

Within a quarter-hour, Louisa felt refreshed, eager to continue her conversation with Lord Boxling. She left her bedchamber and headed down the corridor, only to find Owen waiting for her near the stairs.

"Where were you?" he demanded.

She frowned. "Why, I was changing from my riding habit as the others."

He took her elbow. Heat from him seared into her.

"I meant during the ride."

"Oh, that."

He glared at her. "Yes. That."

"I showed Lord Boxling parts of the estate. The party was so large and I am quite familiar with Cliffside after all my rides about it."

"Was it his idea or yours?"

Louisa's cheeks pinkened. "What do you mean?"

"Did he suggest leaving the group or did you?"

She snorted in exasperation. "Why does that even matter, Owen?"

"Did he kiss you?"

Louisa's eyes went wide. "That is none of your business!" she hissed.

Owen's eyes narrowed. "That means he did," he said grumpily.

"Whether he did or didn't is absolutely none of your concern," she said icily. "Please, release my arm."

He glanced down and saw he was holding her elbow and let go.

"Owen, I know you are my friend—"

"You're damned right I am."

"But friends don't order friends about. You are treating me like one of your soldiers. Snapping your fingers and expecting me to blindly obey any command you give." She crossed her arms. "Well, I won't have it, do you understand that?"

His eyes darkened. "Did he kiss you?" he asked softly.

"*If* he did—and I am saying if—it was because I thought it was a good idea and allowed him to do so. I have told you that Tessa and Adalyn think kissing is important when deciding upon a husband. Even you told me kissing in a marriage is important. If I am to decide whether or not I like a man enough to marry him, then I am going to have to kiss a few of them to find out."

"Did you enjoy his kiss—as much as mine?"

Louisa shook her head. "You . . . are impossible."

She brushed past him and hurried down the stairs.

What right did he think he had to ask her such questions? What if she did kiss Lord Boxling? It was none of his business. At all.

OWEN STOOD ON the terrace and wondered for the tenth time what he had been thinking when he confronted Louisa.

She was right. It was none of his concern if she rode off alone with a handsome rake. If she kissed said rake. If she *liked* kissing said rake.

Anger caused his blood to boil.

"You look as if you could use a bit of punch," Tessa said, pressing a cup upon him. "I know the day is warming up. Hopefully, this will cool you off."

He accepted the cup and quickly drained it of its contents, not tasting anything.

"What's wrong, Owen?"

"Nothing," he said tersely, glancing away and finding Louisa standing in a group with Miss Peterson, Mr. Hampton. And Lord Boxling.

"Nothing—or Louisa?" Tessa ventured.

Whipping his head around, he said, "What did you say? Oh, never mind." He placed his cup on a tray held by a passing footman.

"You are out of sorts," Tessa said. "I don't like to see you this way."

"And I don't like meddling wives."

She frowned. "You think to hurt me when you are the one hurting. Come, Owen, I am one of the few present that you can speak with about this. Or would you rather me call Spencer or Everett over so you men can solve your little problem."

"It's not a little problem, Tessa," he complained. "It shouldn't be a problem at all."

"But it is a very big one. Please, share it with me. I promise you our conversation will go no further. Not even to Louisa."

He harumphed. "It's just that Boxling is interested in her."

Tessa glanced over to the viscount. "Yes, he is a most impressive man. I could tell last night he was interested in Louisa."

"Well, he shouldn't be," growled Owen. "Actually, he should. I can't for the life of me understand why more men haven't been taken with her. But Boxling is not a good sort."

"Spencer did tell me that Lord Boxling was quite the ladies' man during your university days. He has spoken with the viscount, however, and believes with the death of his father, Lord Boxling has put aside his wandering ways. In fact, he disclosed to Spencer last night that he is very interested in finding a wife and the timing of this house party seemed like providence. Even at breakfast this morning, he was speaking fondly of his niece and nephew."

"He damned well better not offer for Louisa."

"Who should, Owen?" Tessa asked innocently.

"Hurley," he sputtered. "The man seems steady as a rock."

"I overheard Lord Hurley tell Louisa at breakfast that he is eager for a family. Perhaps he will offer for her by the end of the house party. Usually, an engagement or two occurs at the end of such affairs."

"They do?"

Tessa nodded. "Very often. You would do well to look over the ladies in attendance, Owen. I think Miss Peterson would be an admirable choice if you are not interested in Louisa."

"I am not interested in Miss Peterson or the idea of matrimony."

"And yet it seems as if you would keep Louisa from it."

"No, I don't want to do that. Just that Lord Boxling is not right for her. And Hampton has no occupation nor a title. Lord Marksbury is—"

"You would be an ideal match for Louisa, Owen," Tessa said quietly. "Spencer and I have talked it over. Everett and Adalyn also believe the two of you are well suited."

Her words angered him. "It is so good to know that my dear friends have my entire life planned out for me, including the woman I should make my countess. Have the four of you discussed where the marriage should take place? How many children we should have? And which of you would comfort my wife when I decided to spend nights with my mistress?"

Tessa scowled at him. "You are being more stubborn than a donkey, Owen Hasbury. Go ahead and brood all you want. If you are the kind of man who would leave a wife such as Louisa for the arms of a mistress, then I don't want you near my cousin. Don't talk to her. Don't flirt with her. And by God, don't you dare offer for her."

With that, Tessa stormed away, past several of the guests, who looked from her to him in confusion.

Spence, who had been talking with Marksbury and Ev, strode over to Owen, anger flashing in his eyes.

"Whatever you did or said to Tessa, you will apologize, Owen," his friend said. "Give her a chance for her temper to cool but know this—I expect an apology."

Spence turned away, leaving Owen standing alone. Here he thought if he didn't become involved with Louisa in any manner that it would be for the best and help him keep his friendships with Ev and Spence. Now, he was alienating his friends and their wives.

And he still didn't have Louisa.

"Bloody hell," he said to himself.

CHAPTER SEVENTEEN

LOUISA CAME TO the bottom of the staircase and realized she was far too agitated to join the other house party guests on the terrace. She headed for Adalyn's study, hoping to get ahold of her emotions in a more private place. Then she realized with the French doors inside it that overlooked the terrace, she might actually be seen.

Instead, she had a better idea.

Making her way to the rear of the house, she took the servants' stairs to the top floor. She would go to the nursery. A visit with Analise would be just the thing to calm her and help her regroup emotionally.

As she made her way along the corridor, she spied Analise's nursery governess leaving. The woman smiled and greeted Louisa as she passed. Wondering why the servant left the baby alone, Louisa hurried inside the nursery.

And found her uncle rocking Analise.

He glanced up and smiled. "Ah, Louisa. It is good to see you, my dear."

"I wasn't expecting to find you here, Uncle Uxbridge," she admitted.

A smile lit his face. "I am practicing on Analise. Adalyn confided to us about the babe. I hope she and His Grace fill this house with children."

Then a shadow crossed his face. Louisa knew he must be thinking back on all the babes that her aunt had lost. Adalyn was the only one to survive to maturity. Upon his death, Lord Uxbridge's title would go to his brother, Edgar, and with Edgar's passing, a distant cousin.

"You have always been a perfectly splendid father—and uncle—and you will be a wonderful grandfather."

"I think so."

She glanced down at the yawning girl, whose eyelids fluttered several times and then closed.

"Ah, I think our little beauty is ready for her nap," he said softly, rising and carrying Analise to the cradle and placing her down gently.

Louisa joined him and they stood gazing at the babe in wonder.

Then he turned to her, taking her arm and leading her away to the window, which looked out over the Cliffside gardens.

"What ails you, Child?" he asked. "Something is definitely amiss."

"It was that obvious?"

He chuckled. "You have never been one who could hide what you were thinking, Louisa. What has upset you? Or rather . . . who?"

She had always liked Uncle Uxbridge and decided to confide in him.

"It is Lord Danbury. He is a close friend of Everett and Spencer. They went to school together and then served in the army alongside each other, as well. His estate lies next to Cliffside."

"So, he is frequently here? And he has you out of sorts."

Louisa nodded. "We have become friendly since I arrived at Cliffside. In fact, Lord Danbury even took me out riding multiple times. Adalyn said that riding would be a big part of this house party. You know I haven't been in the country in years and years so I hadn't ridden in ages. I never do so in town. Lord Danbury was very patient with me and after so many hours in the saddle, I do feel much more confident about my riding skills."

"Then what troubles you."

She sighed. "I think he believes since I have no brothers and Papa is in Vienna that he should take upon himself a role of being my protector. He said that during the house party, he could get to know the eligible bachelors better than I could and would advise me about which ones might make for a suitable husband."

"That sounds reasonable."

"I thought so. Until he started giving me unsolicited advice. He has warned me off one and it looks likely he'll do the same about all the others. Like a protective brother, he is seeing that none of them are good enough for me."

He studied her a long moment. "There is more to this story, Louisa. Does this Lord Danbury fancy you himself?"

She shrugged. "I do find him incredibly attractive, Uncle. He's clever and interesting. But he only recently sold out and claimed his title. His brother was in a coma and Lord Danbury came home to manage the estate on his behalf."

"Ah, Danbury. I recall he and His Grace's brother were attacked."

"Yes, that's correct. Everett's brother died instantly, while Lord Danbury's brother lingered from severe injuries and never awoke. The new earl says that he has much to learn about his earldom and has no interest in a wife now or for several years to come. Even if I did want to consider him as a husband, I am already four and twenty. I don't have the time to wait for years to see if he might be interested in me."

"And yet he doesn't want to seem to allow any other gentleman to be interested in you."

"It is worse, Uncle. We had terrible words just now. He was bossing me about. Practically ordering me not to have anything to do with a gentleman he believes is unsuitable. My opinion of this man is far different."

"Then you should follow your instincts, Louisa. You have always had a maturity about you, even when you were a little girl. If you think this man should be given a chance, do so. Lord Danbury can bugger off."

She laughed and he joined in.

"As far as protecting you, that is my role with your father out of the country. Shall I speak to this earl and set him straight?"

"I don't think that will be necessary, Uncle. I made it perfectly clear to him. If he does become annoying, then I will let you have at him."

"Agreed."

Louisa caught movement from the corners of her eyes and turned, seeing the nursery governess had returned.

"Thank you for allowing me to have a quick cup of tea, my lord."

"I enjoyed the time alone with Analise," he said. "And I got to have a lovely visit with my niece." He looked to Louisa. "We should go downstairs and rejoin the others, however."

She took the arm he offered and they left the nursery.

"Everyone will be on the terrace. Adalyn was serving light refreshments after our ride and before we begin lawn bowling."

They went outside and found the terrace crowded. Immediately, her aunt waved them over, giving Louisa a warm embrace.

"Oh, my dear, I have missed you so. Town wasn't the same without you. I hope you are still coming to Conley Park with us once the house party concludes."

"I am not certain of my plans, Aunt. Adalyn wishes me to stay here with her while she is increasing."

"I understand, dear. Know that you are always welcome to come to us when you are ready. Have you word from your father?"

"Not in two weeks. I should be due for another letter soon."

Lord Hurley joined them. "I do not believe I have been introduced to our newcomers," he said.

"Then I will do the honors, my lord. This is Lord and Lady Uxbridge, Her Grace's parents. This is Lord Hurley, who served with His Grace in the army and has recently assumed his title."

Her uncle brightened. "I do love the military. Wish I could have gone into it myself. Tell us a little about your experiences, Lord Hurley."

As he told several stories, Louisa believed it was a sanitized version of war the viscount spoke of. She glanced about, noticing that Tessa was missing.

And that Owen stood off to himself, apart from the group.

Spencer caught her eye and she excused herself, going to him.

"Is something wrong with Tessa? I see she is not here. Uncle Uxbridge and I just came from the nursery. Analise has gone down for a nap."

"Tessa stormed out of here after having a conversation with Owen. I have already made clear to him that he is to apologize for whatever he said that upset her. Her leaving caused a bit of a stir, which is why I did not follow her. Would you go see if she is all right?"

"Of course."

Louisa slipped from the terrace, wondering where Tessa might have gone. She guessed Adalyn's small parlor and went there first. Sure enough, the door was closed so she knocked softly and heard Tessa bid her to enter.

Her cousin looked out of sorts and she went and gave her a hug.

"I heard Owen upset you somehow. Spencer sent me to find you."

"Oh, that man is bloody pigheaded," Tessa declared.

Her cousin's words surprised Louisa. Tessa had a sweet nature and never spoke ill of anyone.

"What did he say?" she demanded.

"It doesn't matter. I think he's a fool and deserves what he gets. I won't let him upset me anymore and ruin the party. In fact, we should both go back outside."

"Why don't you go and bathe your face in cool water first," she suggested diplomatically.

"That is a good idea. Will you come with me?"

They went to the guest bedchamber Tessa and Spencer were staying in and Tessa washed her face and dabbed a bit of scent on her wrists.

"There. I feel much better. Let us return to the others."

The pair went downstairs and out to the terrace, joining Spencer. He was in conversation with Miss Peterson, Lord Marksbury, and Mr. Hampton.

Spencer slipped an arm about Tessa's waist. She merely nodded at him. Louisa believed all would be well.

At least if Owen apologized and quit irritating her and her cousin.

Footmen began collecting empty punch glasses and plates and Adalyn moved to the center of the terrace.

"We are going to go down to the bowling green for some lawn bowls. I have decided we will play in teams since that will allow more people to participate. It would be good for those who have played before to join with others who haven't. His Grace will explain the rules."

Everett stepped forward and explained what seemed to Louisa to be quite simple rules. She liked that the game would be uncomplicated.

Almost immediately, Lord Hurley appeared at her side.

"Have you played lawn bowls before, Miss Goulding?"

"No, this is my first country house party, my lord."

"Then I would be pleased if you would partner with me. I am an accomplished player."

She laughed. "I hope you don't mind losing. I have never had the so-called beginner's luck at anything I have tried."

He looked at her solemnly. "It isn't always about winning, Miss Goulding. Rather about the fun of the activity—and the company you keep."

"I would be happy to act as your partner, my lord," she assured him, feeling pleased that he had sought her out. While she had enjoyed her time with Lord Boxling, this man also interested her.

The viscount offered her his arm and she took it. They strolled to the bowling green along with the others. On the way, he reiterated the game rules to her.

"The jack—sometimes called the kitty—is a smaller ball than the others in play. It is also white. It is known as the target and is thrown out at the beginning of the game as a target."

"And the point is for the players to see who can get their ball the closest to the jack," she said.

"Exactly. The game has always been popular throughout England's history. In fact, Henry VIII worried that too many of his subjects would start playing lawn bowls instead of practicing archery, which was a necessary element of warfare in those days. The king made it illegal for all but the most wealthy to play. In fact, he made it a law that even the few who were allowed to play could only play on their own estates and even required they pay a licensing fee of one hundred pounds for the bowling greens they created on their lands."

"How absurd," Louisa declared.

Lord Hurley grinned. "Even more absurd? That requirement is still on the books today. His Grace pays the crown in order to have a bowling green at Cliffside."

Louisa shook her head. "Then we better help him get his money's worth," she joked.

They reached the area, which was a large, rectangular, flat piece of land, the lawn manicured and divided into parallel playing strips.

"Those long strips are known as rinks," Lord Hurley informed her. "If we were playing a singles competition, a coin would be flipped to see who wins the mat and starts a segment of the competition. The winner would place the mat and roll the jack to the other end of the green. Once the target—the jack—stops, it must be aligned to the center of the rink. Then the players take turns, rolling their bowls from the mat toward the jack."

"Remind me again about a ball being in play," Louisa said. "I was a bit unclear about that aspect."

"Certainly, Miss Goulding. Once a bowl is rolled, it must stop within the rink boundary in order to remain in play. If it falls into the ditch, that ball is removed from play unless it touched the jack as it rolled."

"His Grace called that a toucher, I believe," she said.

"You are correct. A toucher is marked with chalk and stays in play, thanks to having contact with the jack. And if the jack itself is knocked into the ditch, that becomes a dead end and must be replayed. The jack is placed again in the center of the rink."

"Once everyone has a turn, what then?" she asked.

"In singles play, each player fires off four balls. His Grace said that partners today would also be awarded four balls. We will toss one at a time. I will have two and you will have the same. We will alternate our tosses. Of course, the other players will go between our turns. We won't toss all four of ours in a row."

"That makes sense. Oh, I do hope my tosses won't embarrass me. Or you," she added, testing out one of the side glances Owen had her practice and batting her lashes at the viscount.

She gazed across the huge green. "Then once all the tosses have been made, the distance of the bowls closest to the jack is determined?"

"Yes, then points will be awarded. Play usually goes to twenty-one shots, though sometimes twenty-five is used instead. Points are often called shots." Lord Hurley looked across the green. "This green looks to be fast. I think it will be an excellent competition."

Louisa saw that Owen arrived last and she noted he did not seem to have selected a partner. Adalyn must have also realized that and took Miss Oxford to him, making certain the young lady would not be left out.

"It looks as if we are ready to begin," Everett called. "A prize will be awarded to the winning team."

"What?" cried Lady Sara. "I simply adore prizes."

"Win—and you'll find out," teased Everett. "Let the competition begin."

Louisa felt Owen's gaze upon her and deliberately placed her hand on Lord Hurley's arm.

"I hope we win, my lord," she said, giving him a brilliant smile.

Chapter Eighteen

Owen no longer wanted to be at this house party. He didn't want to do Adalyn a favor and keep her numbers even. He didn't want to be nice to people who were perfect strangers to him. Lady Sara and Miss Oxford got on his nerves with their constant giggling. Miss Rexford kept casting amorous looks his way, which he ignored. Miss Peterson was . . . well, Miss Peterson had said very little to him. She seemed the most sensible of the bunch but, at this moment, all females were getting on his nerves.

He hadn't even known he had nerves until today.

As for the gentlemen, he didn't wish for any friends beyond the Second Sons of London. That is, if he was even still friends with them. Spence was still shooting him daggers, while Tessa ignored Owen. Everett wouldn't be in a friendly frame of mind if Owen up and left for Danfield. Adalyn would be enraged, seeing her plans ruined.

The other gentlemen were not the kind he wanted to be friendly with. Oh, Hampton seemed a good enough sort if a bit young and clueless. Lord Marksbury had a bit of a sly sense of humor but nothing else stood out about him. As for Lord Boxling, he still believed the viscount to be unfit for Louisa.

And Owen was now having his doubts about Lord Hurley.

While he thought he had supported the former military officer's suit, he didn't like how aggressive the man seemed when it came to Louisa. Hurley had already openly discussed with Owen his wish to wed and quickly start a family. He had also made no secret of his interest in Louisa. He had dined with her at breakfast and cozied up to her aunt and uncle upon their arrival. Then when it was announced that they would be divided into partners for the lawn bowling, Hurley had practically run to Louisa's side and stolen her as his partner. Owen had thought he might ask her to play with him so that they could talk. He wanted to make amends for their earlier tiff.

Now, he was stuck with Miss Oxford, thanks to Adalyn's meddling, and would have to watch Louisa and Hurley together the rest of the afternoon. It was enough to bring on a bloody headache. Not that he ever got them.

But there was always a first time.

"My lord, have you played this game before?" asked Miss Oxford, squinting a bit in the sun.

"Yes, of course," he said brusquely. Then he saw her lip tremble and thought if she cried on him, he would have a massive headache. Wanting to forestall her tears and his aching head, he added, "I will be happy to show you what you need to know."

He glanced about and saw that was most likely the point of playing in mixed partners. It would allow the men to help their helpless female partners. He watched Boxling laughing, trying to show Miss Peterson what to do and how she flirted outrageously with him. Now, those two would be a good pair.

"Let me get a few of the bowls and we shall practice."

Owen retrieved several and did his best, trying to walk Miss Oxford through the steps for a good toss. Unfortunately, Lord Hurley was doing the same with Louisa. Her rolls were wild and after each one, she would laugh richly.

He wanted to kiss her into silence. Her seductive laugh was keeping him off-balance. He couldn't even think. Why was this happening? A woman had never affected him in such a way.

Returning his glance to his partner, he saw every attempt had gone into the ditch. "Try again, Miss Oxford. You will get the hang of it, I am certain," he told his companion, doubting the featherhead ever would.

Pretending to watch his partner, Owen instead stole glances at Louisa and Hurley. The damned man handed her a ball and then went behind her, his arms going around her as he instructed her how to hold and roll it, as if she were some drooling idiot and hadn't a clue how to do so.

"In this way, my lord?" Louisa asked, her voice low.

Damnation! She even gave the viscount one of the glances that Owen and she had practiced, fluttering her eyelashes prettily. Rage boiled within him. He forced himself to keep his feet planted instead of charging over there and smashing his fist into Hurley's face.

"I think we are about ready to begin," Ev told the group. "If you will retrieve your bowls, we can start."

After a draw, Lord Boxling won the mat and had the honor of rolling the jack to the other end of the green to serve as the target. He strutted about like a peacock before making an excellent toss, which all the ladies applauded. Owen's gaze met Hampton's and he shrugged.

As expected, his partner's two bowls fell in the ditch. Thankfully, Owen's both made it close to the jack.

"I rather like calling it a kitty," Miss Oxford said to him. "I like that name better than jack."

"Call it whatever you wish, Miss Oxford," he said, trying his best to keep exasperation from his voice as he looked with interest as Hurley and Louisa made their way to the mat.

The viscount allowed Louisa to go first. Surprisingly, her bowl rolled true down the center of the green, the first time that had occurred.

She shouted with glee. "I did it!" Her face glowed with pleasure.

It made him want to kiss her even more.

Hurley made a fine roll, while Louisa's second turn proved as disastrous as Miss Oxford's rolls.

"Oh, well," she said. "I suppose my beginner's luck has come to an end."

After all six teams completed their turns and measurements were taken, two were eliminated, including Hampton and Miss Rexford and Owen and Miss Oxford.

"I suppose we will have to watch the others," Miss Rexford said. "How boring."

Hampton suggested a stroll in the gardens to her and the pair left the others. Owen and Miss Oxford remained behind, cheering on their hosts.

The next round commenced, with the four remaining teams all taking turns and rolling four balls per team. After rolls were made and measurements taken, Ev and Adalyn, as well as Marksbury and Lady Sara, took to the sidelines.

"It's a showdown, Boxling," proclaimed Lord Hurley, who smiled at Louisa. "But I have faith my partner and I will prevail."

"I wouldn't be so certain," Boxling retorted. "Miss Peterson is improving with every roll."

Miss Peterson smiled broadly with the viscount's praise.

The two couples shook hands and Boxling again won the mat and rolled the jack into place.

"A well-placed jack, my lord," Louisa praised.

Jealousy flooded Owen at the smile she gave Boxling.

"Who will we cheer for this round, my lord?" Miss Oxford asked him.

He had forgotten she was still by his side. It would stick in his craw to cheer for either man.

"I don't care. You choose, Miss Oxford."

Worry filled her face. "Oh, I don't know. Both men are so athletic. And Miss Goulding and Miss Peterson have both gotten better as the competition has gone on."

"Then we should cheer all the good rolls and let the best team win," he told his partner.

She brightened. "What a clever idea, my lord." With that, she slipped her hand through his arm.

Maybe she wasn't as much of a featherhead as he had thought.

He hoped Louisa saw the gesture.

No, she was too busy flirting with both Hurley and Boxling. Irritation rippled through him in waves. Why had he thought Hurley a good match for Louisa? He had been wrong about that.

Actually, he had been wrong about other things.

The only thing he wasn't wrong about was wanting Louisa.

For himself.

This arbitrary timeline he had spouted about waiting years to wed was foolish. Tessa—and the others—had been right. Louisa Goulding was perfect for him in every way. Cultured. Polished. Beautiful. Intelligent. Why should he allow one of his peers to snatch such a gem from under his nose when it was obvious they were suited in every way?

Determination filled him. No other man was right for Louisa except him. He would have to let her know that he'd had a change of heart. He would offer for her and make her his countess.

He watched as Miss Peterson rolled her first time, followed by Boxling. Both did well. Louisa came next and surprised him by surpassing Miss Peterson's effort and coming close to where Boxling's bowl had landed. Hurley followed and his bowl came to land a hare's breadth from the jack.

"Are you sorry we aren't in the finals, my lord?" asked Miss Oxford.

"Not at all," he replied, keeping his eyes fixed upon the contestants.

"You like her, don't you?"

"Hmm."

"I said, you *like* her?" Miss Oxford prodded.

"What?"

"Miss Goulding."

"Yes, she is very nice," he said neutrally, not wanting to stir a cat fight between the two women, especially not before he had a chance to get Louisa alone and explain things to her.

"You watch her a lot. She's pretty but too opinionated. In my opinion." She giggled.

Owen focused on his companion a moment. "You are not as witty as you believe, Miss Oxford. My advice to you is to never speak ill of anyone—because you never know if it will come back to haunt you."

Her bottom lip stuck out in a pout. "I don't have a chance with you, do I, my lord."

"Not a one," he assured her.

She appraised him. "Thank you for being so straightforward with me." She slipped her hand from his arm.

He turned his attention back to the bowlers, having missed a couple of rolls. Watching the rest of the match play out, he could see that while Boxling and Hurley had been evenly matched, Louisa had outplayed Miss Peterson.

Ev completed the measurements and looked up, smiling. "It seems as if the victors are Lord Hurley and Miss Goulding!"

Polite applause filled the air, including that from Hampton and Miss Rexford, who had returned from their garden stroll.

"What is the prize, Your Grace?" asked Lady Uxbridge.

"It is a glass vase," Adalyn replied, signaling a footman, who brought the vase to her. "I suggest after tea that our winners go to the gardens and select a few blooms to place in it."

Lord Hurley stepped forward and claimed the vase and then handed it to Louisa. "You are the true winner today, Miss Goulding. You went from knowing nothing of the game to being quite dreadful to actually showing promise at lawn bowling. I believe you should claim this for your progress."

Louisa laughed, the color high on her cheeks, making her very appealing. Owen swallowed, knowing he better speak to her soon.

Perhaps he would tag along when she went to the gardens with Lord Hurley.

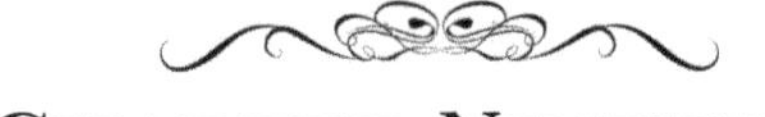

Chapter Nineteen

Louisa went up to her bedchamber to change again. She had had no idea so many gowns would be required at a house party. She thought she had changed gowns often during the Season while in town but this house party was proving to be twice as many times as usual. Tilly, however, was enjoying it and told Louisa to make certain to let her know what tomorrow's activities would involve in order for her to have the correct number of gowns that would be appropriate for each event.

As Tilly fussed with the ribbon on a gown, Louisa washed up, actually thankful to be changing clothes again before going to tea. Lawn bowling had proved to be a bit exerting but she was incredibly pleased at how well she had picked up on the sport. She hoped they would play again before the house party ended so she could practice her new skills some more. Especially after hearing that Everett had to pay the crown a licensing fee to have and maintain his bowling green, she wanted to make certain he got his money's worth.

"After tea, it is just dinner and indoor activities?" Tilly asked.

Louisa nodded. "Yes, and after tea I am to walk in the gardens with Lord Hurley and collect a few flowers for my new vase. Then I will need to freshen up and change again for dinner since it is a formal affair each evening. As far as I know, we will remain indoors after dinner. I believe Her Grace has a few parlor games planned."

"Very well, Miss Goulding. I have laid out the sprigged muslin for now and I think we should go with the blue satin for evening if that is agreeable with you."

"I am always happy to listen to your advice, Tilly. You have quite a sense of fashion, much more so than I ever will."

The maid helped Louisa into her gown, tying the ribbon beneath her bosom into an elaborate bow.

"Perhaps I should wear a fichu with this," she suggested. "The neckline is a bit low for the afternoon.

"Tsk-tsk," Tilly said, shaking her head. "That won't do at all, Miss Goulding. I know you are here to find a husband and one of the first things men do is look at a woman's bosom." Tilly gave her a stern look. "Don't think I am judging you in any way, Miss Goulding. I know the purpose of house parties and there are several good candidates among the men gathered here." She paused and then asked, "Are you interested in any particular gentleman?"

Though Louisa hated to gossip, she was interested in her maid's opinion. They had been together for many years and she trusted the servant.

"Lord Boxling and Lord Hurley have both been quite attentive to me," she began. "Both men have recently come into their titles and have indicated to me they are interested in wedding soon and having a family."

"Oh, Miss, that is wonderful to hear," Tilly exclaimed. "Both viscounts are quite handsome. Do you have a preference between them?"

Louisa did not have an answer for that. "No, not at this time. I am just beginning to know them. Perhaps in another few days, I might be able to answer your question."

"What about the other gentlemen? That Lord Danbury is a handsome devil, he is. It seems the two of you were growing quite friendly before the house party even began."

A wave of disappointment hit Louisa, knowing that Owen

was not considering a bride. She swallowed and said, "Lord Danbury is a good man. However, he is not the one for me. He is in no hurry to wed and, as you know, I am not getting any younger. I need to take the opportunities given to me in hand and hope something comes of them."

"Just asking, Miss Goulding. He always seems to look at you a bit hungrily, if you know what I mean."

Louisa did—because she felt as if she looked at Owen the exact same way. It didn't matter. She had to put those desires behind her and look ahead. Not behind.

"I think I will wear the earrings Papa gave me this evening. Or even now. They would look good with both this gown and that one."

"Of course," Tilly replied, retrieving the earrings and handing them to Louisa so that she might screw them onto her earlobes.

She rose, smoothing her skirts, giving herself one last glance in the mirror.

"You look very pretty, Miss Goulding. I hope you enjoy cutting flowers with Lord Hurley."

The two women left the bedchamber, Louisa turning to the right and Tilly to the left to go down the servants' staircase. As Louisa continued down the corridor, a door opened. Miss Peterson stepped out.

"Miss Goulding, it is so good to see you. Shall we go down to tea together?"

"That will suit me," she said. "How are you enjoying the house party, Miss Peterson?"

"Actually, more than I thought I would," the younger woman said. "I am glad we have struck up a friendship and hope that we might continue it once we leave here. I also have found several of the gentlemen present quite interesting."

"Do you favor any of them?" Louisa asked. "Are you looking for a husband, Miss Peterson?"

Miss Peterson chuckled. "I suppose we all are. I am three and twenty now and despite my bluestocking tendencies, I do long for a husband and a home of my own. Children, as well."

"I am a year your senior and know exactly what you mean," Louisa confided. "I also have a reputation as a bluestocking and have kept numerous men at bay during the Season. However, I have been pleasantly surprised that among the bachelors here, it doesn't seem to be much of an issue. In fact, a few of them have encouraged me and been interested in hearing my opinions."

"I suppose that is because of the men your cousin selected to invite as her guests," Miss Peterson said as they headed down the staircase. "I quite like Her Grace and I believe she likes me, too."

"She has spoken very highly of you," Louisa said, not wanting to tell her new friend that Adalyn had actually considered Miss Peterson at one point to be Everett's duchess.

"Who knows?" Miss Peterson asked. "I have heard that house parties often spark an engagement or two. Wouldn't it be lovely if we each found our match here at Cliffside over the next week?"

They continued to the drawing room, where tea would be served, and entered the room. Immediately, Lord Boxling and Lord Marksbury joined them.

"Congratulations on your victory at lawn bowling today, Miss Goulding," Lord Boxling said, his eyes taking her in with interest.

"Thank you, my lord. I do believe I experienced beginner's luck. It was quite enjoyable, though, and I would be happy to participate in another contest if my cousin decides to hold one."

"Then if that occurs, I am asking you to partner with me, Miss Goulding," the viscount said. "I think as a team we would be unstoppable."

Lord Marksbury looked to Miss Peterson. "Did you enjoy the lawn bowling?"

"I did, my lord," Miss Peterson replied. "I find it invigorating to try new things."

"Then, as Miss Goulding suggested, if there is a second match, I hope you would do me the honor of competing alongside me," the earl said.

Louisa saw the faint blush that tinged Miss Peterson's cheeks as she said, "I would be happy to do so, my lord."

The teacarts arrived and Lord Boxling suggested they take a seat.

Viscount Hurley smiled broadly at her and said, "Come sit with me, Miss Goulding. I believe we have the place of honor, thanks to our resounding victory this afternoon."

She joined him on the settee and said, "I am not quite sure I would call it resounding, my lord. It was most enjoyable, however. I am hoping to be able to bowl again before the house party ends."

Adalyn looked pleased at the remark. "I will be happy to accommodate anyone who wishes for lawn bowling again," she said. "We'll have to think of a new prize to award, however. In the meantime, I have many other things planned. A picnic by the lake. Painting. More riding."

"And I would hope for more musical evenings," Owen interjected, smiling warmly at Louisa.

"Hear, hear!" said several present.

Owen added, "Performances last night were most enjoyable. I am sure the other young ladies present would like a chance to entertain us, as well as hearing encore performances from Lady Sara and Miss Goulding."

"That is easy to arrange," Everett said. "Tonight, however, I believe my wife has planned parlor games. Or was it card games, my love?" He smiled at Adalyn.

"It is card games this evening, Your Grace," she said, returning his smile.

The rest of teatime passed swiftly. The one good thing about this house party was the many conversations. With such a large group, it was natural for people to break off into smaller groups and converse. She found herself in an interesting discussion with Mr. Hampton, Miss Rexford, and Lord Hurley. All the while, she sensed Owen's gaze upon her and deliberately never looked once in his direction. As the old saying went, he had made his bed—

and he could now lie in it. He had told her he was not interested in her or marriage while she'd shared she was looking for a husband. She would not let the handsome earl be a distraction to her.

The nursery governess slipped in with Analise, bringing her not to Tessa but Spencer. The proud papa took his daughter and placed her on his knee.

"See how well she is sitting up?" he asked no one in particular. "She is also crawling faster than I can walk. I can only imagine she will be walking and then running soon."

"She is such a pretty baby," Lady Sara said. "Might I hold her?"

Spencer grinned. "Only for a minute, my lady. I enjoy my time with my daughter."

Lady Sara and then Miss Oxford held Analise for a few minutes each before returning her to Spencer.

When Tessa asked if Miss Rexford or Miss Peterson would like a turn, Miss Peterson declined politely, while Miss Rexford said, "I have yet to hold a child. I suppose one day I shall hold my own. I will wait until that time, if you don't mind."

Louisa thought it poor judgment on Miss Rexford's part to make such an announcement, especially after she saw the look on Lord Boxling's face. If Miss Rexford was interested in finding a husband, her declaration had not won any bachelor present to her side.

Spencer cradled Analise in his arms and as tea finished, he said, "I think we will take a walk, my two girls and I."

Adalyn reminded her guests that dinner would be served at seven, adhering to country hours. She added, "We can gather here in the drawing room again at half-past six for a drink before dinner is served. Cook tells me tonight it will be roast mutton."

Everyone rose and Lord Hurley looked at Louisa. "Are you ready to cut some flowers, Miss Goulding?"

"I should have brought the vase downstairs with me," she said. "Let me fetch it and we should meet in the kitchens. We can leave the vase there and see about gardening shears. I will meet you there in a few minutes."

She left the drawing room and hurried to her bedchamber, retrieving the vase, and exiting the room.

Owen lingered in the hallway, much to her dismay.

"Might I have a word with you, Louisa?" he asked.

"Now is not a convenient time, Owen," she told him.

His gaze pinned hers. "When would be a convenient time then? It is important that we speak soon."

"We spoke quite a bit before the house party, Owen. I don't know how much there is to be said now that it has begun." She gave him a haughty look. "Unless you think to give me more unsolicited advice about the men present? If that is the case, I will remind you that I have my own opinions, strong ones, and I know to follow both my head and my heart."

She turned to move away and he caught her elbow. She glanced at the long tanned fingers resting there, back to his face, arching her brows and waiting.

He released her, his reluctance evident, and said, "This has nothing to do with the bachelors attending Adalyn's house party," he said flatly.

"Then what possibly could we have to speak about?"

Before he could reply, Louisa added, "I am tired of it, Owen. I know because of your friendship with Everett and Spencer—and mine with Tessa and Adalyn—that we will be in each other's lives for years to come. I suggest we limit that proximity as much as possible and when we do find ourselves in each other's company, that we behave civilly. I am afraid that I have nothing else to say to you."

With that, she quickly moved away, hoping he would not follow her. She scurried down the stairs and when she reached the foyer, glanced over her shoulder.

Owen was nowhere in sight.

Disappointment filled her. Why, she couldn't say. Did she think if he chased after her things would change between them?

No, they most certainly would not.

Louisa made her way to the kitchens and gave a scullery maid the vase, telling her to put it in a safe place because soon it would be filled with blossoms from the duke's garden.

She turned and found Lord Hurley standing nearby and he held up a basket.

"Cook gave me this for us to place the flowers in. I also spoke to a gardener." He lifted a pair of shears from the basket. "We may use these to clip whatever flowers you desire."

"You have thought of everything, my lord. I am eager to explore the gardens and see what we can find."

The viscount offered Louisa his arm and she took it. He carried the basket as they left the house and set out toward the gardens. Contrary to what she had just said, Louisa was highly familiar with the gardens, having walked them every day of her visit to Cliffside. She decided she would try to see them with new eyes with this man.

They reached the entrance and he said, "we probably should walk the length of the gardens and see what flowers are now blooming. If we cut too soon, we may find something later that we like better and regret our earlier choices."

"That is an excellent idea, my lord," she said as they moved along the garden path.

Louisa decided she needed to kiss Lord Hurley—and this was the perfect opportunity.

CHAPTER TWENTY

THEY STROLLED SLOWLY along the path. Louisa could feel Lord Hurley's warmth since they stood so close to one another. He smelled merely of soap, not that wonderful combination of scents that Owen seemed to emit.

Stop thinking of Owen.

Think of Lord Hurley.

She noted the viscount's good points. He was very nice-looking, just over six feet with dark blond hair and blue eyes. His frame was solid, his posture straight. He was well-spoken and could carry on a conversation about a good number of topics. He hadn't been the heir apparent. She had discovered many of those sought as a spouse the daughter of a high-ranking peer, while she was merely the daughter of a second son who had been knighted. He was in the market for a wife.

On the other hand, Lord Boxling was also quite handsome. At six feet, his athletic frame appealed to her, as did his dark wavy hair and dark eyes. He also had a sense of fun about him, a wit, as well as intelligence. He kissed well and seemed quite interested in her.

She decided she would definitely kiss Lord Hurley and use the kiss to compare the two men. Now, she only had to find a way to get him to kiss her. She couldn't be so brazen as to kiss him. It had to be his idea.

Or at least Louisa needed to make it seem like his idea.

"Do you know much about flowers?" he asked.

"A little. My aunt, Lady Uxbridge, is fond of gardening and has a large one at Conley Park."

"Are you partial to any particular flowers?"

"I will show you the ones I like as we go."

They strolled the gardens a good half-hour or more. Louisa pointed out the sweet Williams and sweet peas, both in pinks and purples, though the sweet Williams also came in plums and the sweet peas in varying shades of red.

"I also like lilies," she told him.

"Which ones are those?"

"Over there. Those in pinks and oranges."

"They are nice," he agreed.

They reached the end of the gardens and she noted the calendulas.

"I like that golden shade," Lord Hurley said. "It and the orange and yellow ones are quite nice." He paused. "Have you decided which to pluck?"

"Let's take a few of these calendulas and then go back to the lilies. They were in full bloom and I think the prettiest in the garden. Then a few of the sweet Williams as we first entered. That should do it."

The viscount asked, "Do you wish to hold the basket or do the cutting?"

"I would like to cut, my lord."

He handed her the shears and she took a few of the calendulas and then decided to clip a few more. She would have one of the maids put them in a separate vase and have it placed in Lord Hurley's room.

They weaved their way along the path in the reverse direction, stopping at the lilies. Louisa took her time deciding which colors and flowers to cut before placing them in the basket. She decided since the sweet Williams were so close to the entrance to the gardens that she would need to kiss Lord Hurley before they arrived at that point.

And she had the perfect place for that to occur.

When they reached a bench at the halfway point, she sighed.

"Are you tired, Miss Goulding?"

"A little. Do you mind if we pause for a few minutes and catch our breaths?"

He chuckled. "Here is the perfect spot to do so."

They sat on the bench, which was obviously meant for couples to squeeze together. Louisa's thigh and hip were pressed close to Lord Hurley's. She hated that he was so much taller than she because he probably could look down her gown with little effort. Wishing she had worn the fichu despite Tilly's protests, she tried to put that thought from her mind and focus on the task at hand.

Kissing her second viscount in just two days.

"This is a bit cramped," he said, causing her to fear he would stand as he set the basket on the ground beside his feet. Instead, he asked, "Would you mind if I place my arm along the back?"

"That would be perfectly fine, my lord," she told him.

He turned slightly and rested his arm along the back of the bench. It rested partly against her shoulders, which she didn't mind. He seemed at a better angle.

For both talking and kissing.

"I suppose you are feeling the exertion from our lawn bowling."

"That is very true," she agreed. "While I enjoy walking every day and have begun riding daily since I have been at Cliffside, I am not use to lifting bowls and rolling them about."

"You will most likely be sore tomorrow, Miss Goulding. The strain on your muscles having done something they are unused to."

She laughed. "It was worth it because we won."

"It certainly was." His voice was low. His eyes darkened.

Oh, he was going to kiss her. Her heart began racing at the thought.

Then she asked herself if it was because she anticipated the kiss or was excited by the thought of his kiss. She blinked several times, trying not to overthink the situation.

"Do you have something in your eye?" he asked, concerned.

Louisa blinked again and swiped a finger over her lashes. "There. I seem to have gotten it."

"Probably an eyelash."

"No doubt it was," she agreed, moistening her lips and then mentally chastising herself for doing so.

"I am glad Their Graces invited me to this house party," Lord Hurley said.

"Yes, it has already been successful."

"I meant I was glad because *you* are here, Miss Goulding. I would have hated to wait until next Season before having met you."

She merely nodded, not quite sure how she should reply.

His hand smoothed a stray lock from her face and then his palm settled against her cheek. "I am most happy to be in your company now. I would like to see more of you."

Nerves rippled through her. "We can see quite of bit of one another at the house party."

His thumb stroked her cheek. "I would like to see more of you than that."

She knew that he was about to kiss her. His eyes had deepened from blue to almost black and he leaned toward her. Closing her eyes, she waited for his lips on hers.

He kissed her for several minutes, not using his tongue at first, which she thought was nice. His kiss however, left her cold. Nothing sparked between them. It would be foolish to let this go on so she turned her head slightly and opened her eyes.

Lord Hurley looked down at her, desire written across his features.

"I need more," he said, his mouth lowering to hers again.

"No, my lord. I think that is plenty," she said lightly.

His hands clasped her shoulders a bit too tight and she frowned.

"I said I need more." His lips met hers again and Louisa squirmed.

"No. That is enough."

Anger sparked in his eyes as his fingers tightened. "I say when it is enough."

This time, his mouth slammed down on hers, shocking her. She tried to pull away and he held her in place. Irritation filled her. She had said no. He had not stopped.

Lord Hurley was no gentleman.

Louisa brought her palms to his chest and shoved. Hard. It was enough to break his hold on her shoulders and she leaped to her feet.

"I do not want to kiss you anymore, my lord. I have had enough."

He rose, his hands latching on to her elbows, holding her in place.

"You say you want a husband. At your age, you'll have to take who you can get," he said harshly, suddenly becoming a stranger.

"I would rather remain unwed than be taken advantage of," she declared, clawing at his hands, trying to win her release.

"I think your father has granted you too much independence, Miss Goulding. You need a husband to bring you to heel."

Anger surged through her. "I am not some dog to be trained, my lord. I am a rational person with a mind and will of my own. Now, unhand me. Someone could come through and see us."

"Yes, they could," he agreed smugly. "If we were kissing, then you would have to wed me."

With that, he kissed her again. Louisa struggled to free herself, her wrath growing. Words hadn't stopped him.

It was time to take action.

She lifted her knee slightly—and then rammed it full force into his groin.

He shouted something. She thought it might have been *bitch*, which upset her to no end. She watched him fall to the bench, holding himself, a low, guttural sound coming from him.

"I said no more—and I meant it, my lord," she said, her mouth hard, her gaze penetrating his. "I don't want to kiss you ever again. I don't even wish to speak to you again."

Louisa bent and wrapped her fingers around the basket's handle and took off at a brisk pace, leaving behind the cursing viscount.

Lord Hurley's actions made things easy for her. Mentally, she struck a line through his name. He would be the last man she would desire to marry.

She hurried along the winding garden path, her fingers tightening on the basket, her breath coming in gasps.

Mr. Hampton seemed nice but quite bland and the man had absolutely no direction in life. Lord Marksbury was an enigma to her and she felt no desire to try and unravel his layers.

That left Lord Bowling. She would try her best to get to know him better and hope that he was the one for her. If he proved to be unworthy of her, as Lord Hurley had just demonstrated, then she would be happy to remain unwed. Louisa would rather be happy in solitude than miserable with a man who treated her as an object.

She cut through the kitchens, claiming her vase, which a scullery maid filled with water. She stormed up the stairs and to her bedchamber, forcing herself not to slam the door behind her.

Giving herself over to the quiet of the room, she set the basket and the vase down and bathed her face in cool water. It had the expected effect, calming her. She then took a vial of lavender and dabbed a bit on her wrists, rubbing them together before she brought them up and inhaled deeply. As always, lavender brought a sense of tranquility to her.

Not wanting the flowers to wilt, she began placing them one by one into the vase, taking her time in arranging them. When she finished, she nodded to herself, satisfied at how the arrangement had turned out. Louisa placed them on the table and then sat in the chair next to it, staring out the window.

Now, she had two men to avoid during the next week—Owen and Lord Hurley.

At this rate, she might have to leave for the sanctuary of Conley Park sooner rather than later.

Chapter Twenty-One

Owen returned to his room after his confrontation with Louisa.

It did not go as planned.

He had merely wanted to find time to have a decent conversation with her, one where he would admit how utterly foolish he had been. Instead, she had rebuffed him firmly and trounced off to go pick flowers with Hurley. He had considered chasing her down and decided her temper would flare and they might cause a scene.

Instead, he licked his wounds in solitude.

He thought back to their brief time in the corridor together. Louisa had been curt. Not wanting to be touched. She had escaped before he could even get out of her a time they could convene. Then it hit him.

She was brusque and fled because she was hurting. He had been the one to cause that hurt. If she truly was as indifferent to him as she claimed to be, she would have stood her ground and heard him out. Spurned his offer. Then continued on her merry way to her appointment with Lord Hurley.

He smiled. Louisa was far from uninterested and detached. It was because she still cared for him that she reacted in such a gruff manner. Owen decided that life with Louisa would never be dull.

He collapsed in a chair, contemplating his next move. Instead, he kept thinking about Louisa. What it would be like to make love to her. How it would feel to enter a ballroom, with her by his side as his countess. What she would look like as her belly swelled with his child inside her.

Suddenly, he longed for those children. He had never been around any child before Analise, and she was still a babe. Yet he knew instinctively that Louisa would be an excellent mother. He wanted to be a good father. Not a distant, disapproving one as his own father had been. Louisa had said she wanted a man who would spend time with their children.

Owen wanted to be that kind of man for her. In fact, he wanted to be the best husband he could be to her. He had thought he could not be faithful to one woman. That he would become bored and restless. Now, he understood more of what Ev and Spence had. Women who were equals to them. Wives who were fascinating and loyal. More than anything, Owen wanted to please Louisa. And that meant being faithful to her and the vows they would take. He understood now that no woman would ever hold the appeal for him that Louisa Goulding did. Who needed a mistress when he had a woman like Louisa in his bed for all the years to come?

Rising, he decided to head to the gardens. Knowing the little minx, she would most likely kiss Hurley. Owen was absolutely certain she had already kissed Boxling. He was going to put an end to her flirtations. The only man that would ever kiss her again would be him. He wanted to brand her as his. Let the world know how things stood between them.

As soon as he cleared up the tiny misunderstanding that now lay silently in the middle, forcing them apart. Oh, he knew it was of his own making. He would have to eat a huge slice of humble pie. But in the end, it would be worth it. He would have Louisa. Satisfaction filled him at the thought and he grinned like a fool.

His hand came to rest on the doorknob, a frightening thought occurring to him.

Was he in love with Louisa?

Owen shuddered. Then he took a deep breath and exhaled slowly. Would it actually be so bad to love her? He'd witnessed how utterly happy Ev and Spence were in their marriages. While he had teased both men unmercifully, calling them whipped dogs, he saw that they were filled with joy. Both men enjoyed spending time in their wives' company more than anything on earth. Did he feel the same way about Louisa?

Even if he didn't, he liked her a great deal. He couldn't wait to have her in his bed so that he could totally make her his. If love came, then so be it. He would be prepared to be bewitched.

Leaving his room, he moved along the corridor and down the staircase, going out the front doors and heading toward the gardens. At first, he thought of what he might say. What excuse he could give for being there at the same time they were. Then Owen decided he didn't need to give any excuses. He was a guest at Cliffside and free to walk the grounds whenever he saw fit.

He only hoped he arrived before Louisa kissed Hurley. He didn't know if he could stand to see that occur.

Owen entered the gardens, moving quickly through them. About halfway along the path, he heard voices and slowed. Remembering a bench sat there, he believed Louisa and Hurley had paused from their jaunt. Apprehension flooded him. Louisa was already as mad as a wet hen at him. What if he interrupted this interlude? Would it totally be a death knell?

Deciding he couldn't chance it, he moved quietly and then left the path, moving far to the right and then circling around. Sure enough, he spied the pair on a bench.

And they were kissing, just as he suspected they would be.

Except all wasn't perfect in paradise. Louisa shoved at Hurley, bringing a smug feeling to Owen. She shot to her feet and though he couldn't make out what they said to one another, her tone was evident.

Louisa Goulding was not pleased—and she was letting Viscount Hurley know.

Suddenly, Hurley was kissing her again, forcefully, and Louisa was squirming like a fish on a hook trying to get away. Owen would have to take action. He would enjoy taking Hurley apart, piece by piece.

Then his darling hauled off and kneed the man so hard that even Owen sucked in a quick breath. Hurley made a strangled noise and collapsed onto the bench.

Louisa glared down at him like an avenging goddess. Owen didn't know what she said. He only knew how very proud he was of her.

It sounded like the viscount cursed at her as she took off, basket in hand, flowers inside. A few spilled from it as she hurried away.

He wanted to kiss the life out of her for being so brave and strong, standing up to this bully. It was definitely something he would do later.

Now, he would confront Hurley.

Owen moved back around through the woods and returned to the path, heading along it until he came across Hurley.

"Lord Hurley, are you all right?" he asked innocently, doing his best to keep the smirk off his face.

"Quite fine, Danbury," the viscount managed to get out. "Just taking a little breather."

"You were out cutting flowers with Miss Goulding, I believe. For the vase which you'd won," he said. "I passed Miss Goulding on the path a few moments ago. She seemed a bit out of sorts."

"She is a vicious cunt," Hurley spat out.

The man barely got the words out of his mouth when Owen's fist slammed into Hurley's nose. Blood spurted, staining the viscount's shirt.

Owen looked down to the ground, where Hurley now lay cradling his bollocks in one hand and his nose in the other.

"I suggest you never utter those words again about Miss Goulding—or any other lady of the *ton,*" he suggested. "Else I will thrash you within an inch of your life."

"We are military men and should stand together, Danbury.

How dare you take that little trollop's side?" fumed Hurley.

He kicked the fool in the ribs, as hard as he could, and hoped a few of them broke.

Hurley gasped, tears springing to his eyes.

"You were a military man, by God," Owen roared. "You know how to behave as an honorable gentleman. Instead, you have chosen to be a vile, despicable oaf. I suggest you pack your things at once and leave." Owen glared at the man he had once thought would make for a good husband. "If you see me at an event during the Season, never speak to me, Hurley. And if you dare speak to Miss Goulding, I will publicly cut out your tongue."

Owen strode away, shaking with anger. He would have preferred beating the man but refused to go to Louisa with bruised knuckles. In fact, he didn't even want her to know that he had witnessed what had occurred between her and the viscount. Louisa had grown in confidence and he didn't want it shaken.

Returning to his room, he stripped off his clothes and rang for Strunk and hot water for a bath. He sat in the tub until the water had grown tepid, allowing the burn of his temper to cool. His valet dressed Owen for dinner and he returned to the drawing room, hoping a stiff brandy would do him a world of good.

LOUISA DID NOT say a single word as Tilly helped her dress for dinner. She was still shaken by what had happened with Lord Hurley and dreaded seeing him again this evening.

She had no idea how to avoid the man for the next week or more. It would be obvious to the others if she did not speak to him at all. Yet how could she after his atrocious behavior? She wondered if she should leave the house party and avoid any further contact with Lord Hurley. It would defeat the purpose of the gathering—that she was to have a chance to make a match. It would disappoint Adalyn terribly.

She didn't think the connection she had formed with Lord Boxling was strong enough to survive until next spring when the Season began. If she left now, she could see him just as easily pursuing one of the other four unattached females at the party.

What should she do?

She decided to talk it over with Tessa. Adalyn was much too fiery and would probably go and punch Lord Hurley for his ungentlemanly behavior under her roof—or send Everett to do so. Tessa was more a voice of reason and calm and Louisa trusted she could obtain good advice from her cousin.

She thanked Tilly and dismissed the servant, then thought better of it.

"Tilly, would you please go to Lady Middlefield now and ask her to meet me in Her Grace's sitting room as soon as possible?"

Tilly nodded. "Of course, Miss Goulding. I will do so at once."

Louisa left her bedchamber and went downstairs to Adalyn's sitting room, finding it empty as she had expected. She didn't have to wait long. Within minutes, Tessa flew into the room, concern written on her face.

She came straight to Louisa, who stood looking out the French doors, and embraced her. Louisa teared up, her emotions frayed.

Tessa pulled back, taking Louisa's hands in hers. "Tilly said you were out of sorts. What has happened? Has Owen done something to upset you?"

"No, it isn't Owen. It is Lord Hurley. You know we went to walk the gardens and cut flowers for my new vase."

Tessa squeezed Louisa's hands and said, "Yes. Did he behave in an untoward manner to you?" she asked gently.

Louisa's eyes welled with tears and she nodded.

"Come and sit and tell me about it," her cousin said.

Tessa led her to the settee and they both took a seat. Louisa swallowed hard and then cleared her throat.

"First of all, I will tell you that I have kissed Lord Boxling."

Tessa's eyes widened in surprise. "Is that so? How was it?"

"I liked it. I like him. I know you and Adalyn have emphasized the importance of kissing and so I thought to do the same with Lord Hurley Being alone in the gardens seemed a perfect opportunity to do so."

Tessa frowned. "You did not enjoy his kiss?"

Louisa shrugged. "It was . . . oh, I was indifferent. That is the truth. Lord Hurley, however, pressed on when I asked him to stop."

Anger flared in her cousin's beautiful blue eyes. "He kissed you after you asked him not to?"

"Yes, he did. It made me very uncomfortable, Tessa. I pushed him away and yet he still insisted."

"I will have his head on a platter," Tessa declared. "I cannot think of a more ungentlemanly thing to do, ignoring a lady's request in such a situation."

"Then you don't think I was overreacting?"

Tessa's eyes hardened for a moment. "Not in the least, Louisa. If Lord Hurley had any genuine affection for you, he would have stopped the moment you asked him to." She paused. "What happened? Did he hurt you?"

Louisa smiled bleakly. "Actually, I hurt him."

Tessa's jaw dropped. "You didn't. You kneed him, didn't you?" Her cousin grinned. "Good for you."

"I didn't know if he would stop with the unwanted kisses. I was afraid he would take it even further. I decided it was my only option."

"Well, I hope he suffered. I hope he is sore for days to come."

"I told him just what I thought of him, trying to take liberties with me. I also told him I wanted nothing more to do with him during this house party. That leaves me with a dilemma, however. I do not want to ruin Adalyn's party. I know she is giving it for me. Yet, I feel as if I should leave."

"You will not!" Tessa proclaimed. "If anything, it is Lord Hurley who should leave. There is no point to you being gone, especially if you think there is a chance things might progress with Lord Boxling. Also, it would be unwise to have Lord Hurley remain and be a danger to the other females present."

"Then what should I do?" Louisa asked. "If I tell Adalyn what happened, I fear she will physically attack Lord Hurley."

"Leave it to me," Tessa said, taking Louisa's hand and squeezing it reassuringly.

"You aren't going to tell Spencer, are you? Or Everett?"

Or Owen?

As protective as Owen had become of her, Louisa feared what he might do to Lord Hurley.

"I promise not to tell Spencer or Everett," Tessa said. "I do believe that Lord Hurley needs to go, however. Do you trust me?"

"Implicitly," Louisa said.

"Good. Then let me handle this my way." Tessa gave her a hug. "Thank you for sharing this with me, Louisa. I am glad you felt comfortable coming to me. We should go to the drawing room now where the others will assemble. Stay by my side and you will be safe."

They departed the sitting room and went to the drawing room, where Louisa quickly scanned, looking for Lord Hurley. He was not among those who had already gathered but only about half of their number were present.

She accepted a glass of sherry from a footman and sipped on it, hoping it might calm her nerves.

Owen entered the drawing room and surveyed it himself. When their gazes met, he gave her a brief nod and then went and joined Lord Marksbury, Miss Rexford, and Miss Peterson.

Eventually, everyone arrived—except Lord Hurley. Louisa felt her belly twist with anxiety.

Arthur appeared and spoke to Everett a moment. Everett turned to the group and said, "Dinner is now served. Before we go in, however, I will share with you that Lord Hurley has been called away from our gathering. Pressing business at his estate took him from us."

Louisa's eyes flew to Tessa's. Her cousin gave a small shrug, leaning in close and said, "It seems as if our problem has solved itself. I would like to think Lord Hurley realized he had been a cad and gracefully made his exit before his behavior was made public."

Tessa moved away and Spencer claimed her arm to take her in to dinner. Mr. Hampton, who had been engaged in conversation with Spencer, asked, "Might I escort you to dinner, Miss Goulding?"

"Yes, thank you, Mr. Hampton."

They arrived in the dining room and Louisa found Lord Marksbury to her left and Lord Boxling to her right. She had not spent much time with the earl and tried to divide her attention between the pair during dinner.

When it came time for the ladies to leave the men to their port, Lord Boxling helped her from her chair.

"I hear it's card games tonight, Miss Goulding. Whist, in particular. Would it be presumptuous of me to ask you now to be my partner for the evening?"

Relief flooded Louisa, in part because she would not have to leave the house party and the rest happy that Lord Boxling had sought out her company.

"That would be most agreeable, my lord. I will see you in the drawing room."

He smiled at her, a genuine smile, unlike so many social ones she had witnessed during the Season. She was growing to like Lord Boxling a great deal.

CHAPTER TWENTY-TWO

LOUISA JOINED MISS Peterson as they exited the dining room and made their way to the drawing room.

"Do you play whist, Miss Goulding?"

"I do. It is a favorite pastime of mine," she revealed and then added, "Lord Boxling has asked to partner with me."

Her friend nodded thoughtfully. "He seems to be taking quite an interest in you. Is that interest returned?"

"I find him to be a very amiable gentleman," she said, not wanting to commit aloud to anything involving Lord Boxling.

He was nice. She did seem to find him interesting. And he was paying her special attention.

But he wasn't Owen.

Mentally, she chastised herself. Owen could go leap into the lake for all she cared. She needed to focus her attention on Lord Boxling. She truly did believe that they might suit—and that the possibility that he might offer for her before he left Cliffside certainly existed. True, he wasn't Owen. Then again, no man would ever be Owen. If she couldn't have Owen, then Lord Boxling was a wonderful substitute.

Oh, she hated thinking of him that way. He was a lovely man. She thought he could make her happy. If he did extend an offer to her, Louisa would do everything in her power to show him how grateful she was.

The group of women entered the drawing room and took seats. Miss Rexford came and joined them.

"I wonder what business called Lord Hurley away," mused Miss Peterson.

Miss Rexford snorted. "He didn't leave because of any business."

Queasiness filled Louisa. "Why do you say that?" she asked.

"Because I saw him from my window when he departed."

Miss Peterson frowned. "How could seeing him leave allow you to know why he left?" she asked, looking perplexed.

Miss Rexford gave a knowing smile. "Because of how he looked." She smiled enigmatically.

Miss Peterson took the bait. "How did Lord Hurley look? Was he ill?"

"Possibly." Miss Rexford leaned in. "His nose was swollen three times its size. I would say it was broken. And he moved gingerly. As if he had taken a beating."

Louisa flinched. Yes, she had put quite a bit into the thrust of her knee, which might cause Lord Hurley to move carefully. But she hadn't come close to bashing him in the nose. Quickly, she glanced to Tessa, who was talking with Lady Sara. Had her cousin already known of Lord Hurley's injuries? Had Spencer hurt Lord Hurley? She didn't think so. No guests had been in the gardens. No one had seen what had taken place between her and Lord Hurley.

Or had someone watched—and punished Lord Hurley for his misdeeds?

Owen . . .

He would not have hesitated to brutalize Lord Hurley if he had seen what the viscount had done to her. Had it been Owen who had broken the viscount's nose?

For her?

She wanted to ask him and yet dreaded bringing up anything of that nature to him. If he had known, Owen was the type to go after Lord Hurley. And if he had been the one to hurt the viscount, then he had seen what occurred. Seen her humiliation. Was that what he wished to speak to her about?

No, it couldn't be. He had asked for a private word with her before her time in the gardens with Lord Hurley.

She bit her lip, unsure what to do or say.

"You are being awfully quiet, Miss Goulding," Miss Rexford observed. "Did Lord Hurley's leaving the house party upset you? Were the two of you forming an attachment?"

Louisa did not like this woman. "We merely partnered during lawn bowling, Miss Rexford. There is not—and never will be—any attachment between us."

"Hmm." The woman studied her. "I thought he might be growing sweet on you." She paused. "Are *you* the one that punched Lord Hurley in the face?"

"Certainly not," she huffed. "I would hope you wouldn't think to spread that kind of misinformation."

"Perhaps Lord Hurley fell and broke his nose," Miss Peterson suggested, trying to look helpful. "That could account for his injury and any others he might have suffered."

"Louisa, would you like to take a turn about the room with me?" Tessa called. "I want to ask your advice on something"

Relief swept through her as she rose. "Of course, Tessa." She looked to her companions. "If you will excuse me, ladies?"

She hated leaving Miss Peterson with such a viper but was happy to escape Miss Rexford's company.

Linking her arm through Tessa's, they turned away from the women gathered and began to move about the perimeter of the room.

"You looked as if you needed rescuing," her cousin said.

"Miss Rexford was telling us that she saw Lord Hurley before he left. She claimed his absence wasn't because of business, noting that his nose looked to be broken and he moved carefully, as if injured."

"You didn't mention anything about hitting him in the face."

"That's because I didn't," Louisa said. "I fear someone may

have witnessed the incident in the gardens between me and Lord Hurley and doled out a bit of punishment."

"Well, it wasn't Spencer," Tessa declared. "He would have told me if he had seen you in distress, as well as what he had done to Lord Hurley." She thought a moment. "Do you think it was Everett? He is the one who mentioned Lord Hurley leaving for business?"

"I think that was just Everett's way of being kind. I think it might have been Owen. He has been protective of me."

Tessa frowned. "I don't wish to discuss Owen."

"Did he apologize to you as Spencer demanded?"

Her cousin nodded. "He did. I told him I would think about forgiving him once I thought him properly contrite."

"Should I ask Owen if he is responsible for Lord Hurley's absence?" she fretted.

"Do you truly care that Lord Hurley is no longer a part of our company?"

"No."

Tessa nodded wisely. "Then the less said about him, the better."

They continued their stroll about the room until the gentlemen appeared in the doorway.

Adalyn rose. "You can see that I have had tables set up for us to play whist. We will play in foursomes and then have one pair move to the next table after their rubber is completed. Keep track of your points. The couple with the highest total after four rounds of play will name the dessert they wish Cook to prepare for tomorrow's picnic by the lake."

Lord Boxling met her and Tessa. "Lady Middlefield, I am afraid I must steal Miss Goulding away. She has promised to partner with me for this evening's card play."

Tessa smiled graciously at the viscount. "Then you have claimed the best partner in the room, my lord. My cousin is terrific at whist and most competitive."

The viscount smiled at Louisa. "I look forward to our play

together."

He escorted her to one of the tables, where her aunt and uncle were their first competitors. Though she loved them both dearly, Uncle Uxbridge wasn't the brightest of men and her aunt could be a featherhead at times. As she predicted, she and Lord Boxling easily won all three games of the rubber.

They squared off next with Lady Sara and Lord Marksbury. The earl was as clueless as her uncle when it came to play but Lady Sara was a good strategist. Louisa had written off the younger woman as unsophisticated but she now saw a different side to Everett's cousin. Still, she and Lord Boxling won two of the three games they played.

Their third opponents were Everett and Adalyn. She had played whist both with and against each of them and knew they were formidable opponents. Having played with them before, however, would give her insight into their play.

"Follow my lead, my lord," she told her partner as the Camdens took their seats.

"I am happy to do so, Miss Goulding," the viscount replied.

Louisa knew Adalyn always led with her strongest suit and used that knowledge to her advantage. Lord Boxling played brilliantly, allowing her to take the lead and capture several tricks. She nodded to him twice and he understood that he was to take that hand's trick. They won that game handily.

The next proved more difficult, with Adalyn and Everett proving to be the victors. The last game of the match was the closest of the night but she and the viscount claimed their second game and overall victory over their hosts.

"You are a wicked card player, Louisa," Everett proclaimed. "No wonder Lord Boxling wished to ride your coattails."

She merely smiled—until she saw that Miss Rexford and Owen were to be their final opponents. Though she longed to ask Owen if he had been the one to attack Lord Hurley, she agreed with Tessa that it was water under the bridge. Louisa did not want to show any interest, now or in the future, regarding Lord

Hurley.

Owen called out, "Who are the leaders going into this final match?"

Everyone replied and it quickly became apparent that the yet to be named dessert was riding on the outcome of the rubber at their table.

Lord Boxling caught her attention. "Don't worry, Miss Goulding. We will prevail. I guarantee it."

"You are certainly sure of yourself—and your partner—my lord," Miss Rexford said.

"Miss Goulding is a superb player, as I am, Miss Rexford," the viscount said.

Owen frowned at the remark as he shuffled the cards and dealt, revealing the last card of his hand so the table would know which suit would trump. In this instance, it was diamonds.

Since she was sitting on his left, Louisa led, playing the king of spades, and play went clockwise. While the other tables conversed merrily, theirs remained silent. It was obvious the players seated here all wanted to win.

Owen and Miss Rexford took the first game but after claiming five tricks in a row, Louisa and Viscount Boxling won the second game. The winner of this round—and the evening itself—boiled down to this final game of the rubber.

Others had finished and came to stand and watch the play. Thank goodness she had played several games with Lord Boxling before they met these competitors because the two of them had connected. She could glance at him and know when she should pick up the trick or throw away a card and allow him to take it.

In the end, she and the viscount claimed the last game by the narrowest of margins, with those watching applauding their effort.

"What dessert will you choose?" Adalyn asked, smiling at Louisa and then Lord Boxling.

"I believe that should be up to Miss Goulding," her partner said. "Never have I enjoyed whist more than playing with her.

What say you, Miss Goulding?"

She thought a moment. "Since your cook is so talented, Your Grace, I believe I will ask her to make a flummery in the shape of a swan. With lots of cream and fruit." She looked to Lord Boxling. "Would almonds in it be acceptable, my lord?"

"That sounds delightful," he declared.

"Then with almonds and passionfruit if it is available. If not, raspberries will suffice."

"I will go and tell her now," Adalyn said. "Come along, Your Grace."

She and Everett left, as did a few others. Owen and Miss Rexford excused themselves and Louisa remained conversing with Lord Boxling for a few minutes. They talked about how they had been in tune with their play.

Then Louisa noticed more than half the guests had already retired for the evening and started to tell her partner she was ready to do the same when Lord Boxling asked, "May I escort you to your bedchamber, Miss Goulding?"

Her heart fluttered in her chest, wondering if the viscount might kiss her again.

"Of course, my lord."

They quit the room and took their time moving up the staircase.

"This is my door," Louisa told him, her pulse beginning to pound.

Lord Boxling faced her, taking her hands in his. "It was a pleasure partnering with you in cards this evening, Miss Goulding. I hear there will be a picnic tomorrow by the lake. Would you do me the honor of dining with me and possibly going out on the lake with me, as well?"

Louisa smiled warmly at the viscount. "Thank you for asking me to do so, my lord. I would be delighted to spend more time in your company."

He squeezed her hands and then lowered his lips to hers for a tender kiss. It was brief but very sweet.

Lord Boxling broke the kiss and released her hands. "Pleasant dreams, Miss Goulding."

"The same to you," she said.

Turning, she opened the door to her bedchamber and entered, closing it behind her. A lone candle burned on the bedstand. Louisa went to ring for Tilly to assist her in undressing and suddenly stopped in her tracks.

Owen emerged from the shadows in the room.

"What on earth are you doing in here?" she demanded.

"Is this a convenient time to speak, Louisa?"

"It most certainly is not," she said briskly. "I told you we have nothing to discuss. Especially alone at night in my bedchamber."

"What I have to say to you requires privacy. This is the most secluded place I could think of for us to have this conversation."

Anger bubbled up and she told him, "There will be no conversation. Now or ever. I have made my feelings clear to you."

Owen took a few long strides and reached her, his hands taking hers. "But I have not made my feelings clear to you," he stated softly.

Confusion filled her, not just his words, but the feelings that stirred within her as his hands engulfed hers. She looked into his eyes and saw a tenderness there she had never seen before. Her pulse leaped.

"I have not always been good with words, Louisa. From the time I was young, I was a man of action, never more so than on the battlefield. I find myself floundering in a genteel society now. But one thing has become perfectly clear to me.

"I want you."

Disappointment raced through her. "This is just more of the same, Owen," she told him, trying to pull her hands from his. "Yes, I realize we are attracted to one another but it doesn't matter."

His gaze held hers as he said, "But it does matter, Louisa. I have changed. I admit that I am one of the most stubborn men on the planet. At times, my hardheadedness has gotten me into trouble. This time, it almost did me in."

She shook her head, bewildered. "I don't know what you mean."

"Then let me make it perfectly clear to you, Louisa. I want to marry you."

Stunned, her jaw fell open, no words coming out.

It didn't matter, however, because Owen's mouth took hers.

CHAPTER TWENTY-THREE

LOUISA FELT AS if she had come home as Owen's arms encircled her, drawing her against him. His lips caressed hers tenderly, an aching beauty to be found in his kiss.

Then he grew bolder, his mouth pressing hard against hers, quick kisses and breaks, and then more hungry kisses. His hands roamed her back as she clung to him, her fingers tightening on his waistcoat, afraid he would move away and leave her bereft.

The kisses became softer, almost as light as butterflies now, leaving her lips and dancing across her cheeks. Her eyelids. Her brow. Her temple. They trailed to her ear, his breath hot as his tongue dipped into the shell of her ear, causing a jolt to run through her. She made a guttural noise unlike anything that had ever come from her.

And giggled.

He kissed her jawline and between kisses, said, "I have never liked a giggler. Until I heard the sound coming from you. Your giggles are quite intoxicating, Louisa. As you are."

His lips traveled back to hers and his kisses became an assault now, battering against the barrier of her lips until she allowed him entrance. His tongue plunged inside her mouth, claiming her, hot velvet tangling with her tongue, the scent of his soap and maleness wafting about her. His kiss demanded that she submit to him. Louisa wanted to fight it but couldn't. Temptation proved too great and she gave herself over to it.

Owen's body shifted, his hands leaving her back. She wanted to protest but found herself scooped into his arms. He went to the chair beside the window and sat. In his lap now, she wrapped her arms about his neck and lowered her mouth to his. This time, she was the invading force, seeking to dominate him. Their tongues tangled in a war with no losers as those delightful tingles rippled throughout her. At the center of her core, the low, pounding beat of an inner pulse began, drumming steadily, speeding up, crying out in need.

"Touch me!" she cried, breaking the kiss. "I need you . . . to touch me."

A brilliant smile lit Owen's face. "Exactly where would you like me to touch you, Louisa?" he asked, his voice low and seductive.

She felt herself flame with embarrassment. "I can't say it."

He kissed her long and hard. Breaking the kiss, he told her, "Oh, yes, you can. You can say anything to me. Ask anything of me. And know that I will give you satisfaction like no other man can."

She swallowed hard, biting her lip, not knowing how to ask for what she wanted because such thoughts had never come to her before.

"Stop that," he chided lightly. "If anyone is going to sink their teeth into that full, lovely lip, it will be me."

He took her mouth again and she sensed the need driving him. He captured her lip between his teeth, holding it, teasing it with his tongue. Then he released it, soothing it with that same tongue, causing her bones to completely dissolve.

Owen kissed her endlessly, until her heart pounded so hard and fast that she thought it might break through her chest. His lips finally left hers, trailing along the column of her throat, going lower. She knew what would come because he had done this before.

Then he surprised her, rising from the chair and placing her on her feet, spinning her around. His warm fingers moved along the buttons, unfastening them, each time kissing her nape after he freed one. Somehow her gown was gone, followed by her petticoat. Breathless, she felt him loosening her stays before flinging them aside.

His arms came about her, drawing her into him, his hands caressing her belly as his lips caressed her neck. Then he turned her in his arms so that they faced one another and he began a long series of drugging kisses that left her trembling with desire.

Owen took the hem of her chemise and lifted it over her head, tossing it to the floor and then eased off her slippers. He took her hands, lacing his fingers through hers and holding her hands away from her, his eyes feasting upon her. All Louisa wore were her stockings and garters—and a coat of red embarrassment that seemed to color her entire body.

"You are so beautiful," he said softly. "Quit squirming. Let me look at you."

She felt the heat everywhere and it only grew hotter as his gaze swept over her.

"I am a lucky man," he told her. "Because you are going to be mine. Forever."

He pulled her into his arms again, her bare skin against his clothing. The feeling was erotic as she brushed against him. He cupped her buttocks, kneaded them, his lips buried against her throat.

Then she found herself swept up again and he carried her to the bed, placing her upon it sideways, her legs dangling from it.

"Stay there," he ordered, stepping back and unknotting his cravat.

Louisa watched in fascination as Owen stripped his own layers from him, revealing a taut, muscled physique that her fingers itched to touch. She sat up, wanting to go to him.

"No," he ordered, stepping to her and pushing her back against the feathered mattress.

A thrill ran through her as she remembered how he had

touched her before.

"Are you going to . . . put your fingers . . . inside me again?" she asked, hoping he would.

A wicked grin lit his face. "You liked that, didn't you?"

"Yes," she said softly.

"I will put my fingers there if you ask me. And my tongue," he promised. "If you ask."

Heat filled her at his words. She recalled he said that was done but she couldn't imagine it.

Owen leaned over her, his fingers entwining with hers, his hard, muscled torso grazing her flesh. Fire blazed within her. He kissed her slowly, thoroughly, completely.

Breaking the kiss, he smiled at her. "Do you have anything to ask me, Louisa?"

She swallowed hard. "I . . . do."

When she hesitated, he kissed her again. "I need to know you want me as much as I want you, my love."

"Oh!" He called her *my love*. Did that mean he loved her? He had said he wanted to marry her but Owen had said he didn't believe in love. It might just be an endearment. Or it could be—

His pressed his lips against her pulse, which pounded. "You are overthinking things. Talk to me, Louisa. It is important that I know how to please you."

She chuckled. "You are the kind of man who instinctively knows how to please a woman, Owen."

He gazed at her longingly. "I only have one woman I want to please now. You."

His mouth moved to her breast and devoured it hungrily. She whimpered and moved restlessly as he did so. He attacked the other one with equal gusto, sucking, licking, nipping until she thought she had lost her mind.

His mouth came back to hers and tenderly kissed her. "Well?"

Summoning all the bravery she possessed—and knowing that this man was the one to have emboldened her—she said, "I want you to put your fingers *and* your tongue inside me."

Owen beamed at her. "Very well."

His hands skimmed the curve of her hips, going all the way to her knees and then his fingers danced back up her thighs. They teased the seam of her sex, brushing back and forth along it, causing her breath to become shallow spurts. Then he pushed a finger inside her and she sucked in that breath.

"You are so wet for me, love. That means you do want me."

His fingers worked the same magic as before and soon Louisa writhed on the bed, clutching the bedclothes as that fullness grew and grew and spilled forth. She bucked against his hand, riding the waves as they crested and fell, crested and fell. Finally, she grew still.

His tongue circled her belly button and began sliding lower. Panic shot through her and she pushed up to a sitting position.

Owen gave her a disdainful look and pushed her back down, one large hand pressing against her belly to keep her in place. Then he lowered his head between her legs and she felt something. Something wicked and wonderful. Something beyond wicked and wonderful.

His hands moved to her ankles. He brought them to the bed and placed them on the edge.

"Keep them here for now."

He then took her knees in hand and pulled them away from her body, parting her thighs. She realized this gave him better access. His tongue plunged inside her and stroked her, moving in and out in varying speeds. That fullness came quickly and she cried out as he feasted upon her. Her fingers pushed into his hair and clutched it as he had his way with her. Her orgasm came so hard and fast that when it ended, she lay limp and unmoving.

Owen lifted her until her head touched the pillows.

"I can't move," she said, her eyelids drooping. "I can barely speak."

He hovered over her again. "You are sated," he said. "But it can be even better."

"I don't see how," she mumbled.

His hands began stroking her body. She opened her eyes and saw he now straddled her.

"You do want to wed me?" he asked, uncertainty on his face.

Louisa smiled. "I do."

"This will sting for a moment. It never hurts after that," he said.

He cradled her face, kissing her deeply, then broke the kiss. She glanced down and saw his manhood jutting toward her. It was enormous.

"You think that will fit inside me?" she asked, alarmed.

"I do."

Owen continued his caresses and then she felt his cock brushing against her. Suddenly, a slice of pain rippled through her. Before she cried out, his mouth covered hers, soothing her with drugging kisses.

"Is it better now?" he asked, concern on his face.

"I feel . . . full. Definitely full. But it doesn't hurt anymore."

"Good."

He rocked against her.

Now, that felt good. No, better than good.

"I'm glad you think so."

"Did I say that aloud?" she fretted.

He kissed her. "You did."

Owen moved again, withdrawing and plunging inside her. Soon, the rhythm became a dance they shared, an intimate dance which allowed her to shed her inhibitions and dance with joy and abandon. Soon, that marvelous feeling filled her again and as she cried out, so did he.

He collapsed atop her, his weight driving her into the mattress. She stroked his broad back, welcoming the feel of him. Then he rolled to his side and brought her against him, his arms protecting her from everything. Her ear nestled against his chest and she heard his strong heart pounding rapidly, then slowly as they lay together for several minutes.

Rising, he dropped a kiss upon her brow and retrieved a basin and cloth, dipping it into the water and then using it to clean her. Louisa should have been embarrassed and found she was the opposite. She reveled in the intimate gesture.

He dried her and then returned to her bed, slipping in behind her and pulling her next to him so that they nestled together as close as spoons.

It was heavenly.

She must have slept for she opened her eyes and saw the faint light of day beginning to peek through the window. Owen was already dressing. She watched him, a thrill of possession sweeping through her. This handsome, perfect man was going to be her husband.

Her husband . . .

He turned and smiled. Coming to the bed, he sat upon it, brushing the hair from her cheek and kissing her.

"I hope I did not awaken you. Go back to sleep."

"I need to put on my night rail," she told him. "I cannot have Tilly coming in and finding me lying naked in bed."

"All right."

He stood and pulled her from the bed, into his arms for another long, deep kiss. She broke it and found her night rail and he helped her into it. She noticed all her clothes, down to her stockings, now lay neatly across the chair.

"I will see you later. Adalyn mentioned a picnic. I know there are rowboats we can take out."

Louisa frowned. "Oh, dear. I promised Lord Boxling that I would eat with him and let him row me across the lake. I cannot break my word to him."

Owen looked lost in thought a moment. "No, enjoy the picnic. We will talk later. We have much to discuss."

He led her back to the bed and tucked her in, dropping a sweet kiss upon her lips.

"Go back to sleep."

"All right," she muttered, drifting away.

Into dreams of Owen.

Chapter Twenty-Four

OWEN SLOWLY OPENED his eyes, a warmth filling him. It was the warmth of happiness. How long had it been since he had awakened in such a state?

Perhaps never.

Oh, he was an optimistic fellow, as much so as the next man, but he realized in this moment that he had never truly been happy. Nothing had brought him this inner glow. Only Louisa filled an empty space inside him that he hadn't even known needed filling. He longed to spend every waking moment with her and then cradle her in his arms, holding her close even in sleep. In some wonderful way, she completed him. As an earl. As a man.

And soon, as a husband.

He wished for them to wed immediately. That would mean a special license. He decided he would go into London today and purchase it. That way, once the house party concluded, they could be married since their closest friends and her aunt and uncle would be here. He hoped that she wouldn't insist on her father being present at the ceremony. Sir Edgar might still be in Vienna for months to come.

Owen wasn't willing to wait that long. A week would be too long but he would do so.

That didn't mean he wouldn't want Louisa in his bed each

night. Now that he had his taste of her, he craved her. He wanted all of her. It might shock Strunk and her maid but he decided he would insist that they spend the next several nights together since they would be wed within a week.

He wondered if he should speak to Lord Uxbridge before he departed for London and decided it could wait until he returned with the special license in hand. He could see no reason for Louisa's uncle to deny her hand in marriage, especially to a fellow earl. Besides, Louisa was of age and could make her own decisions. To be safe, though, he would speak to Lord Uxbridge upon his return.

Now, he needed to share with Ev and Adalyn his plans. They were already down one male guest at the house party with Lord Hurley's departure. Owen hoped today wouldn't be too awkward with him gone, as well. At least the remaining bachelors would receive their fair share of attention from the ladies present.

It irked him a bit that Louisa would be spending most of today with Lord Boxling. While he knew nothing untoward would occur, he didn't like his betrothed spending time with the handsome, easygoing viscount. He wondered if he should pull Boxling aside and ask him to step away. No, he didn't want to intrude upon Louisa's decision. She might herself share the news with Boxling of her betrothal in order for the viscount not to take any liberties with her during the picnic.

He rang for Strunk and the valet entered with a steaming bowl of hot water for Owen's shave.

"Good morning, Strunk," he called cheerily, padding over to a chair and sitting so that his valet could shave him.

He closed his eyes and thought of Louisa, wishing he could ask her to accompany him to London. He thought of all the wicked things they could so in his carriage during the journey but decided he couldn't have her come with him. It wouldn't do for an unwed female, albeit a betrothed one, to spend that many hours unchaperoned with her fiancé.

Owen shrugged into his shirt and trousers and allowed Strunk to help him into his waistcoat and coat. He pulled on his boots.

"You certainly seem in high spirits today, my lord," Stunk noted. "The smile hasn't left your face—and you were even whistling when I first arrived."

He decided to share his news. "You may take the day off, Strunk. I am going to London and won't return until early evening." He paused. "I plan to purchase a special license while I am there."

The valet grinned. "Congratulations, my lord. Might it be Miss Goulding?"

"It is," he confirmed. "She agreed to marry me last night."

Strunk's grin broadened. "Miss Goulding is a favorite with the staff at Cliffside, my lord. They say she is sweet as the day is long. You have made an excellent choice for your countess, if you don't mind my saying so."

"I totally agree Strunk. Please go to the stables now and have them saddle Galahad for me. I will ride him back to Danfield and take my carriage into London."

"Very good, my lord."

Strunk left and Owen brushed his hair quickly, ready to seek out Ev and Adalyn. He opened the door and stepped into the hall, crashing into someone. Quickly, he clasped their elbows to keep them—and him—from falling.

To his surprise, it was Miss Rexford. Before he could apologize for running in to her, she clutched the lapels to his coat and yanked hard, pulling his head down, his lips crashing into hers.

For a moment, Owen froze, not comprehending what was happening. Then he quickly lifted his head and thrust her away, taking two steps back.

"I say, Miss Rexford, that—"

"That is the problem, my lord. You haven't said or done anything," she pouted. "That is why I decided I should be the one to take action and let you know of my interest in you." She batted her eyelashes prettily at him, wetting her lips.

He cleared his throat. "If this had been in the past, Miss Rexford, I can assure you I would have been more than interested in you. Things have changed, however. I have asked Miss Goulding to be my wife and am leaving now for London in order to purchase a special license."

"Oh," she said, her disappointment obvious. "I am sorry to hear that. I thought that we could have quite a bit of fun together."

"You'll have to look to someone else. Perhaps Lord Boxling," he suggested, hoping to keep the viscount away from Louisa.

"If you change your mind, let me know," she said huskily.

"I won't," he said firmly, letting her know where he stood.

Owen watched her retreat, thinking Miss Rexford was exactly his type before he met Louisa. He would have enjoyed romping with her, knowing nothing serious would come from the relationship. Now, though, everything had changed. Louisa had opened his eyes to a new world. He wanted to build upon the intimacy that had begun between them last night. Build a life with her. Have children and play with them, teach them, watch them grow into adulthood.

He loved Louisa. This is what it meant. To commit to another in heart, mind, body, and soul. He couldn't imagine spending time with any woman other than Louisa. He would love her until his dying day—and beyond.

Closing his bedchamber door, he ventured down the hall, hoping to avoid Miss Rexford. He arrived in the dining room and saw Lady Sara, Miss Oxford, and Lord Marksbury eating together, deep in conversation. Ev approached the buffet and Owen hurried toward him.

"Might I have a private word with you, Ev?" he asked.

His friend nodded. "We can go to my study." He set the plate down.

When they arrived, Ev closed the door. "What is this about?"

"I wanted to let you and Adalyn know that I will be missing from the house party today. I am traveling to London." He paused. "To purchase a special license."

Hope sprang in Ev's eyes. "Is it what I think?"

Owen nodded. "Louisa agreed to be my wife last night."

Ev captured him in a bear hug, slapping Owen on the back. "This is the best news possible. Adalyn will be over the moon that her house party brought the two of you together."

"Could you keep this to yourself until I return? Merely tell Adalyn that I had business to attend to at Danfield and that I will return in time for dinner this evening? I would rather share the news with Louisa by my side." He chuckled. "Of course, she may decide to tell Adalyn and Tessa on her own. We haven't really talked about how to share our good news."

"Have you discussed a date? With the special license, you will have a month."

"I would like to do so after the house party concludes. Once your guests leave, our closest friends, along with Lord and Lady Uxbridge, could stay."

"I think that a fine idea, Owen." Ev paused and then asked, "Do you love Louisa? She deserves nothing less."

"I do. I haven't told her in words, hoping my actions spoke what was in my heart, but I know women like to hear that. I cannot believe how deliriously happy I am, Ev."

His friend smiled. "Then it most certainly is love. We have been blessed—you, Spence, and I—to find remarkable women and love."

"I will let you get back to your breakfast. I'll ride Galahad back to Danfield and take my carriage into London. Keep an eye on Louisa today for me if you will."

"I can do that." Ev thrust out his hand and Owen took it. They shook firmly, both men beaming.

He went immediately to the stables and found Galahad saddled and waiting for him. The short ride to Danfield only took a quarter-hour and once at the stables, he called for his carriage and driver. Settling against the cushions, he closed his eyes, ready to catch a nap after last night's exertion with Louisa.

Owen fell asleep with a smile playing about his lips.

LOUISA AWOKE AND stretched lazily. She was a little sore but in a good way.

She hoped Owen would come to her bed again tonight. The intimacy they had shared was surprising. Lovemaking was passionate and volatile, but it was also tender and moving. She knew she still had much to learn and her fiancé would be a master teacher.

Papa would adore Owen. She wished her father could be here when she wed. They had discussed that very thing before he had left for Vienna. He knew she would be going to a full slate of Season events and the possibility existed that she might receive an offer of marriage. He had encouraged her to accept it if she wished and had asked his brother to step in and handle any arrangements necessary as far as a wedding was concerned.

Perhaps she and Owen might travel to Vienna on their honeymoon so that he could meet Papa. She would ask him today. They had a dozen things to talk about, including when the wedding should take place. As far as Louisa was concerned, the sooner the better. She would impatiently wait as the banns were read and then be happy to take Owen as her husband once that three-week waiting period had passed. She wondered if he would wish to wed at Danfield. At least Adalyn and Everett would be on the neighboring estate and Tessa and Spencer only a little more than an hour's carriage ride away.

Should she share the good news with her friends while the house party continued? Or would Owen wish to wait until after its conclusion? There was so much to decide.

One thing she determined was to inform Lord Boxling that she was no longer unattached. It would be unfair to the kind, handsome viscount for her to monopolize his time today when he could be spending it with one of the other female guests. Though she had told Owen she would go ahead and spend today in Lord Boxling's company, it didn't set well with her now.

Especially when she wanted to spend every waking moment with Owen.

Already, she longed for his kiss. His touch. She found she even wished for the picnickers to go ahead without them, in order for her to spend time with her betrothed.

A light knock sounded and Tilly quickly entered, looking a bit flustered.

"Oh, Miss Goulding, I am ever so sorry I did not help you prepare for bed last night. I waited for your summons and then I rested my eyes for a few minutes. I regret that I fell asleep and slept through the bell."

Louisa sat up. "Not to worry, Tilly. I did not ring for you."

Confusion filled the maid's face. "Then how did you undress?"

Hoping she wouldn't blush, Louisa said, "I stayed up rather late talking with Miss Peterson. She came back with me and helped me to unbutton my gown because I did not want to inconvenience. I laid everything out on the chair there," indicating where Owen had placed all her various layers of clothing.

"Oh, that's good to hear, Miss Goulding, but don't worry about that in the future. It's my duty to see to your needs."

"I will keep that in mind."

She rose from the bed and washed with the water Tilly had brought then dressed in her riding habit. Louisa knew she would be the only female present in the dining room wearing one but she thought it foolish to wear a gown down to breakfast for an hour and then have to change. Since plans had been made for those who wanted to ride to do so after breakfast, she decided she would simply wear the riding habit to the meal.

Tilly dressed Louisa's hair and then excused herself. Louisa gazed at her image, wondering what Owen saw in her that he didn't in other women. She did have a glow about her today.

And knew it was the glow of love.

Owen hadn't said anything about love last night and she didn't want to be the first to bring it up. He had said he didn't truly believe in it. His actions last night, though, made her feel loved and cherished. She hoped, in time, that he might come around and actually love her. For now, she would keep those feelings to herself and be happy that she was marrying such a wonderful man.

It was still a bit early but she decided to go down for breakfast anyway, knowing the buffet would just now be placed out by servants. Louisa left her bedchamber and went down the corridor. She turned the corner.

And froze.

Owen was in the hall with Miss Rexford. He held her elbows. She jerked him down for a hard kiss.

Bile rose in Louisa's throat as she forced her feet to move, retreating to her bedchamber. She flung the door open and closed it quickly, leaning against it for support. Slowly, she slid the length of it, hitting the ground.

No tears came. Instead, a cold filled her, numbing her.

He hadn't changed.

Owen was the rake she had always known he was.

His betrayal, so soon after leaving her bed, caused her belly to roil. Her heart seemed to twist within her, causing her physical pain.

She had once thought that she would turn the other way if her husband strayed from their marital vows. That thought—with Owen as her husband—had seemed inconceivable. Fidelity was something she would have expected, especially after what had passed between them last night. But tigers could neither change nor ignore their stripes. Owen was what he was—a dissolute rake of the first sort. He hadn't even the decency to hide what he did with another woman. Why, any servant or houseguest could have seen him kissing Miss Rexford, just as Louisa had.

She could not marry him. Ever. The fleeting happiness she

had felt upon awakening evaporated faster than morning dew as the sun rose high in the sky. She had to protect herself. Protect her heart at all costs.

Should she flee Cliffside? She could ask Uncle Uxbridge for the use of his carriage and return to Conley Park in order to lick her wounds. She wouldn't want her aunt and uncle to have to leave the house party so soon, not after they had been looking forward to spending time with Adalyn. But running wouldn't solve anything. Owen might even follow her and she couldn't have that. He would most likely ply her with kisses and convince her to change her mind.

No, she was stronger now. The Louisa from before would have left, defeated. One thing Owen had done for her was help her see her own worth. He had empowered her and she valued herself now more than she ever had. Why should she leave a house party because of his actions? She was here to make friends.

And possibly find a husband.

Lord Boxling came to mind. When she had thought Owen wanted nothing to do with her, the handsome viscount had been a worthy suitor. He still was. Louisa didn't think she would ever love him. Despite his betrayal, Owen would always own her heart. But Lord Boxling was kind. Affable. He truly seemed interested in her. She would not go into hiding. Instead, she would let the rest of the party play out. Spend more time with Lord Boxling and see if they might have enough in common to make a go of a marriage. She liked his character. His intelligence. The fact that he wanted a family. If this house party ended with a betrothal to the viscount, it would be better than she had hoped for.

Louisa went to the mirror. A ghost stared back at her. She sat at the dressing table and opened the pot of seldom-used rouge. Dipping her finger into it, she rubbed some on her cheeks, hoping the color would prevent others from seeing the hurt in her heart.

Owen had crushed the dream she had of marrying him. Of loving him and raising children with him. But dreams faded and reality took their place. The fact of the matter was that nothing was wrong with her. It was Owen lacking in character and morals. She had nothing to be ashamed of.

She would need to have one final conversation with him, though. She would tell him after careful consideration that she had decided they would not suit after all. If he pressed her, she would reveal what she had seen and explain that she would not tolerate his perfidy. He might plead with her to change her mind but one thing was certain.

She would not be marrying the Earl of Danbury.

CHAPTER TWENTY-FIVE

LOUISA WENT DOWN to breakfast, finding most of the guests already present at the table. Lord Boxling sat with Lord Marksbury, Lady Sara, and Miss Oxford.

She went through the buffet with Mr. Hampton and then joined him, sitting next to Miss Peterson and across from Miss Rexford. She said good morning to them and then focused on buttering her toast points, not thinking she could stand to look at Miss Rexford.

Owen was nowhere in sight.

Forcing herself to take a bite, she sipped on her tea, trying to get the toast down. Thankfully, no one was really looking at her. All attention was on Mr. Hampton, who was telling an amusing story from his university days.

Her gaze wandered about the room and she found Everett smiling broadly at her. She nodded politely to him, wondering what was on his mind. Probably sheer happiness because he was wed to Adalyn and she was expecting their first child. Once again, Louisa was grateful that she and Everett had quickly figured out they would not make for a good husband and wife, clearing the way for him to pursue Adalyn with a passion.

Mr. Hampton's lengthy story came to an end and he dug into his plate. Miss Peterson excused herself to go change for riding.

Miss Rexford said, "How are you doing this morning, Miss

Goulding? Anything exciting to report?"

She met the woman's eyes and saw the mirth in them.

"Not a thing, Miss Rexford. All is as it was when I left our group last night."

"Oh," she said, sounding disappointment. "I felt for certain you might have news to share."

Louisa shook her head and looked at her food, not thinking she could get down another bite. Had Owen told Miss Rexford of their betrothal? Was that why she asked what she did? It cut her to the quick that not only had Owen already cheated on her, but it seemed as if he had told Miss Rexford about their engagement. Oh, how Miss Rexford must be laughing at her now. Louisa only wished she could set the woman straight and tell her she could have Owen all to herself.

She wouldn't do that, though. She would speak to him first and break off things with him. If he chose to discuss that with Miss Rexford, that was his business. Certainly not hers.

Once the others started leaving the table, Louisa left with them, heading down to the stables. She spent a few minutes currying Fancy and then summoned Georgie to saddle the horse.

"I'll bring Fancy right out to you, Miss Goulding," the young groom promised.

Wandering from the stables, she found Lord Boxling and Lord Marksbury outside, along with Miss Peterson and Miss Oxford.

Everett strode toward them and said, "This seems to be all in our party this morning. Her Grace, Lady Sara, and Miss Rexford said they all had letters to write. Mr. Hampton went to his brother's house to check on things but he will return in time for the picnic."

Everett didn't mention Owen and Louisa wondered where he was. Since no one else asked, she decided to put thoughts of him from her mind and enjoy the ride.

Lord Boxling stepped up to her. "It is a fine day for a ride, as well as our planned picnic."

"It is indeed a lovely day, my lord."

"His Grace told me they have six rowboats stationed near the lake so there will be plenty to take out on the water." He regarded her hopefully. "Do you still wish to go out with me?"

"I am looking most forward to it," she told him, forcing herself to smile. This man had done nothing wrong. In fact, he had done everything right. He had paid attention to her. He had asked before he kissed her. He was a gentleman in every sense of the word.

Then why was she so miserable?

Louisa decided it was because her heartache was fresh. That she had opened her heart and loved Owen with everything she had. With time—and distance—she would recover. She would be wiser in affairs of the heart. For now, she must be open to the possibility of a future with Lord Boxling.

They rode for close to two hours and by the time they returned to Cliffside, she was ready for a little time to herself. She called for a bath and scrubbed herself clean, washing way any traces of Owen from her skin. Tilly dressed her in a gown of light blue and swept her hair away from her face.

"Be sure and take this bonnet, Miss Goulding," her maid warned. "The summer sun is strong today. You want to protect yourself."

The servant handed Louisa a parasol. "Take this, as well. You will be glad for its shade."

She went downstairs and met the others in the foyer. Still, no Owen. Louisa made her way toward Everett, who chatted with Tessa and Spencer. She wouldn't directly ask where Owen was but she might glean some information from his friends about his sudden disappearance.

"I do love a picnic," Tessa said as Louisa joined them. "Adalyn has already gone ahead and is supervising the servants. She told me she is having them erect a tent and the food will be placed under it and out of the hot sun. There will also be blankets for us to sit on."

"Is Analise coming?" she asked.

"Not the entire time. Spencer says it is too hot for her. Analise is so fair and he doesn't wish for her to be burned. He told her nursery governess that she could bring her down for a few minutes."

Louisa glanced around. "I suppose everyone is here?" she asked.

Everett surveyed the foyer. "It seems they are. Except for Owen. He returned to Danfield for the day but will be back with us by dinner tonight."

At least that explained his absence. She felt a little miffed that he had gone without telling her. Not that she would have wanted him to explain his whereabouts every minute of the day if they had remained engaged. It would have been courteous, however, if he had at least left her a note as to why he was absent from the activities today. Just another reason she should be glad they would not wed. He only thought of himself and not others. She didn't need a husband who would be so selfish and unthoughtful.

Everett got everyone's attention. "There is a carriage if any of you would like it to take you down to the lake. Otherwise, we shall stroll there as a group and enjoy this wonderful weather."

"I would rather ride," Miss Rexford said. "Walking bores me." She glanced to Lord Boxling. "Would you care to keep me company, my lord?"

"I am sorry, Miss Rexford, but I already promised Miss Goulding that I would escort her." He glanced to his right. "Hampton? Why don't you accompany Miss Rexford?"

"I would be happy to," the young man replied.

They left the foyer and Lord Boxling swiftly came to her, offering his arm.

"I hope you don't think me too bold, Miss Goulding, but I did not feel comfortable riding with Miss Rexford. She is a bit . . . forward."

"Not at all, my lord. I am happy for your company."

Louisa was. She truly was. At least she kept telling herself that. Lord Boxling had made a very favorable impression upon her, more so than any man from the past Season. She would give him every chance to continue to do so.

Despite her low spirits, the afternoon turned out well. The food tasted marvelous. The weather was splendid. Analise arrived after they had eaten and Louisa got a turn holding her before Spencer claimed his daughter.

Lord Boxling led her down to the rowboats and he and Everett carried one to the water, returning several times to bring more to the water's edge. Then he took her hand and helped her into it.

"Have you ever ridden in a rowboat before?" he asked.

"No, I haven't."

"My best advice is to stay seated in the center. It will rock a bit from side to side but that is nothing for you to worry about." He paused. "Do you mind if I discard my coat? It will be easier to row that way."

"Be my guest."

The viscount stripped off the coat and Louisa saw his large biceps. He started to place the coat on the ground and she told him that she would hold it. That seemed to please him. He helped her into the boat and she centered herself. Handing her the coat, she draped it over her lap.

Lord Boxling pushed the boat from the shore and jumped into it, picking up the oars and slipping them through a notch. Taking the handles, he began an easy motion, propelling them far from the shore. After a few minutes, he paused and lifted the oars, placing them back in the boat.

"I thought we could drift for a while," he told her.

"This is nice," she said. "I have never been out on water before."

"Not even the Thames?"

"No. I am afraid I have devoted the last few years of my life to my father and his work. With him gone to Vienna, I decided it was time to enjoy life for myself."

He gazed at her intensely. "I am enjoying the time in your

company, Miss Goulding. Very much."

Louisa couldn't do this. It wasn't fair to him. She couldn't allow him to be a substitute for Owen. This man deserved a woman who would fully commit to him.

"What's wrong?" he asked, picking up on her changing mood.

"Nothing—and everything," she admitted to him. "I have found it to be most pleasant being in your company, my lord. You possess many of the traits that I am looking for in a husband."

"But I am not Lord Danbury."

His words startled her.

He smiled ruefully. "I have seen how he looks at you, Miss Goulding."

"He is a rake," she said flatly. "He looks at all women that way."

Lord Boxling shook his head. "I disagree. It is different with you."

"I can't speak to that, my lord. I will say that I have a bruised heart now and am not good company for anyone. I sincerely hoped that things might work out between us."

"But your heart lies elsewhere," he said softly.

"It does. It may always. I cannot say. I will not see you abused, though, by my indecision. I have never been fickle and do not plan to become so." Louisa paused, meeting his gaze. "I would ask that you be kind to me but that you no longer pay any special attention to me."

"You are saying there is no chance of a future for us?"

"Probably not. I would not want to keep your hopes up. You are a wonderful man, my lord. Any woman would be lucky to claim your attention."

"I understand," he said, defeat in his voice.

Louisa said, "I hate hurting you, my lord. I hate that I am ending any chance I have with you. I think it better though, that I remain alone than lead you on. I would not want us to wed and me never be able to give you my heart. You deserve more than that."

He reached for her hand and squeezed it. "You are very special, Miss Goulding. I hope that your heart will heal and that one day you will find the happiness I believe you richly deserve."

Picking up the oars, he said, "Shall we row back to shore? I think I should give another young lady a turn about the lake."

"Thank you for understanding," she told him.

The viscount used long, deep strokes and had them back to shore in no time.

As they reached it, he called out, "Any other takers? I am happy to bring someone else out on the water? What do you say, Lady Sara?"

The young woman stood. "I would enjoy that, my lord."

Lord Boxling helped Louisa from the rowboat, their eyes meeting in understanding. He squeezed her hand and then released it.

"I will take your coat with me," she told him. "You can claim it when you are finished."

He nodded and then put on a bright smile, taking Lady Sara's hand and assisting her into the boat.

Louisa returned to where the blankets were spread out. Analise and her nursemaid were about to leave.

"I think I will accompany you back to Cliffside," she said. "I have a bit of a headache."

"Oh, I am sorry to hear that," Tessa said.

"Ask Bridget for one of my headache powders," Adalyn suggested. "It will help you to sleep. Hopefully, you can join us for dinner."

"I plan on it," she said.

Louisa would definitely attend dinner. Because she needed to speak to Owen and make certain he understood that no betrothal would be announced.

Chapter Twenty-Six

OWEN CHOMPED AT the bit as his carriage turned into the lane leading up to Cliffside. He would arrive just after drinks were being served in the drawing room. The trip to London usually took three and a half hours or so. He had been at Doctors' Commons for close to two hours, doing his best to try and speed along the process. Some things couldn't be hurried, however.

He touched his hand to his breast pocket for at least the tenth time since he had left London, making certain the special license was still there. It had been worth every guinea he'd paid for it and allowed Louisa and him to wed any place of their choosing.

He raked his fingers through his hair, thinking they still had so much to talk about. Would she want the wedding ceremony held in a church? Or would she allow Ev and Adalyn to host it as he had thought upon the conclusion of the house party? He knew women were always talking about gowns and how long it took elaborate ones to be made up. Would Louisa need a new gown for their wedding and cause further delay or could she be happy marrying him in one she already possessed?

Owen intended to get the answers to all his questions very soon. He began to think where they might honeymoon. With Bonaparte now in custody, Paris might actually be a city Louisa would enjoy seeing. Or would she prefer they travel to Vienna and try to visit some with her father? He sighed in frustration. All he seemed to know was that he loved Louisa and was ready to marry her on a moment's notice.

He wondered about the time she had spent with Lord Boxling today. If Owen hadn't been vying with the viscount for Louisa's hand, Owen might consider the man as a friend. He possessed an easy assurance and was quite intelligent. Besting him, though, and claiming Louisa as his countess would most likely put an end to any friendship between the two men. It didn't matter. He had Ev and Spence nearby and hopefully Win and Percy would be able to take some time away from the army and visit in the near future.

The vehicle began to slow and excitement filled Owen. Having spent most of the day away from Louisa had been torture. He would make it up to himself—and her—tonight. He planned to ravish her until the wee hours of the morning. In fact, he would start with kissing every inch of her beautiful body. That might take a good hour or more.

The carriage came to a halt and he threw open the door, bounding down before the stairs could be placed down for him.

Looking to his driver, he said, "Return to Danfield. Have a groom ride Galahad over before eight o'clock tomorrow morning so that he will be available to me to ride after breakfast tomorrow."

"Yes, my lord."

Owen hurried toward the house, realizing he would need to change into more formal wear for dinner. He cursed under his breath and opened the front door, hurrying up the stairs to his bedchamber. When he opened the door, he saw Strunk awaited him. All his clothes were laid out on the bed.

"Thank you, Strunk," he said, quickly unknotting and discarding his cravat.

"We will have you ready in no time, my lord," the valet promised.

Even with the efficient Strunk aiding him, Owen knew he had most likely missed out on seeing Louisa in the drawing room. As he rushed down the stairs, he saw Ev and Adalyn leading the way to the dining room, their guests trailing behind them.

Ev saw Owen and called out to him. He joined them, glancing over his shoulder and seeing Louisa on Hampton's arm. The young man also escorted Miss Peterson.

"Did your business go as planned?" his friend asked, his lips twitching in amusement.

"Yes, it did. Everything that needed to be accomplished was."

Adalyn frowned. "What was so important at Danfield that your steward could not handle it? You were missed today."

"It is good to hear that," he told her. He paused, believing that Louisa had actually kept their secret, else Adalyn would have been pumping him for details about the upcoming marriage.

They entered the dining room and everyone took their places. Owen inwardly breathed a sigh of relief. It was the first time he had been seated next to Louisa.

She took her seat and he leaned over. "Good evening," he said huskily, inhaling the lavender that clung to her skin.

"Good evening," she said curtly, a wintry look in her sapphire eyes, immediately turning to Spencer, who was on her right.

He was a blithering idiot. Louisa was mad at him. Of course, she was. He had spent the night in her bed, taking her virginity. He had offered marriage to her. Then he had absented himself for an entire day, leaving no word with her that he would be gone for the day. No wonder she had given him the cold shoulder.

At least he knew how to warm her up.

Owen turned to Miss Peterson, who was on his left.

"Did you enjoy the picnic today, Miss Peterson?"

She spoke of the day and he tried to relax and not worry about Louisa's behavior. He deserved being ignored. He would accept his punishment as a man. But he definitely planned to end the frost between them after dinner.

As he spent much of the meal conversing with Miss Peterson, he could see why Louisa liked her so much. Owen hoped that Lord Boxling wouldn't be a fool and walk away from this house party without having made an offer to this woman. She was bright, entertaining and quite pretty, with her lively blue eyes and trim figure. He recalled that Miss Peterson was one of the candidates Adalyn had put forward to Ev before Ev let it be known that he wanted Adalyn and no other.

The meal concluded and Adalyn led the women from the room, promising there would be music and dancing if the gentlemen could finish their port in a timely fashion. Owen longed to hold Louisa in his arms and dancing would be a perfect way to start what he hoped would be a long night together.

He left with the others to head to the ballroom after they had finished their port. Lord Boxling fell into step with Owen.

"A word, my lord?" the viscount asked.

He wondered what the man wanted and nodded, slowing his pace so that they fell behind the others.

Boxling looked at him sternly. "I did not take you for a fool, Lord Danbury."

"And you do now?" he asked, put out.

"Yes," Boxling said succinctly. "You have the heart of an amazing woman. I cannot for the life of me understand why you have wounded Miss Goulding so."

"Wounded her?" he asked, mystified by the viscount's words. "Why, I have offered for her—and she accepted."

Now, Boxling looked utterly confused. "I do not understand. It makes no sense."

"What?" Owen asked, impatient.

"When I tried to make my feelings known to Miss Goulding this afternoon, she very gently and kindly turned me away. She said her heart belonged to another but it had been bruised. She did not want to lead me on in any way and suggested I look to other female guests at the house party." Boxling paused. "Why would she speak as if she did not have an offer from you?"

Clueless, Owen shrugged. "I will get to the bottom of this, Boxling. Know that I was absent from Cliffside today because I was at Doctors' Commons purchasing a special license. I intend to wed Miss Goulding as soon as possible."

The viscount visibly relaxed. "Then that is good news, my lord. I hope you will quickly clear up whatever misunderstanding there is between you."

Boxling nodded brusquely and strode off, leaving Owen to remain behind. He couldn't think why Louisa would tell the viscount her heart had been hurt. Not after he had made known his intention to wed her. Not after the night they had spent together.

Then it slammed into him, like a blacksmith bringing down his hammer on his anvil.

Louisa had seen Miss Rexford kissing him.

It was the only possibility that would make her doubt him. Owen had to speak to her now. Before she threw up an impenetrable wall.

He rushed down the corridor, running full speed, passing all of the men heading to the drawing room. Bursting into the room, he raced inside, seeing every woman's jaw drop at his appearance.

Except Louisa's. She looked at him with dull eyes.

"We must talk," he said, moving toward her.

She rose, her chin raising a notch, a bit of defiance coming into her eyes. "Yes, I agree."

Owen strode toward her with purpose—and swept her off her feet.

"What are you doing?" she squeaked as he started carrying her across the room. "Put me down at once."

He paused, his gaze pinning hers. "No," he said firmly. Glancing at the astonished group, he added, "Nothing to worry about. Miss Goulding and I are to be wed."

"We are not going to wed," she said, her voice raised.

"Oh, yes, we are, sweetheart."

Owen exited the room, tuning out Louisa's pleas to set her down. Instead, he tightened his grip on her because she was squirming and didn't want to lose his grasp on her.

He took her to his bedchamber, flinging open the door and

slamming it behind him. He threw the lock and then crossed the room, tossing her onto his bed.

Immediately, she scrambled off it—but he blocked her way. His hands went to her waist to hold her in place as his mouth crashed against hers. Her fists beat on his back as she tried to free herself.

That wasn't going to happen.

Owen kissed her deeply, dominating her, hoping she would submit. She responded by stopping her fist pounding and going utterly still. She did not react to his kiss. Then she thrust her knee hard into his bollocks.

White-hot pain shot through him as he gasped, releasing her and stumbling back. Tears stung his eyes and he blinked, trying to see.

Louisa was hurrying to the door. He couldn't let her leave.

Bent over, cradling himself, he limped awkwardly after her. "Wait," he cried hoarsely. "Don't leave."

She reached the door and turned, fury in her eyes now. "I won't leave until I say what I need to say. I will never marry you, Owen. I knew you were a rake. I *knew* it—and I still let myself fall in love with you. You will never change. You will never be the husband I need or deserve. You—"

"You love me?" he asked, the pain still reverberating through him.

"Unfortunately, I do," she admitted. "I don't know exactly how I fell in love and I don't know how I will fall out of it—but I must. I cannot love a man I do not trust."

"It's because of Miss Rexford, isn't it?" he managed to get out.

"Yes!" she cried. "I saw you kissing her. In the corridor, Owen. Anyone could have seen you. You had barely left my bed. You had pledged yourself to me. *Me!* Yet I stumble across you kissing her."

He managed to rise a bit. "She was kissing me."

Louisa snorted. "Oh, there is a difference?"

"Yes. I opened my door and stepped out, running into someone. I didn't know if they were male or female. I clutched at them so as not to knock them down and realized it was Miss Rexford. She jerked on my waistcoat and, suddenly, my lips were against hers. The moment I realized what was going on, I thrust her away. I swear it is true, Louisa. I would never betray you. I love you."

Owen saw her begin to tremble. "I love you," he repeated. "I didn't think I would ever love anyone but you have changed me in ways I am only beginning to see. You have brought love and laughter into my life. I yearn to spend all my waking hours with you. Raise our children. I want to learn everything I can about you. Your favorite food and flower. How many times you sneeze in a row. Whether you prefer Haydn or Handel. If your feet are ticklish."

He loped toward her and took her hands in his. "I love you, Louisa Goulding. I am becoming a better man because I know you. I hope I will continue to be a better man because of your influence on me. I will be more faithful to you than Ev is to Adalyn or Spence is to Tessa. *That* is how much I love you."

Lifting her hands to his lips, he kissed them tenderly. "There is no other woman for me, Louisa. You alone are my one true love. I journeyed to London today in order to purchase our special license."

Owen released her hands and withdrew the license, handing it to her. "We can wed wherever and whenever we choose, thanks to this. I had hoped to do so by the end of the house party since our friends and your aunt and uncle are here."

He dropped to his knees. "Say you still wish to marry me, my love."

Tears streamed down her cheeks as she looked from the special license to him. Louisa fell to her knees, setting the document next to her. She grabbed on to his lapels.

"I am so sorry that I doubted you, Owen. Can you ever forgive me?"

Cradling her face in his hands, he kissed her tenderly. "There is nothing to forgive, my sweetest love." Then he grinned wickedly. "However, I think I will demand that you stay in my bed tonight—and every night. I am not sure I can perform the way I wish just yet but I would like to fall asleep with my fiancée in my arms."

"I love you so much, Owen," she said. She winced. "And I am very sorry that I kneed you." She grinned. "But I will always need you, my lord. Forever and ever."

"This is embarrassing but will you help me up?" he asked.

Louisa rose and took his elbows, helping him to his feet.

"I suppose you are going to teach that little trick to our daughters," he mused.

She laughed. "I certainly intend to."

"Come to the bed then," he said. "We have much to talk about."

They helped each other remove the layers of clothing they wore and climbed into Owen's bed. He held Louisa next to him, stroking her hair. They talked for hours about themselves and what they wanted for their shared future.

Eventually, Owen recovered and made tender love to the woman who had captured his heart and soul. Spent, they lay together.

Just before sleep came, he asked, "When will you marry me?"

"I think tomorrow," she replied. "And then we will go home to Danfield. It is the place we will learn to be married."

He pressed a kiss against her temple—and they both tumbled into a deep sleep.

Epilogue

Danfield—August 1815

"WHAT THE BLOODY hell is taking so long?" Owen demanded.

Ev looked up from his newspaper and sighed. "You're going to wear holes in the carpet from pacing so much."

He saw Spence enter, Analise riding on top of her father's shoulders.

"Uncle O!" she cried, seeing him. "Uncle Ev!" she added after spying Ev. "Down, Papa," she ordered.

Spence lifted her to the ground and Owen knelt, holding out his arms to her. Analise flew into them and gave him a very slopping kiss on his cheek.

"New baby?" she asked.

Owen sighed. "Not yet. Soon, I hope."

She wriggled away and raced to Ev, who set aside his newspaper and scooped her into his lap.

"I want a story," Analise told him. "Princess."

"I can do that."

Ev launched into a story and Spence took a seat, motioning for Own to join him.

"I know you are worried," his friend said. "But these things take time." He looked across the room and smiled at his daughter. "They are well worth the wait. Tessa assures me come November, the second babe will not take nearly as long to come as Analise did. First babies can take a day or more, Owen."

"I know," he grumbled. "Louisa warned me. But I want to be with her, Spence."

"She has Tessa and Adalyn with her. Remember, Louisa was also with Adalyn when she gave birth to Edwin in February. She is familiar with the process. The three cousins will always be there to support one another."

The grandfather clock struck four. Owen swallowed. "It's already been sixteen hours, Spence. I cannot help it. I want to be there with Louisa."

"Then go to her," Spence advised.

"The midwife banned me from the bedchamber," he complained.

Spence's brows arched. "You are an earl, Owen. Danfield is your home. If you want to be with your wife, do so."

That was all Owen needed to hear. He raced from the room, running along the corridor and up the stairs, taking them two at a time. Louisa was in the bedchamber designated for the Countess of Danbury, which she only used for storing her clothes and dressing. All her nights were spent with Owen.

As he skidded to a stop, the door opened. Tessa appeared. The moment she saw him, she grinned.

"I was just coming to get the new father," she said.

"Louisa?" he asked, his voice breaking.

"She came through without any complications."

Owen's eyes brimmed with tears. "And the babe?"

"Why don't you go inside and have your wife introduce the two of you?"

He needed no further advice and entered the room. A maid, holding a set of rolled-up sheets, passed him, cheekily giving him a wink.

"Congratulations, my lord," she said.

His eyes flew to the bed, where Louisa lay propped up against a bevy of pillows. Her hair was damp with sweat and it was obvious she was exhausted, but she had a glow about her.

Quickly, he strode to the bed, sitting next to her, his hands smoothing her hair.

"How are you, my love?" he asked, his throat thick with emotion.

Louisa cupped his cheek. "I am fine, Owen. I told you I would be."

"And the babe?"

"See for yourself," she said, looking over his shoulder.

Adalyn appeared next to him, a bundle in her arms. "Would you like to hold your daughter, Owen?"

"It's a girl?"

"It is," Adalyn confirmed. "And she is a beauty."

She carefully handed the infant to him. Owen gazed down at perfection.

"Hello, little one," he said softly, turning slightly so Louisa could also see the babe.

They stared at her in wonder. Then his gaze turned to his beloved wife and Owen leaned over and pressed a soft kiss against her lips.

"You have made me a father," he said, turning back to the child. "She is lovely. And so tiny."

Louisa laughed. "Not that tiny," she proclaimed. "At least it didn't seem so as she came out of me."

Owen dropped a light kiss upon his daughter's brow. "We never spoke of names."

"I know. I have a suggestion."

"Whatever you choose is fine with me, Louisa. You have done all the work these past months and spent a hard day in labor."

"I think I would like to name her Margaret, after my mother."

He nodded. "That is a beautiful name. Hello, Margaret. It is your papa and mama."

The babe, whose eyes had been closed, opened them sleepily.

She blinked a few times, studying him, and then her eyes closed again.

Adalyn appeared. "She needs to nurse before she sleeps. The wet nurse is waiting."

Hating to give her up, Owen kissed his girl again and then handed her to Adalyn. He turned his full attention to Louisa.

"I love you so very much," he told her. "I hope that we will be blessed many times over in this same way."

"That is my greatest wish," she replied.

Owen captured her hands in his and raised them to his lips, placing a fervent kiss against her knuckles.

"You changed everything about me, Louisa. Every breath I take is for you—and now for Margaret, too."

"I love you so much, Owen," she said sleepily.

He kissed her and then turned, stretching out beside her. His arm came around her, drawing her to him.

Kissing the top of her head, he said, "Go to sleep, my love. You've earned your rest."

As Louisa fell asleep, Owen counted his many blessings.

About the Author

Award-winning and internationally bestselling author Alexa Aston's historical romances use history as a backdrop to place her characters in extraordinary circumstances, where their intense desire for one another grows into the treasured gift of love.

She is the author of Regency and Medieval romance, including: Dukes of Distinction; Soldiers & Soulmates; The St. Clairs; The King's Cousins; and The Knights of Honor.

A native Texan, Alexa lives with her husband in a Dallas suburb, where she eats her fair share of dark chocolate and plots out stories while she walks every morning. She enjoys a good Netflix binge; travel; seafood; and can't get enough of *Survivor* or *The Crown*.